She  **in wet sand**

A golden furry creature loomed over her, staring with large contrite eyes.

"Galahad!" A horrified voice reached her ears.

Running beside the water was the cause of *all* her troubles—Paul Sherwood. She cringed.

"Lauren," he said. "My God, I'm sorry."

"This is a public beach and a person ought to be able to enjoy the view without a hurtling, furry object—" Switching her gaze from the dog, to her ruined suit, then back to Paul, the humor of the situation struck her.

Here she was, covered with sand, facing a legendary financial wizard. She broke into uncontrolled laughter.

"What's so funny?"

"All I could think was..." she answered "...we've got to stop meeting like this."

Dear Reader,

Four more fabulous WOMEN WHO DARE are heading your way!

In May, you'll thrill to the time-travel tale Lynn Erickson spins in *Paradox*. When loan executive Emily Jacoby is catapulted back in time during a train wreck, she is thoroughly unnerved by the fate that awaits her. In 1893, Colorado is a harsh and rugged land. Women's rights have yet to be invented, and Will Dutcher, Emily's reluctant host, is making her question her desire to return to her own time.

In June, you'll be reminded that courage can strike at any age. Our heroine in Peg Sutherland's *Late Bloomer* discovers unplumbed depths at the age of forty. After a lifetime of living for others, she realizes that she wants something for herself—college, a career, a *life*. But when a mysterious stranger drifts into town, she discovers to her shock that she also wants *him!*

Sharon Brondos introduces us to spunky Allison Glass in our July WOMEN WHO DARE title, *The Marriage Ticket*. Allison stands up for what she believes in. And she believes in playing fair. Unfortunately, some of her community's leaders don't have the same scruples, and going head-to-head with them lands her in serious trouble.

You'll never forget Leah Temple, the heroine of August's *Another Woman*, by Margot Dalton. This riveting tale of a wife with her husband's murder on her mind will hold you spellbound...and surprised! Don't miss it!

Some of your favorite Superromance authors have also contributed to our spring and summer lineup. Look for books by Pamela Bauer, Debbi Bedford, Dawn Stewardson, Jane Silverwood, Sally Garrett, Bobby Hutchinson and Judith Arnold...to name just a few! Some wonderful Superromance reading awaits you!

Marsha Zinberg
Senior Editor

P.S. Don't forget that you can write to your favorite author

    c/o Harlequin Reader Service
    P.O. Box 1297
    Buffalo, New York 14240
    U.S.A.

Casey Roberts
SHENANIGANS

Harlequin Books

TORONTO • NEW YORK • LONDON
AMSTERDAM • PARIS • SYDNEY • HAMBURG
STOCKHOLM • ATHENS • TOKYO • MILAN
MADRID • WARSAW • BUDAPEST • AUCKLAND

Published May 1993

ISBN 0-373-70547-6

SHENANIGANS

ABOUT THE AUTHOR

"I was home one evening watching an episode of 'Santa Barbara' when the idea behind *Shenanigans* was born," says Casey Roberts. "The episode had nothing to do with corporate takeovers, but it got me thinking about a company I used to work for, which went through a merger. Of course, my company was not family owned, but then again, the corporate raider involved didn't look like my hero, Paul Marshall, either."

Casey Roberts makes her home in Scottsdale, Arizona, with her new husband of one year. She has two grown children and three grandchildren.

Books by Casey Roberts

HARLEQUIN SUPERROMANCE
429—HOMECOMING
493—WALKING ON AIR

To Neil—

You are the wind beneath *my* wings.

And to Pam—

My eternal gratitude. Without your input, I might have been compelled to jump myself.

CHAPTER ONE

"TRUST ME, FRED. Everything will work out."

Lauren Afton didn't believe a word she'd said, but Fred looked so dejected—his shoulders slumped, his head resting on his hands—that she felt compelled to comfort him with white lies.

"I've been stalling for months," Fred said wearily. "Then today they insisted. Cash On Delivery, or nothing."

"It's not your fault. The thing is, I'm puzzled." She ran a finger across her lower lip, trying to find the best way to phrase her question. "Why didn't you tell me sooner?"

"Er, yes, it's just that... Well, Miss Cheri didn't much like to be bothered with, uh, little details. I thought you might feel the same."

"I handle things a bit differently than my mother." Hoping she'd hidden her irritation—this wasn't the first time she'd heard that justification during the past three months—Lauren walked from behind his desk and went to the door. "I'll make a few phone calls, work something out. In the meantime, it's not your worry anymore. You've done a fantastic job already."

Fred's shoulders straightened and a wan smile appeared on his face. "Thanks. I needed that."

Lauren forced a responding smile, then headed for her office, deep in thought. How many other ugly surprises were still waiting? There seemed to be a new one every day. The question generated a spurt of anger that she quickly shoved away.

As she entered her office, still reflecting, she was jolted by an unexpected presence.

"Excuse me, are you lost?"

A man stood by the window, looking out. He turned at her question and flashed a dazzling smile. Staring into his undeniably attractive face, Lauren was momentarily struck speechless.

He wasn't classically handsome. He was unusually tall—six-four or better—and though his suit was perfectly tailored to his large frame, Lauren somehow felt that a sudden move of his broad shoulders would rip his seams. His tawny blond hair appeared sun-streaked, as though he spent a great deal of time outside. A square jaw and a prominent bump on his slightly broad nose added to the impression that he'd be more at home in the great outdoors than in a boardroom, that he'd look more natural in a casual flannel shirt than in his European-cut pinstripe.

But it was his eyes that had robbed her of speech. Dark, smoky blue and full of avid interest, they compelled the viewer to give full attention to him. This man had *presence,* thought Lauren. There was no other word for it.

"Ms. Afton?" His voice, too, had presence. Deep, resonant, filling the room. He moved closer, extending his hand. "I'm Paul Sherwood. I've been wanting to talk to you for a long time."

Lauren blew out a breath, her awe changing to exasperation. This was all she needed to cap off a perfectly awful day!

"We've received your letters," she said in an inflectionless tone. "I thought our answers made it perfectly clear we don't care to pursue this matter."

"Doesn't money interest you, Lauren?"

Lauren wanted to fidget and tear her eyes from Paul Sherwood's penetrating gaze, but fearing that nervous movement would betray her internal fragility, she returned his stare with icy steadiness.

"I don't think so, Mr. Sherwood." Her choice of words displeased her. Too vague. And rather stupid. Of course, money interested her. Especially now. Why hadn't she simply said, *Not your money, Mr. Sherwood?* Lord knows, the words had been on the tip of her tongue and would have left no room for discussion.

"It doesn't?" He lifted his thick eyebrows skeptically, while casually seating himself in a side chair as though he owned the office.

"Not when the money comes from a Greek bearing gifts."

Paul Sherwood laughed a delighted sound, and for a moment it shattered the image he'd created—that of a domineering, powerful businessman. Now he seemed like a boy. Young, carefree, mischievous.

Did he think this was a game?

He leaned back in the tiny chair. It occurred to Lauren that a man his size should be miserably uncomfortable sitting there. But if he was, it didn't show as he lifted an ankle and placed it on the opposite knee. Now that he wasn't towering over her, Lauren felt more at ease and she stepped behind her desk to sit down.

"I've tried to reach you by phone," he said. "Since I couldn't get through, I decided to pop in, see you in person."

"My family isn't interested in selling," Lauren answered in what she hoped was a strong, firm voice. "Especially not to someone who will simply tear the company apart and barter off the pieces. Cheri Lee Cosmetics is a family-oriented company. We offer secure jobs to competent people. Some have been with us for nearly thirty years. Their security is important and I'll do nothing to put them in jeopardy."

Quite a long speech, thought Paul, struggling to maintain his studiously contrived, albeit torturous, position in the silly mauve armchair. It was built for a midget, and was as inflexible as its owner.

Everything about Lauren Afton was studiously controlled, from her artfully applied makeup to the light blond hair pulled severely off her face. Her gray-blue eyes nailed him like silver darts. Her pink suit looked as if it didn't dare wrinkle. She was also a knockout. Sleek, elegant, like a highbred racehorse. The kind of woman that would turn his head in a crowded room. But this was a business meeting, not a cocktail party, Paul reminded himself as he hurried to reassure her.

"I understand your concern. Still, it could be in your best interests to hear me out. I've done projected revenues for Cheri Lee Cosmetics, and if current trends continue, you have less than a year before you're in serious trouble. I'm offering a way to prevent that."

Without waiting for her answer, Paul sat up and reached for his briefcase. He pulled out a glossy portfolio tied with a black ribbon, which he opened and set on Lauren's desk. The desk was a clear acrylic slab, spotless, and almost bare. He briefly wondered where she kept her files and supplies, then discarded that thought as he continued his presentation.

Lauren's impassive face made Paul wonder what she was thinking. She would make a hell of a poker player—although she probably wouldn't stoop to such a down-and-dirty game.

"This is a chart of projected revenue," Paul said, pointing to a red line that slanted downward, bisecting a graph showing seven years of business activity. "Research shows that your market consists mainly of the blue-haired elderly. Young women think of your line as face powder, cold cream, and lavender water."

"Things are hardly that bad. We've recently added a number of up-to-date products."

"Product aside," Paul continued, giving little attention to her objection, "image is the foremost problem. To be candid, your market share is literally dying off."

"At the risk of repeating myself, Cheri Lee Cosmetics is not for sale. We do not need your money." Her face registered scorn as she brushed back an errant strand of hair.

Paul merely nodded. This woman was lying about needing his money, and he planned to use that to his advantage. Boldness was his trademark. It was time to put it to use.

"This deal could infuse a large amount of capital into your firm. Enough to wage an advertising campaign to change your image. Enough to secure the company's future for both your family and your employees."

"How could I secure our future with a company we no longer own?"

"What if you still retained ownership?"

The scorn vanished, and Paul remained silent. A printer clattered efficiently in a distant room, while the air around them crackled with tension. The stillness grew in length. Finally Lauren moved, placing a finger on her lips, and Paul knew he'd struck a nerve.

"What are you proposing?" Lauren wanted to shoot herself for blurting out the question, but considering the news Fred had just delivered, she could barely help herself. Once a supplier put a firm on COD, others followed suit.

"I'm very aware that a total buyout is unacceptable. I'm suggesting a partnership."

Trying to squelch a disbelieving smile, she glanced down, her eyes resting on Paul's crossed ankle. His trouser leg had crept up, revealing a dark blue sock, which merged almost seamlessly with his suit.

Then her eyes widened in surprise.

Embroidered on his sock was what looked like a . . .

Not quite trusting her vision and certain she'd been gawking, she lifted her head to find herself staring into eyes that reminded her of a stormy afternoon sky. For a moment, their gazes locked and held, creating an unsettling intimacy. She broke away, her thoughts again focusing on Paul as a person.

His appearance said "rugged male." His manner, "high-powered businessman." His socks, "mischievous boy." Which was he?

Why should she care? She'd listen politely, send him on his way, never see him again.

"A partnership," she repeated, then laughed scornfully. "Do you think I don't know about your association with J. Mitchell Cotton? Do you consider me naive, Mr. Sherwood?"

"Not at all." His grin widened. "And call me Paul." Then the smile was gone, giving Lauren a mysterious hollow feeling. "To answer your first concern, Mitch Cotton and I parted ways more than two years ago over, uh, a basic difference in philosophy...." Paul paused momentarily, his eyes darkening with an unidentifiable emotion. In a flash, he recovered and continued. "Cheri Lee Cosmetics has great potential, and I'm aware that your family won't consider an outright sale. This is my alternative." He flipped the top page of charts over. "Let me show you."

She settled into her chair as Paul began. He was polished, yet not slick, with just the right amount of informality. This didn't seem the kind of man who would buy a company, lay off its employees, and sell the assets for more than the price of the whole. Beneath his powerful air, Lauren saw a gentle vulnerability that she found herself wanting to explore. Where had he come from, this man who'd made himself a financial legend while he was still not much more than a boy?

Yet, as she listened to the last of his proposal, Lauren reminded herself that no matter what he seemed, Paul Sherwood was still a corporate raider.

"Very informative," she said when he'd finished, carefully hiding her interest. "You seem to know more about my company than I do." She rose, suddenly wanting to get away from him. Too attractive to ignore, his offer made her uneasy. Had it been a mistake to let him make his presentation? Despite all his glowing plans, he hadn't assured her he wouldn't liquidate Cheri Lee Cosmetics sometime down the road.

But the amount of money he discussed so casually made her mouth water.

"Leave your business card and the packet," she said tonelessly. "I'll let you know."

"I understand." He wore a polite smile, and if disappointed, he didn't reveal it. Standing, he thanked her and formally shook her hand, again seeming more mature than a man in his late twenties, which she knew him to be. When he reached the door, he turned back and gave a boyish wave. "See you, Lauren," he murmured, before walking out.

Once the door clicked shut, Lauren plopped back in her chair and smoothed her blond hair, wondering what her mother would think of the way she'd handled Paul Sherwood.

It was only three months since her mother's stroke, three months since Lauren had taken control of the company. Yet it seemed an eternity.

She'd been groomed to take command all of her thirty-one years, and she'd thought she was ready for the challenges that came with the territory. Still, as each day passed she'd learned her job was even bigger than she'd ever imagined. How had her mother managed to hide the problems? Self-doubt consumed her. True, during these past few months she'd managed to slow down the financial losses—but not nearly enough. And dealing with so many upset or irate people was a constant test of her ability.

How had she fared this morning? Had she presented the correct image to Paul—that of a firm businesswoman, totally in control? Had she faltered?

Appeared weak? Or lived up to her family's expectations?

What if she'd failed in her duty?

She got up and walked to her window and stood staring out over the mountain of trees. A bird—perhaps a sparrow?—alighted on the frond of a tall palm, then fluttered its wings a few times. The movement of air delicately lifted the bird's feathers before it again took flight. A fleeting sense of envy gripped her. Oh, to be that free!

Then she turned her attention back to Paul's offer. She reviewed his proposal—the advertising campaign, the designs for trendier containers, the suggestion for a lower-priced, more affordable product line. It was good. Very good. Exactly what she already had in mind.

She smiled with gratification. Her security measures must be working. If Paul, despite his thorough research, hadn't got wind that a new down-scale line was in production, then neither had the cosmetic industry. That's what she'd wanted. This turn-on-a-dime shift in direction would make their quality products affordable by a new and younger market, making Cheri Lee Cosmetics a threat to competitors who'd never before considered them one.

Moving to a glass étagère that tastefully displayed the company's products, Lauren picked up a studded milk-glass jar of cold cream.

Cold cream. No one even called it that anymore. Lauren craved to revamp the old line at the same time she announced a new one. Sleeker containers; lighter, less greasy bases. Another one of Paul's suggestions that echoed her own desires.

But new designs took money. And Cheri Lee Cosmetics had just been placed on COD. Would everything crumble before she could put her ideas into action?

Twenty-five million dollars! The answer to her prayers.

Why had that answer come in the form of a corporate raider? Cheri Lee Cosmetics's assets were worth four times Paul's offer price. A very tempting amount, tempting enough to lure many people into liquidating. Did a man with Paul's background truly want to enter management? Or was this just a ruse to get his foot in the door?

Business aside, Paul was likable. He had an easy, masculine charm. And even as she told herself this wasn't part of the problem, his blue eyes and white smile flashed in her head.

Suddenly she remembered that ridiculous sock. After her initial disbelief, she was certain of what she'd seen. Embroidered on his overpriced stocking had been a Teenage Mutant Ninja Turtle. A small one, to be sure, much like the tasteful emblems that often appeared on upscale men's hosiery, but a turtle nonetheless.

Why would a grown man wear something like that?

Strangely, the recollection brought an amused smile to her face. Although he was clearly competent at what he did—too competent for Lauren's comfort—the sock showed he also had a playful side that she found immensely appealing.

Lately she'd been plagued by urges to throw aside the mold she'd so carefully cast for herself. To do something crazy, take a risk, allow her sometimes-irreverent thoughts to flow from her mind and out her mouth. Her smile widened as she thought of Jessie. Wouldn't her sister love Lauren's new impulses? Approve heartily? Maybe she'd tell her someday. But not now, with these obligations hanging so heavily over her head.

Returning to her desk, she picked up the telephone receiver and punched in an extension. A familiar voice answered.'

"E.J.," she said. "Can you come to my office? Something very important has surfaced."

PAUL SMILED AT LAUREN'S assistant before turning to face the elevator. He kept his shoulders square, confident, and waited for the door to open. Inside, and facing forward, he flashed another smile.

The door slid shut and he slumped against the wall. "Damn! Damn!" Somehow his gambit had failed. How easy it had been to set up, and it should have been foolproof. Surely, he'd thought, once he'd arranged for Lauren's major supplier to put her on COD, she would snap up his offer. Was this yet *another* deal that wouldn't pan out?

Since he'd quit being J. Mitchell Cotton's flunky two years ago, Paul and his partner had made mountains of money, closing three deals in their first thirteen months together. Then everything turned sour. Their last two attempts had fizzled into nothing, severely denting Paul's reserves. But worse, they'd shaken the confidence of his backers—the mortgage and investment bankers on whose goodwill he depended.

If he didn't produce a turnaround quickly, those money men would soon pretend they'd never heard of him.

For a moment he wondered if he could have done anything differently, then dismissed that line of thought as futile. Those aborted deals were history. Tomorrow was another day, and Lauren's delaying maneuver no more than a minor obstacle to success. He'd play this out like a Monopoly game, as he'd always done. If he won, he won. If not, he'd find another game. Besides, wasn't uncertainty part of the thrill?

The elevator came to a stop and the door opened. Paul got out and walked quickly to the parking lot, the wheels of his mind still turning, searching for a new tactic. His thoughts were interrupted by a soft bark.

"Miss me, Galahad?" Paul moved toward his silver-gray Mercedes convertible. The top was down and a large collie sat in the front seat, its tail whopping against the leather. Paul always laughed when people said he was a fool for leaving an expensive dog in an expensive car, unlocked and unguarded; Galahad was the best theft protection a man could ask for.

Slipping into the driver's seat, he lifted an arm so the dog could slip under it. Galahad gave his cheek a cool, wet nudge, then lowered his head. "Good boy," Paul crooned. "Kept everything safe and sound, didn't you?"

Galahad made an appreciative sound low in his throat, a combination growl and whimper, then settled back into the passenger seat.

Paul opened the glove compartment and pulled out a Milk Bone biscuit, offering it to the collie. Gripping it lightly between his teeth, Galahad lowered his head onto his paws and crunched politely.

"Getting some manners in your old age?" Paul remembered a time when Galahad would have devoured the treat in one gulp. His old pup definitely wasn't getting enough exercise. Since he'd been neglecting his own workouts, too, Paul decided to head for his club, do a few sets, then take Galahad to the beach for a run. It would do them both good.

Starting the car, he thought about Lauren. Paul had encountered other sellers with her protective attitude toward their companies, and it always puzzled him. Why this sentimental attachment? A company was just an organization designed to make money. And if you could make more money by selling it than by keeping it going, why not sell? He'd have to convince her she was being unrealistic.

And that was a pleasant prospect. Lauren intrigued him. If he'd been an introspective man he might have wondered why he was so drawn to polished, controlled women when the let-it-all-hang-out types suited his personality better. But Paul never found time for introspection. He only knew that Lauren's coolness presented a challenge—a challenge almost as interesting as taking over her company.

But one challenge at a time was enough. And as he pulled onto Highway 8, he reminded himself he was walking a tightrope these days and needed to watch his step.

He increased his driving speed, and the wind whipped his hair across his forehead. Although it was mid-October, the temperature in Southern California was comfortably warm. Galahad seemed to like the day also. He sat with his head hanging over the window frame, his coat rippling like a field of wheat.

Paul had missed this weather during the years he'd spent in New York. He'd always thought Cotton was a fool to believe you couldn't make money unless you lived on the Eastern seaboard; to think that the wealthy must ride in limousines and live in ivory towers. Paul loved proving him wrong, loved the freedom of driving his own car and living like an ordinary person.

Maybe not quite ordinary. He frequently had to remind himself that not everyone owned a Mercedes, a yacht, several condos and a ranch.

Still, a convertible, a faithful dog, and the warm breeze of a balmy San Diego day. What more did a man need? Unless it was the love of a good woman.

The thought made him laugh out loud.

JESSIE AFTON, TOO, loved the wind in her hair. But she preferred a more modest means of transportation. Her Suzuki Samurai four-wheel drive, a twenty-first birthday present from her father, purred as she crossed the bridge to Coronado Island. Even though her mother often told her she should trade it in, Jessie loved this squat little all-terrain baby. A part of her savored the small tremble of the steering wheel beneath her hands as she speculated on her upcoming meeting. Or, more precisely, on the *man* she'd be meeting.

What a cutie he was. Sort of courtly and dapper. It puzzled Jessie that she found him so appealing, but she was never one to examine her impulses too closely. Just go with it—that's what she always said.

So he wanted to buy her stocks, did he? A grin crossed her face. Of course, she'd never part with them. Cheri Lee would disown her if she did. But she'd string Bill along until she found out if he measured up to her first impression.

Crossing the bridge to the island, she glanced at a small notebook on the passenger seat to recheck the address. A few minutes later she pulled in behind a Spanish-style office complex. It was old-California tasteful, typical of Bill Rosen, she thought. Before jumping out of the Samurai, she reapplied her lipstick and lifted her braids over her shoulders in studied casualness. Ready, she walked briskly to the suite number Bill had given her and entered.

A young woman, busy on the phone, gestured that she'd be with Jessie in a moment. She was a perky girl with bouffed hair and big eyes. A nameplate on her desk said she was Carol Walgren. As Jessie waited, she glanced around the reception area. It, too, was tasteful. Southwestern pastel colors and great leafy plants gave it a relaxed atmosphere, although it was a bit on the dull side. Jessie longed to jazz it up—add a few bright colors and maybe one of those big quirky coyotes. As she was pondering how she'd redecorate, Bill entered the room.

"Jessie, what a pleasure," he said cordially, offering his hand as he approached.

"It's nice to see you again, Bill." She took his hand and shook it firmly. He then turned and introduced her to Carol. As Jessie exchanged pleasantries with the woman she kept an eye on Bill. His subdued gray suit was perfectly pressed and the red pocket handkerchief that matched his tie looked like it had spent quite a while under an iron. Lord, he was so relentlessly well-bred.

As if to prove it, he plucked the handkerchief from his suit pocket, removed his wire-rimmed glasses and polished the lenses. His eyes were a deep rich brown and had that slightly out-of-focus look common to myopics.

"Would you like something? Coffee? A cola?" He replaced his glasses as he spoke, then meticulously folded his handkerchief. Tucking it smoothly into his pocket, he brushed back his close-cropped brown hair.

"Coffee, please. Black."

"I'll get it for you," offered Carol. Bill thanked her, then returned his attention to Jessie.

"This way." He guided her into a hallway with a nearly imperceptible touch. They passed a large office where a half-dozen or so men and women hunched over computers and talked on phones.

"The bull pen," Bill commented. "The analysts who work here spend all day tracking investments and determining the profitability of possible new ones."

"Hmm," replied Jessie, without much interest.

Dear God, thought Bill. This was going to be even more difficult than he'd expected. He'd known from the moment they'd met that Jessie Afton was cut from a different pattern than most. Her hair alone proved that. Few woman her age wore Raggedy Ann doll pigtails, although he had to grudgingly admit she looked good in them.

But why had she dressed that way? The ragged holes in her denim shorts revealed patches of lace as if her underwear was showing. And he could barely resist the compulsion to catch the neckline of her fleece top before it fell down to her waist, revealing God-knows-what. Her choice of clothes loudly stated that she wasn't taking this meeting seriously. She already seemed bored. Whatever would he chat about with this alien person while he was trying to close this deal?

When they entered Bill's office she solved that problem for him. "Oh, you have some of Lisa Bentoni's paintings. How marvelous!" She glided toward a leather sling sofa where a vivid abstract hung. "Don't you just love her?"

She looked at Bill with an expression of lively interest. For an instant, he was struck by her immense vitality, her spontaneous appetite for life.

"Although, from my first impression, I'd never have guessed you to be a Bentoni aficionado," she added.

Bill laughed lightly. "You aren't the first to say that. But her bold use of color appeals to me."

"Ah, it speaks to some unexpressed portion of your soul."

"Umm, perhaps."

Carol chose just that moment to bring in their coffee, for which Bill was immensely grateful.

He settled Jessie on the sling sofa, then pulled up a matching chair. His discomfort was increasing and he wanted to keep a distance between them. The best way to do that was to get back to his area of expertise.

"Before we have lunch, why don't we go over my proposal? As I told you at the Turnbows' cocktail party, my associates and I are very interested in your Cheri Lee Cosmetics shares. I'd like to show how this could benefit you."

Jessie leaned back and crossed her long, tanned legs, then took a lackadaisical sip of coffee. "Will this take long? I'm not much for business."

"So you've told me." Bill forced a smile. This woman didn't seem to care how rich she was. Or could be. "Can you give me ten minutes?"

"I'll be timing you." She flashed him a brilliant smile.

"Fair enough. Now, I'm prepared to offer you ten times current earnings divided by the total number of outstanding shares—"

"What would you do with them?"

"The shares?" What an odd question. Most people would ask how much money they were talking about. But he'd already determined she wasn't like most people.

Jessie nodded, so he launched into his rehearsed explanation.

"My associates are interested in safety and solid earnings. Stock-market conditions are highly unstable right now. Since privately-owned companies aren't subject to the vagaries of daily trading and speculation, they're looking more attractive than public companies these days."

"Who are your associates?" Her tone was light, as though she really didn't care, but Bill began to wonder if she wasn't more aware of her financial affairs than he'd credited her for.

"They prefer that their identities remain private, for now. Is that a problem?"

She didn't answer immediately, took another sip of coffee, this time more lustily. Then she said, "Guess not. Show me what you have."

Bill suppressed his sigh of relief. For a moment he'd thought the deal was already dead. He opened a slick presentation portfolio that he'd placed on the coffee table before Jessie's arrival and went quickly through the salient points—more quickly than he'd prefer, but he could see Jessie was impatient. Considering she'd kept him waiting over half an hour, her impatience annoyed him.

When he'd covered the details on the last graph, he closed the packet with a snap. "Now, that wasn't so bad, was it? What do you think?"

"Interesting. But now I think I'd like lunch."

What? He'd just offered her nearly twelve million dollars and she wanted lunch? He stopped himself before his mouth dropped open, then stood as smoothly as he could, considering the rage boiling in his veins.

"Of course," he agreed stiffly. "It is getting late. We can discuss this over our meal."

"I prefer not to talk business while I eat. But tell you what, Bill. Why don't we meet again? Say, Thursday night, dinner at my place? In the meantime, I'll think the offer over." She got up, standing very close to Bill now, then reached out and patted his cheek.

Bill's skin seemed suddenly warmer after that fleeting touch. Uncertain if the heat came from embarrassment or his struggle with his anger, he stepped back a few paces.

"Of course," he repeated. "Thursday night. In the meantime, I've made reservations at a nice place in La Jolla. Is that all right?"

"Of course," she replied.

Bill noticed her copycat intonation and knew he was being mocked. *This woman is going to drive me mad,* he thought.

Clenching his teeth, he followed Jessie through the door, wondering where he would find the strength to carry out his task.

CHAPTER TWO

HIS HAIR STILL DAMP from his shower, Paul walked into the country-club dining room. Since he knew Galahad was peacefully snoozing in the back seat of his car down in the parking lot, he'd decided to stop for a stiff Jack Daniel's bourbon to ease the raw edge on his nerves.

"Would you like the dining room or the bar, Paul?" asked a pretty hostess whom he recognized from previous visits.

"Is the Lakers–Suns game playing?"

"Sure is." The woman's interested expression revealed that she found him attractive, which at another time Paul might have encouraged. The attention of pretty women always pleased him. But tonight he was preoccupied.

Responding with a courteous but distant smile, he said, "Then I guess it's the bar."

She took the hint and guided him to a stool where she discreetly placed his tab against the leather backstop of the oak bar. A television set glowed in the otherwise dim room. Paul ordered, then immersed himself in the basketball game. Soon he was caught up in the competition.

Twenty-eight to thirty, thirty-one to thirty-four—the score changed continuously, with the Lakers staying just in front. The other patrons cheered accordingly, since most seemed to be Lakers fans, but Paul rather liked the Suns.

For kicks, he began cheering whenever the Suns scored. As expected, he soon became the target of lively catcalls and jeers. He fell easily into the banter and accepted a few small bets, this being a form of male bonding that he understood and greatly enjoyed.

His faith was justified. The Suns won the game, and at the ending buzzer, Paul jumped off his stool with a roaring whoop, amid a burst of opposing boos. Although a few disgruntled fans grumbled about their losses, they settled down when Paul ordered a round for the bar.

He was just signing his tab, feeling much restored and ready for a good night's sleep, when *he* appeared.

"Quite a game, wasn't it, Paul?"

The room tilted as Paul smothered his impulse to whirl toward the familiar voice. Instead, he looked casually over his shoulder into the face of J. Mitchell Cotton.

"If it isn't King Cotton," he said, over the pounding in his ears. "What brings you down from your castle?"

Cotton smiled, a smile as thin as the no-color hair on his head. "That's your problem, kid," he replied, ignoring Paul's gibe. "You always root for the underdog. How many times have I told you the only way to win is to back a sure thing?"

"How much did you lose?" Paul smiled, too, with a genuine pleasure that diluted the adrenaline in his blood. This was a typical Cotton ploy—to attack the opposition when he was losing himself.

"More than you made on your last deal." Cotton patted his ample stomach and added, "But less than I paid for tonight's dinner."

"You always did have a big appetite." Yet Paul wondered if Cotton really did know something about the last deal or was just blowing smoke. Setting his mind to the task of finding a subtle way to dig out that information, he stalled by asking, "What brings you to the land of barbarians?"

"Sun and fun. Hear you're living on Coronado Island these days."

"Yeah, I have a little condo on the ocean." *Sun and fun, my eye,* thought Paul. To Cotton, fun was a four-letter word. Still, tingles of apprehension prickled Paul's skin, troubling him. Hadn't his need for Cotton's approval vanished long ago? Of course it had. He'd even convinced himself he would relish the opportunity to face Cotton head-to-head. And here it was. So why did he feel like a cat with its tail on fire?

"Little condo? This modesty doesn't become you, Paul. A top-floor suite is hardly 'little.' "

"I get by." An internal alarm sounded, and the tingling sensation increased. His breathing roared in his ears like a hurricane, and his fingers, resting on his cotton slacks, could feel each fiber with amazing clarity. How the hell did Cotton know so much about him? Paul's mind whirled with the implications. "I get by," he repeated.

"With a little help from your friends." Cotton smiled with condescension. "You do still have some friends, don't you?"

Anger gripped Paul's chest with sickening force. During their bitter parting argument, Cotton had coldly predicted Paul would become a penniless outcast in less than a year. But Paul had already proved him wrong, so why did the man seem to be rubbing it in?

Determined not to allow Cotton to carve holes in his confidence the way he once had, Paul stood, dismayed to find his legs unsteady. He forced himself to speak evenly.

"Look, Cotton, I was on my way out. Let me buy you a drink before I say good-night."

"Thanks, but I never accept drinks from an opponent."

The gauntlet was down, the challenge made.

"That's smart." Paul's anger slowly turned to cold, protective steel. His legs steadied beneath him. Cotton would never bring him under his thumb again, no matter what. With that in mind, Paul added, "Just remember. The Suns *did* win the game."

With a curt nod, he walked out of the bar, struggling not to look back. He hadn't looked back the day he'd left Cotton's employ and he wasn't going to start now.

His mind raced. What strategy was his ex-employer planning? Obviously Cotton had someone keeping tabs on him. But who? And why was he here now? Usually he hired minions to do his dirty work.

Paul continued toward his car, his mind examining this problem from every angle. As he got inside, glancing at Galahad who lifted a sleepy head in his direction, he remembered his earlier thoughts about one challenge at a time. It seemed he wouldn't be allowed that luxury, and he wished with all his heart it wasn't so.

During the short drive to his apartment he replayed the conversation. He'd worked for Cotton for over eight years. Cotton had liked to say that they worked together, but Paul had never doubted who was in charge. Still, during that time he'd learned his boss's habits well, and this visit to the West Coast wasn't something Cotton would do if he hadn't already laid lots of groundwork.

It was as if Cotton had stepped in for the finale of a well-plotted play, and Paul didn't even know what had gone on in the first two acts. It was time he found out. So instead of driving into the underground garage of his building, Paul passed on, heading toward the bridge, toward his suite of offices.

As he pulled into the parking lot, he noticed a light on inside. Perhaps his partner was there, although perhaps not. The man seldom worked this late, preferring the early-morning hours.

Leaving Galahad asleep in the car, Paul hurried, wanting to get the records he needed, make a quick phone call, then return home for the sleep he seldom got these days.

As he entered the office he saw the office manager slipping some documents into her desk drawer.

"Hi," Paul said. "You're here kind of late, aren't you?"

"Jim was feeling particularly lousy today so I left early." The woman looked wan, her skin sallow beneath the fluorescent lights. "After I got him settled I came back to catch up."

"You didn't have to do that. The work would have waited until tomorrow." Paul knew her husband was seriously ill. She'd been honest about that when they'd hired her, telling them she'd do her best not to let it conflict with the job.

"No. I'm getting too far behind." She fetched her purse from the floor and got up. "But I'm done now. Is there anything you need before I leave?"

"No, I'll be fine," Paul said. This was work he had to do himself. Besides, the poor woman seemed exhausted. "Go home. Get some rest."

"Thanks." But her grateful smile was sad as she turned to leave. "Night, then."

"Night." When she was gone, Paul headed for his spacious office, went to a file cabinet and pulled out several reports. With lightning speed he flipped through page after page, searching for a clue somewhere in the records of his last two failed acquisition attempts. It surfaced like a cork.

Of course! The sudden heavy stock trading, coming from a dozen small buyers—or so the analysts had said. It had made the first acquisition unprofitably expensive. Then, miraculously, the second company's management had found an endless fountain of money. Why hadn't he recognized the heavy hand of Mitchell Cotton?

The discovery caused a leaden ball to form in his stomach, along with the answer to his question. He hadn't wanted to believe Cotton would do this, no matter what he might have threatened. When they'd met on the floor of the Chicago Mercantile Exchange, Cotton had said he wanted to nurture the raw talent he'd seen in Paul, teach him everything he knew as he would the son he'd never had.

In turn, Paul had made Cotton his hero, thought he could do no wrong. Later, Paul began seeing flaws in his idol. Yet their heated quarrels over acquisition strategies hadn't dimmed his loyalty. Cotton had been the only father figure Paul had ever known, and if he questioned Cotton's ethics at times, it had never occurred to him to doubt the older man's affection.

Would a father destroy his offspring?

Apparently, yes. And all over one stinking deal.

The Plymouth bond offering. They'd feuded for weeks after Paul pointed out that the offer implied that the bonds were secured. . . .

"They are," Cotton stubbornly insisted.

"Sure," Paul countered. "With property and equipment so heavily financed, there's no equity left. In my book, that's the same as no security at all. In fact, the Securities Commission might call it fraud."

"Look, kid," Cotton said, dragging deep on his thick cigar before continuing. "Without a little glossing over, no one would ever buy these bonds. It's a fine line, but we're not actually lying about them."

"The line's a little too fine for my comfort." Paul paced the floor, stopped a moment to stare out over the Manhattan skyline from his boss's panoramic window. He flicked the edges of a thick document in his hand, thinking, then turned. "We used to do real takeovers, Cotton. Buy saggy, moribund businesses and make money with them. Now all we do is sell securities—ones that are none too secure. I'm afraid someone's going to get hurt."

"Your East L.A. roots are showing, Paul. This offer's going out the way it's written." Cotton leaned forward, pushed a button on a speakerphone, and asked his secretary to bring him a document, effectively dismissing Paul.

"Not with my name on it!" Paul slammed his fist on Cotton's polished mahogany desk. "Dammit, Cotton. You won't blow me off like this! This offering is highly questionable, probably illegal."

"You're getting on my nerves, kid. I pulled you out of the grain ghetto in Chicago and made you a millionaire. Is it too much to ask that you follow a few orders?"

"When it might cost people's life's savings, yes." Paul's heart thudded, his pulse raced, and his breathing was uneven. He hadn't wanted to do this. He'd hoped to sway Cotton. Now it seemed that edges were blurring—coming into sharp focus, then blurring again—and he was seeing Cotton clearly for the first time.

"You've now got my resignation," he said evenly. "I'll give you a week to change this bond offering so that it's no longer misleading, or I'm filing this paper with the Securities Exchange Commission."

Paul slapped the document he'd been holding down on the desk, and Cotton flipped through the pages, slowly, as though carefully reviewing each one. But Paul knew it was an act, and when his boss looked up with venom in his eyes, Paul broadened his stance. This time he wasn't backing down.

"This opinion paper doesn't worry me, Paul. I've got connections. Go cool off, think things over. I'm sure you'll soon regret your actions."

"No regrets, Cotton. Not now. Not later. My resignation stands."

Paul whirled on his heel and stormed out, slamming the door behind him, and marched from Cotton's thirty-story building. He never returned. Cotton did not changed the offer packet and Paul filed the paper with the SEC, in spite of Cotton's threats to ruin him....

Nothing had come of it. Paul had never been contacted and, because he'd had so many mixed emotions about it in the first place, he never followed up. Until tonight, he'd almost forgotten about it.

Obviously, Cotton had not.

Now, the memory vividly revived, Paul reached for the telephone to call his lead analyst. It was after eleven, but this was too important to wait. Important enough that Mike Armstrong was going to have to lose a little sleep.

When a groggy voice answered, Paul said, "Sorry to wake you, Mike, but we need to dig into Cotton's activities. Right away. He's planted someone in San Diego to watch me." Then he quickly covered the events of the night.

"Has he done any damage yet?" Mike asked.

"That's what I want you to find out. Find out more about what happened during the last two deals. Check my other investments, too. Make sure nothing funny is going on. And let's keep this just between you and me."

"You bet," Mike replied. "It looks like we don't know who we can trust."

"Isn't that the truth." As Paul hung up, he wondered why he felt so desolate. This used to be fun. Outmaneuvering the opposition, beating them to the punch. Lately, though, the game had seemed less challenging, less . . . alluring.

But there wasn't any time to wonder if he was having fun yet. He had work to do. If the cool, collected Ms. Afton didn't contact him within the next day or so, he'd have to find another way to buy a big chunk of her company. He already had one in mind, but had planned to wait a couple of weeks before using it.

Waiting was now an unaffordable luxury. If he didn't act soon he'd be annihilated. No matter what

Lauren Afton might want, Paul would own Cheri Lee Cosmetics. Soon. Very, very soon.

PAUL PULLED HIS convertible into a parking place, inhaling the crisp, salty air of the ocean, allowing himself to be soothed by the gentle roar of the surf.

He fumbled behind his seat for Galahad's Frisbee, then climbed from the car and headed for the other side to let him out. Galahad got to his feet, ears lifted, tail wagging. His tongue lolled lazily from his mouth.

"Come on, Galahad, let's romp." The collie looked at him without much enthusiasm. "Come on," Paul repeated, in more cajoling tones. Lazily, Galahad jumped over the door, making a clumsy landing at Paul's feet. Paul smiled, somewhat relieved. It had been several months since he'd been able to persuade Galahad to jump. Must have been off his feed, Paul thought, because today he acted like a big, healthy puppy.

He headed for the boardwalk, walking briskly. Galahad fell into an easy trot behind him as they wove their way among joggers, bicyclists and skaters. Paul looked for the pavilion where he'd been told E. J. Afton ate his lunch every day, and soon spotted it. Although he'd never met E.J., he was confident he'd recognize him from pictures in Cheri Lee Cosmetics's promotional brochures.

As planned, he was about a half-hour early. He'd be busy playing with Galahad when Lauren's brother arrived. What better excuse could a man have for being at the beach than exercising his dog? He took a short bank of stairs down to the shoreline, enjoying the gentle resistance of the sand beneath his deck shoes. A few sunbathers dotted the landscape, but it was otherwise empty, giving him and Galahad plenty of room to play. With a soft clucking sound, he tossed the Frisbee and cried, ''Fetch!''

Galahad bounded after the Frisbee, caught it mid-air, then ambled leisurely back to Paul with the disk held delicately in his mouth. Dropping it at Paul's feet, he looked up expectantly.

Paul smiled, love for this dog filling his heart. Galahad had been a present from his mother when he'd received his bachelor's degree, and over the past twelve years, had earned numerous ribbons and sired dozens of championship pups. Paul took him everywhere.

Paul tossed the Frisbee again. To his dismay, it veered off toward the ocean, with Galahad bravely bounding after it. Directly in the dog's path, a woman wearing a crisp yellow suit stood at the water's edge, gazing out over the sea.

Oh, no! It couldn't be!

WHAM! HE CAME OUT OF nowhere.

One moment Lauren had been standing sedately, playing with the idea of stripping off her clothes and diving into the foamy surf, but telling herself that even Jessie wouldn't skinny-dip in broad daylight. The next moment, she lay flat on her back, wallowing in wet sand. A golden furry creature loomed over her, staring with large contrite eyes, its breath brushing her face.

''Shoo, shoo!'' Lauren squeaked. The dog backed away, cringing as if he knew he was in big trouble. Lauren pushed herself to a sitting position.

''Damn!'' she sputtered, trying to brush sand from her shoulders. Her messy fingers made things worse, and she looked down at her smeared shoulder in disgust. "This is all I need," she grumbled, glaring at the cowering ball of fuzz in front of her.

"Galahad!" A horrified voice reached her ears. A *familiar* horrified voice.

Oh, no! It couldn't be.

Running beside the water was the cause of her unlikely visit to the ocean. She cringed. Just moments before, she had been contemplating his offer—and her inconvenient personal interest in him. Now, here he was. Paul Sherwood, the disturber of her peace of mind, the man she'd come here to discuss with E.J.

"Lauren!" he said. "My God, I'm sorry."

He grabbed her arm, jerking her to her feet before she was ready to stand. She stumbled, righting herself with a hand on Paul's shoulder, and glared at him. "Why don't you control your dog, Mr. Sherwood?"

"It's my fault, not Galahad's," Paul explained hastily, trying with frantic strokes to brush sand from Lauren's shoulders.

She ungraciously pushed him away. "I can do it myself, thank you."

Scrubbing her hands together with short, irritated movements, Lauren attempted to dislodge the sand, disgruntled because it clung to her so stubbornly. This was outrageous! She was covered with soppy sand, her suit was smudged beyond repair. Changing clothes would take over an hour from her already busy day. And it was all Paul's fault!

She gaped at her hands in revulsion, then looked up at Paul as she continued her rebuke. "This is a public beach and a person ought to be able to enjoy the view without a hurtling, furry object—"

It was his penitent expression that stopped her. Once again he looked like a young boy, vulnerable and as contrite as his animal. He wore a boating shirt over rolled-up cotton slacks. Deck shoes, laces untied, enclosed his sockless feet.

"My dog was just obeying my command." As Paul spoke he picked up her shoulder bag, which had flown off during the collision. "And I didn't look before I threw. I'm sorry. I'll get your suit cleaned."

Here she was, covered with sand, facing a legendary financial wizard, whose blue eyes were saucers of dismay. With her purse clutched in his hands, he looked like a kindergarten boy caught eating another kid's lunch.

And that dog! Lauren wouldn't have been surprised to see a conciliatory bouquet materialize in its paws.

What would Mother think? At the responding image of her mother's delicately raised eyebrows, a delighted giggle bubbled in her throat.

Trying to swallow it and remain stern, she said, "I suppose it could have been worse. I could have ended up in the ocean."

Paul smiled tentatively, appearing unsure if she were accepting his apology. The uncertain gesture crumbled her composure. The bubble in her throat exploded, and, as Paul's smile vanished, to be replaced by bewilderment, it then returned full force and Lauren broke into uncontrolled laughter.

Unable to resist her infectious giggles, he found himself joining in. Hearing him, she caught his eye, then nearly doubled over as she held her sides, unable to fight her hilarity. Strands of her hair floated like a silver halo around her face, and her cool gray-blue eyes had warmed to a brilliant azure. *She's so beauti-*

ful, Paul thought, his laughter dying as his appreciation grew. A strange awe encompassed him.

As his laughter subsided, so did hers. Straightening, she again attempted to brush off the sand. Paul moved behind her, began helping. Touching her, even in this impersonal way, felt intensely pleasant. "Your suit is ruined," he commented.

"Nothing a good dry cleaner can't fix." She tipped her head back, glancing at him.

"What was so funny?"

"All I could—could think," she answered, between short bursts of giggling. "Was, we've got to stop meeting like this. Imagine what the papers would say. Corporate Officials Clinch Deal In Sand. Dog Only Witness. It's all so undignified. I couldn't help thinking how my mother's eyebrows would arch when she read those headlines." Realizing what she'd just said, Lauren abruptly stopped laughing.

What was she doing? Why had she shared this unflattering side of her mother with a stranger? And why did an eerie flutter plague her body at his every touch?

His hand still rested on her shoulder, and she shrugged it off. Paul's smile slowly faded, and a small furrow appeared between his brows. She saw a flicker in his eyes. Hurt. Had she hurt his feelings?

She turned away then, looking out over the ocean. Parachutes dotted the horizon like random pushpins on a corkboard. Briefly, Lauren wondered—not for the first time—what it would be like to do something as risky as parachuting.

"Did I say something wrong?"

At Paul's question, Lauren turned to face him, her impassive mask safely in place. "No, no," she said vaguely, looking off toward the boardwalk. Paul suspected she was deliberately avoiding his gaze. "I'm supposed to meet my brother and he should be here by now."

E.J.! Paul had almost forgotten him. Now he had a new problem because he hadn't anticipated Lauren's presence. As he tried to find a polite way to invite himself along, Lauren said, "You might as well come with me. You're bound to meet him someday. Today's as good as any."

Not the most gracious invitation, but Paul thought it would do. He called Galahad to follow, then walked with Lauren to the boardwalk.

"What's your linebacker's name?" Lauren asked, after a moment of uneasy silence.

"Lineback—? Oh, you mean Galahad. His full name is Sir Galahad of Sherwood."

A smile returned to her face—one that looked as if she knew something he didn't. "Oh? Do you also plan to name your first son after you?"

"Well, I think *Sir* Paul Sherwood II has a nice ring. Don't you?"

Lauren's smile changed to genuine amusement. Licking her finger, she pulled it through the air as if drawing on a blackboard. "Your point."

"I think it's an even match."

"This time, maybe. Next time, I'll win."

"Don't count on it." But even as Paul said those words he felt doubt. Never underestimate your opponent, Cotton had always warned him. For the second time in as many days, Lauren had unwittingly reminded him that he was about to make that fatal mistake. A chill rushed down his spine.

"There's E.J.," Lauren said. Her playful air vanished, and she resumed that efficient, businesslike air, appearing completely composed.

As composed as one could be while covered with sand, Lauren thought, struggling to regain her dignity. What had come over her? Had she really licked her finger? She'd acted cocky and, well, almost provocative—more like Jessie than herself. She had to pull herself together for E.J.'s sake. It was her responsibility to set the right tone.

Something inside her squirmed at the thought of her responsibilities. For an instant, she felt tremendously burdened, but then refocused on her more immediate problem.

Paul's presence put a kink in her hopes of discussing the merger proposal with E.J. today. Not that Lauren believed for one moment that Paul's appearance was a chance encounter. This wasn't a man who left anything to chance. She would stake her life on that.

E.J. caught sight of them and waved, and as they drew closer, Lauren could see the amused expression on his face. She prayed, without much hope, that he wouldn't make a big deal of her appearance, but his face-splitting grin told her there was no chance of that.

"What happened to you?" He followed the question with an outrageous hoot, then added, "Somehow I prefer this to the dress-for-success look."

You would, she thought testily, and was about to answer more appropriately when Paul said, "She got in the way of a long pass."

"Huh?"

"Galahad was chasing his Frisbee, and caught me instead," Lauren explained, gesturing toward the dog.

She could tell Paul was trying to spare her embarrassment and was surprised by this unexpected protective gesture. It warred with her impression of what his kind of man should be. The dog didn't fit, either. Somehow she'd never thought of corporate raiders as having dogs—or even loving mothers, for that matter.

Crouching next to the collie, she scratched his neck. His long coat felt like silk beneath her fingers, and he tilted back his head as if about to purr. When she moved her hand to his ears, he deposited a sloppy kiss on her wrist, catching the sleeve of her jacket with his tongue.

"No licking!" Paul corrected, then looked at Lauren. "If you aren't careful, that suit will be beyond help."

"I don't mind. Really." Lauren was thoroughly enjoying petting Galahad. She'd never been around dogs much because Cheri Lee disliked the shedding and the odor.

"Oh, I'm sorry," she said, realizing she'd forgotten her manners. "I haven't introduced you two. E.J., I'd like you to meet Paul Sherwood."

"I recognize you from your pictures," Paul said as the men shook hands.

"So you're the marauder," E.J. replied without malice, while Lauren cringed inside. "Somehow I expected you to look older."

"Did Lauren say I was a dishonest, potbellied wheeler-dealer?"

"Oh, she made much worse accusations than that."

Lauren stifled a reprimanding retort. Why couldn't E.J. just keep some things to himself?

Paul laughed, and his genuine amusement made Lauren realize he didn't quite see himself the way she saw him. "Actually, E.J., I'm just a businessman, doing what businessmen do."

"And doing it better than most, I'd say."

"I do okay." Paul laughed again as he meandered over to the bench. He didn't sit down and Lauren was certain it was because she was still standing. Good breeding, she thought.

It made her uncomfortable to see this human side of Paul. Like yesterday, when she'd noticed those silly socks he'd worn. Ninja Turtles on a grown man! Ridiculous!

So, why had she found it so charming?

"Don't you think so, Lauren?" Paul asked.

Think what? Was he reading her mind? She rearranged her features into her usual mask and tried to come up with a neutral comment.

"It depends."

"Exactly what does it being a nice day depend on?" Paul's mouth curved up, revealing his perfect teeth.

"Lauren's doing one of her quick recoveries," E.J. commented. A flush crept up her neck, and she became acutely aware of the scratchy sand inside her collar.

"I'm sorry," she said, fighting her embarrassment, and suddenly feeling grubby and defenseless. "I wasn't following."

"Well, it's still a nice day, don't you think?"

"Yes, perfectly lovely. But I think I'd better drive home and get out of this suit." Despite her misgivings about letting the two men talk alone, the damage was already done. In response to E.J's bewildered look, she added, "I'll call you. We can talk over dinner."

"Suits me, sis," E.J. replied, eyeing her speculatively.

She turned back to Paul, partly to avoid E.J.'s scrutiny. Her brother had an uncanny way of reading her mind. She thrust out a hand. "It was nice to see you again, Paul."

"You, too, Lauren." He held her hand a little longer than necessary, and said her name softly, faintly slurring the *r*. She'd never heard it spoken quite so beautifully, and her breath abruptly stopped.

Without another word, she swiveled on her heel and raced down the boardwalk. Off in the distance, parachutes still cluttered the skyline. An almost-painful yearning filled her chest.

"My sister is a remarkable woman," said E.J.

"Yes. I can see that," Paul agreed absently as he watched Lauren walk away. Her hips swayed seductively, at odds with the controlled image she presented.

"So, do you want to get down to business?" E.J. asked.

Paul snapped to attention. Business. Yes. That's what he was here for. "On the boardwalk at the beach?"

"Why not? Better than those stuffy conference rooms. Anyway, isn't that why you came here?"

"You've found me out." Paul grinned. He liked E. J. Afton. This was the kind of man he could make deals with.

"Not a brilliant deduction. I read a biography about you once. It mentioned you liked to approach people in their leisure time. Something about their being more amiable.''

''Well, are you?'' Paul asked.

''More amiable?''

Paul nodded at E.J.'s question. This was going even better than he'd hoped.

''No more than I would have been at the office.'' E.J., suddenly all business, wasn't teasing anymore. ''I see the merits in your offer, Paul, and I'm willing to examine it. But we have immense family loyalty—and loyalty to our employees, as well. Some of them have been with the company since the beginning. Besides, Lauren opposes it. She's worried you'll sell us out, and she's very influential with Mother. So, no matter what I think, you'll also have to win her over. That won't be easy.''

Again Paul nodded. True, it wouldn't be easy, but he was sure to win. Then an odd uncertainty gripped him. After encountering Cotton, he could no longer kid himself that this deal was only one of several, that failing wouldn't be the end of him. All his assets were heavily mortgaged. All his stocks had been purchased at maximum margin, and the smallest downward movement of the market would prompt a call from his broker asking for repayment of the loaned money. Paul teetered on the edge of bankruptcy and Cheri Lee Cosmetics was the only thing that could save him.

But today he'd seen a different side of Lauren. Her contagious laughter had poured over him like sparkling water, flooding into dark, empty places inside him that he'd never known existed. He wanted to see that side of her more often. Horning in on her company was a sure way to guarantee he wouldn't.

As he strained to banish this train of thought, a question came out of the blue. Was his interest in Lauren Afton strictly business?

The answer came just as quickly. If it wasn't, it had better be. His future depended upon it.

CHAPTER THREE

"IT WOULD REALLY HELP if you could come down to-day, Jessie. We have some business stuff to talk over." Lauren had been trying to reach her sister since the previous afternoon. This time she'd been lucky, managing to catch Jessie between excursions.

"Today's inconvenient, Lor. I have this fab date tonight and I'm cooking up something exotic." Jessie laughed. "To serve for dinner, of course."

Lauren smiled but refused to be swerved by her elusive sister. The matter of Paul Sherwood and his mouth-watering offer was too vital to be brushed off. "It's important. Otherwise, I wouldn't even ask."

"Couldn't we meet for lunch or something? You know I hate that place. Those smells make me sick."

"They're called fragrances, Jess." Lauren's grin widened as she recalled other, similar conversations.

"All I know is they turn my stomach. Lipstick, a little perfume—that's all the cosmetics any woman needs. I don't know how we even make a living selling all that other stuff."

"Well, fortunately for you, we do make a living. And it might not be a bad idea if—"

Her door opened and E.J. walked in carrying a stack of computer printouts that he unceremoniously dumped on her desk.

"Hold a sec," she said, looking up at her brother with a question in her eye. She signaled to E.J. to wait.

"Anyway, Jess, we've got to talk."

Jessie sniffed loudly. "Oh, Lord. Something's burning. I gotta go, sis. Get back to me and we can talk over lunch. Okay?"

Before Lauren could say another word, a dial tone buzzed in her ear. She sighed, knowing she'd probably never pin Jessie down. Hanging up the phone, she stared down at the printouts.

"What are these?"

"Financial statements for our last quarter." E.J. sat in a chair, looking at her expectantly. "They're a mess."

"That's old news. We talked about it over dinner last night, remember?"

"Sure, I do. But you left as stubborn as ever. I thought you needed a reminder." E.J. adjusted his white lab jacket and looked uncustomarily tense. "Lauren, you can't ignore the disaster we had with the Nebulae line. It cost the company a bundle and hurt our reputation, too. It was my mistake. I accept that. Now this is my chance to correct it."

"But, E.J., hundreds of people depend on us. Think of all those women who have devoted their lives to selling our product. If we let Paul Sherwood get a foot in the door, we risk losing this company. Then, where will all those people be?"

"Think of all the commissions due next quarter, Lauren. Over a half-million dollars' worth. Paul's right about one thing: we're losing our market. No matter how much you deny it, this company's headed for big trouble."

"The new Minx line will pull us out." Lauren didn't believe this for a moment, but hoped her brother would.

"Not if our suppliers keep collecting on delivery," E.J. countered.

A wry smile twisted Lauren's face. "Here I used to worry about you, buried in your lab. Poor E.J., I always say, he's the original absentminded professor. I never realized you were so up on profits, sales figures and expenses."

He'd never been before, and Lauren knew exactly where he'd gotten his information.

"Uh . . . Paul filled me in." E.J. shifted uncomfortably in his chair. "We met this morning. It was a real eye-opener."

"Did it ever occur to you his figures might be false?"

"No, he seems too up-front for that. Are they?"

Now it was Lauren's turn to shift. She smoothed down the lapel of her suit, then picked up a paperweight, a glass prototype of the container design for the ill-fated Nebulae product. She shifted this weighty symbol of their failing business from hand to hand before answering. "His numbers are pretty much on target."

Lauren knew E.J. would strike at this weakness in her position. He didn't disappoint her. "According to Paul, within a year or so we'll be lucky to find a buyer."

"We'll be lucky to *last* a year," she mumbled, running her hands wearily over her face. Then, even as she saw E.J.'s stunned expression, a rush of relief washed away her queasiness.

"Oh my God, Lauren," E.J. gasped. "I had no idea things were that bad. Does Mother know?"

E.J.'s question brought Lauren to a sudden realization. Part of the reason she'd kept this to herself was that it reflected so badly on their mother. But it would come out anyway, and she needed all the help she could get.

"She must know. But we've never talked about it." She set the paperweight down, stared into its glass depths a minute, then looked back up. "The stroke..."

"Yeah," E.J. said quietly. "Can I do anything, Lor?"

"At the moment you can just listen." Lauren then filled him in on the many problems she'd encountered since taking over her office, from data-processing snafus to inventory mix-ups. She talked about shortages and overstocks, inaccurate records, Equal Employment Opportunity Commission violations.

Afterward, feeling greatly unburdened, she pulled a file from a credenza behind her desk and handed it to E.J. Her business plan for Cheri Lee Cosmetics.

E.J. looked it over and whistled. "This is very good, Lauren. I'm impressed."

"Thanks," she said, smiling with pleasure. "As you can see, I already plan to do a lot of what Paul's proposing. But my first priority is getting the Minx product ready for market and pulling us out of the red."

"All the more reason to let Sherwood in," E.J. replied. "He has the financial backing and the know-how to help you."

Lauren sighed loudly. "He's a corporate raider! He learned at the knee of one of the biggest pirates of all time. I don't want him anywhere near our company."

She leaned forward earnestly, prepared to talk until midnight if that's what it took to turn E.J. around.

Unexpectedly, an image of Paul flitted through her mind. It occurred to her that, if not for him, she and E.J. wouldn't be having this conversation. Perhaps he'd done her a favor.

But could they trust him? She didn't think so.

"E.J., I agree that we need an investor. But not Paul. I'm convinced he'll sell us out."

"I don't think he will."

"Did he say so?"

"No, but—"

"But he'll sell in a flash," Lauren interrupted. "I'll never agree to giving him a controlling interest, and I can guarantee you Mother won't, either."

E.J. nodded. "That's what I told Paul. He didn't appear surprised. Said he'd settle for thirty-five percent."

Lauren ran a finger over her lip, thinking. So Paul was serious about the partnership. Or pretending to be. And he really couldn't wreak much havoc without a majority of the shares. But clearly, this wasn't a decision she could make without consulting the family.

With grave misgivings, she said, "Okay, E.J. I'll set up a shareholders' meeting. But only for the purpose of investigating Paul's offer. Don't count on anything. I'm going to do my best to get Mother to vote against it."

"That's what I told Paul. But he's persistent." E.J. stood and headed for the door. "He won't give up easily."

"Neither will I."

"Yeah. He's prepared for a duel of wits, but I asked him to be gentle...you being unarmed and all." Grinning devilishly, E.J. slipped out the door.

Would she feel better if she indulged her urge to throw the paperweight at the door? Deciding she wouldn't, Lauren smiled. They sometimes butted heads, she and E.J., but his offbeat humor also cheered her up. And she needed that, for there wasn't much to smile about at Cheri Lee Cosmetics these days.

E.J. had been gone less than ten minutes when Lauren's assistant buzzed. "Paul Sherwood's on line one."

Lauren slapped a fist into her open palm, certain E.J. had put Paul up to this call. Inhaling sharply, she picked up the phone. "This is Lauren."

"I had hoped so," Paul's husky voice said at the other end. "How are you today?"

"Fine," she replied, without much warmth.

"I know you must be busy. But I looked out my window and saw this wonderful day. The weekend's expected to be just as nice. I have a little boat moored on the island. How would you like to putt up the coast with me on Saturday and have lunch at my ranch?"

"I have lots of work to do this weekend and really don't have time." His offer was tempting. Their encounter on the beach showed her that Paul could be delightful company. But allowing herself to submit to that temptation would be foolish. She and Paul were opponents. That's the way it was, had to be.

"Surely you can take a Saturday off now and then, Lauren." Paul's voice, soft and persuasive, purred in her ear, weakening her resolve. "Don't you ever have fun?"

Fun? Deep in her head a puny voice asked when she'd last done that, and its plaintive echo caused a responding ache. She felt herself sink, losing control, and it frightened her.

"Come on, Lauren," Paul continued before she could answer. "We can talk about the partnership, so the day won't be a total waste."

The partnership. They could discuss the partnership. A new strategy formed in Lauren's mind. Yes, she'd go on that voyage. And when it was over, Paul Sherwood and his questionable offer would be history.

The throb in her chest eased, although which decision had done the trick—agreeing to spend the day with Paul, or realizing she'd found a way to defeat him—eluded her.

"I guess you're right. The day wouldn't be a total waste. What time do you have in mind?"

"Seven in the morning. Dress casual."

Trying to disguise her enthusiasm, Lauren agreed, then said goodbye. Receiver still in hand, she leaned back in her chair and stared thoughtfully across the room.

Clearly, she'd made a mistake by hiding the firm's unstable financial position. She'd tell Paul all—maybe even exaggerate a bit—for he'd certainly withdraw his offer when he realized how close they were to collapse. Then she and E.J. would quickly find another investor. A trustworthy one. She found herself looking forward to telling Paul about her troubles and seeing the interest fade from his eyes.

Then her thoughts drifted to their conversation at the beach. Although her undignified behavior had embarrassed her, the exchange of barbs had made her feel gloriously unchained. His wit was sharp, yet also gentle, with more maturity than she'd expected, given his boyish ways. Thinking about going another round made her feel alive, electric, empowered. One thing was certain—tomorrow would be anything but another dull day. A delicious shiver of excitement raced down her back.

And even as she mulled over the clever remarks she would use to send him on his way, her puny voice spoke again.

Afterward, she'd never see him again.

"MORE WINE?" JESSIE leaned over Bill Rosen's shoulder, holding a bottle aloft. The scent of spices—cinnamon, cloves—wafted from her body, overpowering the aroma of the stuffed capon on his plate. Strangely, he liked the way she smelled, even though he'd always been an outspoken critic of heavy perfume.

But everything about this evening was strange. This was supposed to have been a business dinner. He'd expected to discuss price/earning ratios, interest rates and amortization schedules: expected that she'd greet him in some sloppy outfit like the one she'd worn to lunch.

Instead, she wore a silky hostess set in an exotic print. A little overdone but, like the perfume, he discovered he liked it.

"Just a little," Bill replied, knowing he should refuse. He'd already had more than his quota of wine tonight. But he liked the way she kind of hovered over him, making him feel special, wanted. Yet it made him nervous, too and took his mind off the subject he'd come to discuss.

The stock. Her twenty-two plus percentage of Cheri Lee Cosmetics.

"Sit down, Jessie," he said. "You don't have to wait on me."

"It's my pleasure," Jessie replied, but she took her seat anyway and delicately picked up a knife and fork, then speared her capon with a vengeance. He wondered if she did everything like that—with a vengeance.

Bill found himself wanting to do the same. He didn't think he'd ever done anything intensely in his life. But now wasn't the time to start. There was, after all, this business matter.

He noticed she still wore no makeup. Or if she did, it was so subtle it didn't show. She really didn't need it. Her coloring was golden, with peachlike blushes on her cheeks. Her eyelashes, lowered now as she concentrated on the capon, were long and dark, fluttering against her cheeks.

A sudden heat flooded his body, and he shifted uncomfortably in his chair, wondering if he'd be able to eat this wonderful meal she'd prepared.

Get back to business, that was the ticket. Back to business.

"Have you had a chance to review the income figures I sent over?"

She looked up and he noticed the green flecks in her golden irises. They reminded him of a cat he'd once owned, back before he'd decided pets were impractical.

"Yes. They look good."

It had been a lovely cat.

"Good enough to make you interested?"

Lovely. Just like Jessie.

She didn't answer, but gestured for him to wait, then got up and went to a CD player to put in a disc. She moved like a cat, too, with long sinewy movements.

The music was decidedly New Age—flute and stormy surf—and as the sweet notes filled the air, Bill sank into the seductive melody while reminding himself he didn't like New Age music.

"Let's talk about the stock later," she said. "We have all night." Her voice harmonized with the music, was just as seductive. "Have you ever seen *The Rocky Horror Picture Show?*"

The question was enough to snap Bill out of his pleasant lethargy.

"The Rocky Horror Picture Show?" No, he'd never seen that movie. Never wanted to. The idea of sitting in a theater with hundreds of costumed kids who would chant and throw toilet paper horrified him.

Jessie laughed. "Goodness. You'd think I was suggesting a porno flick. Have you led a sheltered life?"

"Not that sheltered," he replied, squaring his shoulders. Her question made him feel old and out-of-it, even though he knew Jessie was no more than five years younger than he. "Are you suggesting we go?"

"If you can stay up that late. There's a midnight showing at the mall down the street. It could be fun." Her smile was slightly taunting, but in a gentle way.

"I think I can manage." He smiled also, suddenly pleased with himself. Could be he might enjoy the film very much. Especially with Jessie. And, the good Lord knew, he'd done crazier things in the course of wooing a reluctant seller.

Later, though, he wasn't sure if he had ever done anything crazier. Jessie had made him remove his coat and tie, had then unbuttoned his shirt collar and rolled up his sleeves. Even now, as they entered the theater and he tried not to stare at the girls in their black corsets, garter belts and theatrical makeup, he could feel the warmth of her fingers on his skin where she'd touched him nearly an hour earlier. Was this woman some kind of sorceress? He felt totally in her power.

But what amazed him more was how much he enjoyed himself. He chanted in unison with Jessie and the crowd during appropriate lines of the movie, and even laughed when a roll of toilet paper landed on his head and he become tangled in the sheets.

"Goodness, I've been tepee'd," he'd wisecracked.

Jessie laughed uproariously—a lusty, contagious laugh—and Bill found himself wondering about a woman who was independently wealthy and had no apparent goals. What kind of life would that be? All he knew was she seemed to enjoy it.

Later—at nearly three in the morning—they stood at the door of Jessie's second-story garage apartment. Her cheeks were still flushed with laughter, and as Bill gazed into eyes that were reflecting the moon, he wondered about the apartment, too. Why would she live in what was clearly the servants' quarters? Wouldn't she be more comfortable in the house with her mother?

But as these thoughts flitted through his mind, the silence between them grew longer, and he realized that while he was lost in her eyes, Jessie was regarding him with open curiosity.

"Repressed," she said. "You've just been repressed." She moved an inch closer. Bill could feel her breath against the skin left bare by his open collar.

"Repressed? I suppose that's one way of looking at it." Not that he hadn't been called that before, but this was the first time he'd ever taken it seriously. Or considered it might be a flaw. He found himself wanting to prove to Jessie that he wasn't repressed. At the same time, his rigid, "repressed" self kept reminding him this was a business meeting.

"Jessie," he said, meaning to ask her about the stock.

"Yes?" she answered breathily. Her lips parted in what looked like anticipation.

"Nothing," Bill said, and before he knew what he was doing, he placed his hands on her shoulders, pulled her against him and smothered her open mouth with his own.

She tasted as exotic as she looked—of schnapps and peppermint candy. He slid his tongue tentatively between her open lips, and her own entwined with it. He exploded at that aggressiveness, never having experienced it before, and ran his hands down the full length of her spine, bringing her close, close, closer. A faint rumble of pleasure purred in her throat and the nearly intangible vibrations seemed to shatter his body.

And as the kiss deepened, so did a gut-level fear. This woman was impossible. Impertinent. Unconventional. Everything he'd never wanted. But he wanted her now, with a vengeance.

Vengeance. Passion. Now he knew what they were. Dear God, he hoped he'd survive. He struggled to regain reason.

Finally, it returned. Although it was Jessie who ended the kiss, not he. She didn't step out of his arms. He didn't release her.

"You are the cutest thing I've ever seen," she murmured against his throat.

"You, too," he muttered, hating himself for meaning it. This was just some kind of hot flame, he reassured himself. It would burn itself out. But, for now, he had to remember to complete his mission.

"Jessie, this may be a bad time...."

She tilted her head and looked at him questioningly.

"But have you decided about the stock yet?"

He saw her eyes darken in the moonlight. The green flecks vanished and a sheen covered their surface.

She pulled away and searched through her little bag for keys. He started to take them from her, to offer to open the door, terribly sorry he'd brought up the subject. He'd hurt her. He hadn't meant to do that, only to be true to who he was.

"I can do it." She pulled back from his grip, not angrily, just firmly, then turned and unlatched the door. Opening it, she stepped inside.

"Good night, Bill."

"Jessie—"

"I told you, I want to think about it. I'll get back to you after I have." She closed the door and left him standing alone on the little square landing.

He felt like a total heel.

PAUL HAD PREDICTED correctly, Lauren thought. The morning was beautiful, even though November was fast approaching. She suspected the fog would burn off completely by the time they launched.

He'd picked her up promptly at seven and had successfully hidden his smile at the huge carryall she toted. Almost.

"What all's in here?" he asked, as he stowed it in the trunk.

"Oh, sunscreen, a change of shoes, a heavier jacket and a few odds and ends."

"I think you've worn everything you need. We've got most of that other stuff on the boat. Sorry I forgot to tell you."

His comment made Lauren feel overdressed. So did his attire. She had on perfectly creased white slacks, a spiffy tank top with skinny blue stripes, and a darker blue nautical jacket. The ultimate boating outfit, she had thought.

In contrast, Paul's clothing was similar to what he'd worn that day on the beach, although he'd thrown on a rather scruffy sweat jacket over it all. Lauren considered inconspicuously shedding her jacket but decided it was too cold. As she waited for Paul to open her door, she told herself that *he* was the one who had dressed inappropriately. After all, this was a business meeting.

"You look absolutely gorgeous!" Paul said as he seated her in his Mercedes. The genuine admiration in his tone halted Lauren's internal grumbling, and she looked up at him in surprise. Seeing his blue eyes sparkle with appreciation, Lauren smiled. Paul certainly injected enthusiasm into everything he did, including his compliments.

The smile remained on her face as Paul shut the door and headed for the other side, and widened when she felt a soft nudge on the back of her neck.

"Galahad! How ya doing, boy?"

The tom-tom flopping of his tail told her he was doing fine, and she turned, burying her head in his coat, forgetting for a moment that she might muss her hair.

Paul smiled, too, as he got into the driver's seat. Now that was a sight he'd never expected to see—Lauren Afton with her arms around his dog, her perfect face lost amid Galahad's fluffy coat. He hoped she didn't smear her makeup, but then, on second thought, maybe he hoped she would. She seemed more human to him when she was slightly flawed, the way she'd been on the beach with her suit all sandy and her hair disheveled.

When she'd answered the door of her upscale patio home, his heart had leaped a trillion miles. Lord, she'd looked lovely. And very shipshape. He'd felt like a country bumpkin and had wished he'd taken more care with his own appearance. Yet he'd noticed her uneasiness when he'd commented on her bag. It struck him, suddenly, that maybe Lauren wasn't quite as confident and in control as she seemed.

How could that be? How could this vision beside him lack confidence?

For the first time since they'd met, Paul began consciously considering Lauren Afton, the person, instead of Lauren Afton, chief executive officer of Cheri Lee Cosmetics. What kind of childhood had she had? Was Cheri Afton a loving mother? Had Ellis, Sr., been an attentive father? Had she been devastated when he'd died? Did she have a pet?

The questions paraded through Paul's head until he impatiently smothered them. He'd invited Lauren on this cruise to nail down the stock acquisition. Why was he suddenly so interested in delving beneath the surface of her personality? It was the surface Lauren who would "yea" or "nay" this deal.

He turned, intent on asking a leading question about her business activities.

"Do you have any pets?" he asked instead.

What a curious expression he wore, thought Lauren. A slightly baffled, possibly annoyed frown creased his forehead. Had she done something to cause it?

"No," she replied, noting Paul's quick recovery and concluding she wasn't the cause for his frown. How could she have been? She hadn't said a word to him since he'd gotten into the car. "Not unless you consider a small tank of tropical fish, pets. It doesn't seem fair to have a cat or dog when I'm home so little."

"An aquarium? I have a large one at the ranch. Maybe you'd like to see it when we're there?"

Lauren said she would and they entered an interesting discussion about fish, coral, tropical reefs and various methods of seasoning tanks. At his suggestion, Lauren considered adding a few fish to balance out her little "ecosystem," as Paul called it.

Before she knew it they were at a pier near the tip of Coronado Island and Paul had pulled into a parking lot.

"Here we are," he announced, opening his door and getting out. Without waiting, Lauren opened her side, stood and stretched, then inhaled the air. She felt excited about the day ahead. Paul might be lots of things, but boring wasn't one of them.

While she waited, Paul got her carryall, then lowered the front seat for Galahad. The dog lumbered out and Lauren detected a lack of energy in his movements. The poor thing seemed tired.

"Don't you feel good, Galahad?" She bent and stroked his fur.

"He's just groggy from the ride," Paul commented quickly. Too quickly, and with just an edge of testiness. Was something wrong with Galahad? The possibility made Lauren's chest ache, and she decided not to ask.

Paul slung her bag over his shoulder and called for Galahad to heel. "This way," he said as he approached her. He placed a giant hand on her back and gently guided her to the pier. "My boat's down there." He nodded to his right, where several enormous yachts were moored. Lauren was sure he didn't mean one of those. His boat must be hidden between them.

She yielded to the pressure on her waist and accompanied Paul onto the pier. "Here we are," he said, stopping. "Welcome to the *Gypsy Rose*."

"'Little boat'!" Lauren said in amazement. "My Lord, that thing must be a hundred feet long."

"One hundred twenty-three, precisely. But I don't like to brag." A teasing smile played around Paul's lips.

"I guess not." Lauren laughed, unable to help herself. When he'd asked her to cruise with him, she'd pictured a modest cabin cruiser, not this behemoth. "Truth is, I've never been on a private boat this big. How large is the crew?"

"Four, including the cook and cabin boy. But they're very unobtrusive."

Unobtrusive? What did Paul have in mind? What was this thrill of anticipation permeating her body? Her chest tightened and she fought an urge to take a very deep breath.

"Not too unobtrusive, I hope," she said stiffly.

Uh-oh, I've done it, thought Paul. He hadn't meant to sound suggestive, but looking at Lauren's instant wooden reaction, he realized that's how he'd come across.

"They won't be listening when we talk business. I was sure you might worry about that." *Quick recovery, Paul,* he told himself, pleased when Lauren's expression relaxed.

"Very thoughtful. Shall we board?"

Paul nodded and led her up the ramp. Her playful moods were so fleeting and fragile, as if some unseen hand were wagging an admonishing finger, reminding her to stick to business. Did she ever just go with the flow? Somehow he doubted it, and wondered why he found her so fascinating. He wanted to churn that whimsy inside her, let it bubble into a burst of spontaneity. Ah, how delightful that would be.

These impulses disturbed him. His plans for Cheri Lee Cosmetics were entirely at odds with hers. Eventually she would despise him. Unfortunately, he wasn't good at ignoring his desires, even when they were counterproductive. But this time, he told himself firmly, he would play it smart, squelch this attraction immediately, and keep his attention on his goal.

That way, no one would get hurt.

Only an act of will kept him from physically jumping. Where had that weird thought come from? Of course, no one would get hurt. This wasn't about people, it was about property. But as he looked down at Lauren, a feeling of remorse seeped through his body.

He knew then that he never wanted to cause her pain. But so much was at stake. This challenge was bigger than he'd ever imagined. Maybe so big it would bury him.

Ridiculous! This was all a high-stakes game. In the long run it meant nothing. He smiled at Lauren.

"Race you to the top," he challenged.

At her bemused nod, he took off running.

CHAPTER FOUR

PAUL GAVE LAUREN a steaming cup of coffee, then settled her on the top deck while he saw to casting off. He offered to stow her carryall for her, but she clung to it like a lifeline. It contained her company's salvation. She'd stayed up late the night before, doing creative accounting. A few debts here, a few losses there, and Cheri Lee Cosmetics's profitability was reduced by a staggering amount. Surely this would do the trick, put Paul Sherwood on a new track, far away from Cheri Lee Cosmetics.

As she waited, the boat set out. She sipped her coffee, taking in the majestic beauty of the ocean. *The free-fallers must be out early,* she thought, noting the familiar puffs of parachutes on the horizon.

"Pretty, isn't it?" Paul's voice came from behind her. She looked over her shoulder at him.

"I was watching the sky divers. I've always wanted to do that, but never had the nerve."

"Really?" asked Paul, taking a seat across from her. "I could take you up someday if you'd like."

"Oh, sure," Lauren said, then laughed. "Anytime." So he was also a pilot. Somehow that didn't surprise her. "How long have you been flying?"

"I don't fly. I jump."

"You jump?" A nervous titter escaped Lauren's lips.

"Uh-huh. So you see, I really *could* take you up. What do you say? First you'd need a little ground training. But that doesn't take long."

Lauren looked away, thinking of that day. Remembering her paralyzing fear, trembling limbs, frozen face. Should she confess? She had never told anyone, not even Jessie or E.J. Continuing to watch the jumpers in the distance, she said hesitantly, "I tried it once...."

"Didn't you like it?" Paul stared at her with avid interest, something akin to surprise on his face.

"I...uh...I backed out at the last minute." She had no idea why she was telling Paul. "I was always sorry."

An understanding smile crossed his face. "Happens to a lot of people. You know what they say. Try, try again."

"Maybe..."

"Well, my offer's for real, Lauren. If you change your mind, want to try it again, just let me know. But don't feel bad about backing out. The first jump scared the bejabbers out of me."

"But what was it like? After, I mean. While you were up there, looking down."

"Incredible. Absolutely incredible."

Paul grinned, and his eyes, dreamy with pleasant memories, told Lauren all. She had missed a transcendent experience. Still, she'd been so frightened. "Maybe I'll do it...someday."

"You won't be disappointed, I promise." He turned his head in the direction of footsteps. A white-jacketed young man approached. "Manuel, my man. Glad to see you." Then his attention returned to Lauren.

"Breakfast's here. It's nearly five hours to my ranch. We might as well dig in, enjoy ourselves."

Five hours! Lauren's heart took a nosedive. She'd planned to cruise up there, have lunch, show Paul the documents, then skip out as quickly as possible. But they'd be together until after dinner. Should she wait until then or get it over with now? And, Lord, what would she do for the next twelve hours or so? Every time the man got within ten feet of her, her heart skipped ridiculously.

Fortunately, Manuel's activities allowed her to collect her thoughts before being expected to resume conversation. After setting their places, Manuel unobtrusively put bowls of fruit—lush strawberries, ripe melons, grapes—and baskets of various breads on the table, then disappeared. Lauren chose to eat first, decide later.

Just gazing at the spread of food made her mouth water. The strawberries nearly overflowed their container, glistening with moisture, little seeds standing out in shallow bas-relief. Lauren leaned forward, picked up one of the deliciously swollen fruits, and closed her teeth around it.

The tart flavor stung her taste buds, and she closed her eyes in appreciation. Pure heaven. She lost herself in the flavor. She hadn't tasted a strawberry like this in years. Its generous juices filled her mouth, and then, to her horror, trickled down her chin.

Paul stared in utter fascination as Lauren's even teeth clamped down on the strawberry. In that moment, with her eyes lidded, a halo of hair blowing about her face, she exuded an unrestrained sensuality.

As he watched crimson juices etch a narrow path near the corner of her mouth, he felt a thrust of desire, a stirring between his legs, that nearly overcame him. Aghast, Paul plucked a linen napkin from the table, then reached out to dab at the spot.

Lauren's eyes shot open. She brought her hand sharply to her mouth and it collided with Paul's. An embarrassed flush rising to her face, she hastily pulled away. Paul grinned lazily.

"Looks like you're already starting," he said, dabbing at the offending juices on her skin. His voice seemed to envelop her. As Lauren's senses heightened, she knew her flush didn't stem purely from embarrassment.

"St-starting what?" There she was, losing control again. It was frightening. Exhilarating. Just like skydiving.

"To enjoy yourself." Finished with his task, he carelessly dropped the napkin back onto the table. Then, reaching for a berry, he said, "Here, have another."

"Uh, no, thank you. One was enough." Lauren could hear the tenseness in her voice and hoped Paul wouldn't notice. In an effort to distract him, she rushed on, her postponed decision now made. "I think this would be the perfect time to go over your offer again."

Paul felt his smile fade as he straightened his posture. He'd seen a spirit of adventure in her when she'd spoken about skydiving. He'd seen anger, seen humor, that day at the beach. And now he'd seen sensuality.

But it was merely an illusion. This woman didn't know how to simply enjoy. Business was all she thought about. And he really wasn't experiencing this disappointment—it was only that she'd caught him off guard.

"Now's as good a time as any, I suppose," he replied offhandedly, wondering why he felt reluctant to discuss something so important to him. This was the reason he'd invited her aboard, wasn't it? "I'm assuming E.J. discussed our conversation with you. If so, I'm curious about your reaction."

"Are you sure you want to do this, Paul?"

"What a strange question," he said bluntly, still struggling with his annoyance. She stroked the curve of her upper lip, as Paul had often observed her doing. His annoyance disappeared as he imagined feeling those smooth fingers stroking *his* lip. "I wouldn't have made the offer if I wasn't sure," he added, forcing his attention back to their discussion.

"There are some things you probably don't know, since our financial records aren't made public." Lauren leaned over and pulled a folder from her carryall. With a sphinxlike smile she handed it to him, then relaxed into her chair. "After you've seen this, you might change your mind."

Keeping an eye on Paul with her peripheral vision, she pretended to be taking in the view. These papers would do the job, she was sure of it. All she needed to do was appear indifferent. Indifference, however, wasn't easy. As he read, his head was silhouetted against the morning sky, emphasizing the strong angle of his brow, the rugged lines of his chin.

In a matter of minutes he snapped the folder shut. Lauren returned her gaze to him, firmly yanking her thoughts back to the subject. "Well?"

"I already know this, except for a couple of surprises. Maybe I'll check them out, maybe not. Nevertheless, my offer still holds." He looked at her with steady eyes, his face impassive, and Lauren was taken aback by his unusually forceful delivery. "Thirty-five percent of Cheri Lee Cosmetics. In return you get twenty-five million. Considering what I've seen here, I don't see how you can refuse."

She felt as if he were moving in for the kill, ready to rip her throat out, and now she knew why he was considered so formidable. She also knew, with a sudden flash of insight, that his prime intention was, and always had been, to sell off the company assets. Why else would he want to buy into a nearly bankrupt firm?

"Why do you do this, Paul?"

"What? Offer you a ton of money?" Paul drew his brows together. "You make it sound sinful."

"No. Why do you push yourself in where you're not wanted? Force people to sell when they don't want to?" And why, she asked herself, did understanding Paul matter so much?

"They're only companies." Paul plucked a grape from a basket, placed it in his mouth, staring at Lauren quizzically as he chewed. "I'm not selling anyone into slavery. What's the big deal?"

"What about people's jobs?" She brushed back her hair, a losing battle on the windy deck.

"They find other jobs. Or more often, keep the same job. Different employer, that's all."

He picked up another grape, and Lauren sensed he was attempting to avoid this conversation. Had he glimpsed the ramifications of what he did and been unable to face them?

"Look, Lauren. The object is making money. But the main thing is the game. The bottom line is, it's damned exciting. You deal yourself in, it's hard to deal out. It's the lure of the game that keeps me."

"The lure of the game?" Lauren deliberately became as forceful as Paul had been earlier. "I'm *so* reassured by your lofty motives. But Cheri Lee Cosmetics is not a pawn to me, nor are my employees. We're a family, working together. And I promise you, Paul, I will not let you tear it apart. I *can* refuse your offer. I *do* refuse your offer."

"Whoa, Lauren." Paul raised a placating hand. There was a quiet power in his gesture that was both controlled and menacing. "I didn't mean to offend you. But look what I can do for you. Once word's out I'm backing you, you'll return to thirty-day payment status with your suppliers. Your banks will increase your lines of credit. Even without the money I'll invest, your cash flow will immediately improve. Besides," Paul continued, "E.J. already favors this merger. I think he's going to push for a shareholders' vote on the matter."

Oh, Paul was persuasive. And everything he said was true.

She'd lost this round. What was her next move? This was just another deal to Paul. To Lauren, the company was her life. Could she use it as a bet in a whirling, high-stakes game?

Did she have a choice?

Her mind spun, reviewing the benefits Paul had stated. Suddenly, an idea formed: Paul was clearly trying to use her, to use E.J., to use the company.

Then her idea crystallized.

What if I use him instead?

Paul's name and reputation would open up credit and restore credibility with their suppliers. If she could keep him hanging around for just a little while, she'd have all the resources she needed to carry out her business plan. Then she could send Paul packing. Because—no matter how attractive, how charming, how interesting Paul was; no matter that she felt this frequent impulse to throw herself in his arms; no matter how profitable his offer might be—she would never sell him any part of Cheri Lee Cosmetics. Not for love or money.

Lauren tilted her head provocatively. "Believe it or not, Paul, you've convinced me."

"I have?" Paul jerked his head in her direction, dropping the grape onto his plate.

"Yes," she said definitively, ignoring the little stab of guilt her lie spawned. "I'm going to recommend we accept your offer. However—" Lauren paused, finding her guilt dissipating and beginning to enjoy Paul's bemused expression "—what I suggest is that you begin working inside the company right away. Get familiar with how we do things while we work out the details of the merger. The truth is, it may take some time convincing my mother."

"How much time?" Paul lifted a thick, blond eyebrow.

"Oh, not long," Lauren replied blithely. "We should have the deal done by, say, the first of the year."

Two months! Paul struggled to hide his dismay, knowing he should be overjoyed. He hadn't expected Lauren to concede this much, had thought his success rested with E.J. But the time frame could be a killer.

He needed some demonstrable proof that he was on track to give to his nervous investors.

"Fair," he finally said, picking up the grape he'd dropped and rolling it between his fingers. "We've got a deal. I'll place an announcement in the trade papers." *That should make my investors happy.*

Lauren nodded her agreement. *That should make my creditors happy.* "Just make sure it's clear that we're *negotiating* an agreement."

"What else?" Paul swiveled and raised an arm, then turned back to Lauren. "Since that's decided, let's eat breakfast."

Within a few moments, Manuel brought a tempting array of eggs, pancakes, sausage and plenty of steaming syrup.

As she settled in to eat, the only blot on Lauren's victory was the periodic niggle of guilt in her conscience. She soothed it by telling herself that failure wouldn't hurt Paul. After all, who got serious about a game? And he was already richer than sin. He didn't need her company to get any richer.

Finally convinced, she dug into her meal, highly pleased with herself. As they ate, Paul turned the conversation to lighter topics, and Lauren discovered that he liked baseball, liked ballet and was a diehard James Michener fan.

Lauren responded that she had a hard time getting excited about the labor pains of an island, and preferred Stephen King, herself.

Paul made a disgusted face. Lauren laughed, and for the rest of the trip they never stopped talking—or laughing. As the sun reached its apex, the boat pulled into a small harbor that was actually the border of Paul's ranch. He seemed pleased to be there, and as

Lauren gazed at his happy face it occurred to her that he'd be in her life for at least two more months.

Her heart leaped gladly.

LAUREN STOOD AT THE railing, propping her elbows on the polished brass of the *Gypsy Rose,* feeling snug and warm inside a full-length down coat that Paul had dug up for her. A breeze, cool on her cheeks, filled her with amazing energy, even though it was well after midnight. Their return cruise was almost over and the lights of the San Diego shoreline competed with a brilliant blanket of stars in the sky.

She looked over at Paul, who was standing beside her in a nearly identical posture, and wondered if Jessie's "fab" date had been anywhere as glorious as hers. A little internal start reminded her that this wasn't a *date,* it was a business meeting. But it felt like a date. Behind them, an empty champagne bottle still jutted from its cooler, drained glasses sitting on either side. The day had never slowed down. They'd talked, they'd laughed, they'd even danced to music piped up from below.

Lunch had been perfect, served by Paul's unobtrusive help, but for the life of her, Lauren could no longer remember what they'd eaten. He'd shown her his aquarium—a full wall of tropical reefs that put her little freestanding unit to shame. Then, somehow, he'd found riding clothes that fit her, and they'd gone on horseback to tour his ranch, then visited his kennels where she'd romped with his collies.

Now, as she stood here sharing the horizon with him in a silence that was as comfortable as their conversations, she became caught up in admiration of his rugged good looks. The wind brushed his hair, baring his forehead and revealing his forceful profile, which reminded Lauren of a head on a Roman coin. Her stomach fluttered and she became acutely aware that her excitement was escalating to full-fledged anticipation.

Paul, now aware she was looking at him, turned his head and a slow, pleased smile spread across his face, bringing another flutter to her stomach. His approving gaze warmed Lauren in a way she hadn't felt in a long time. There had been no one in her life for several years. Not since she'd broken her engagement to a man who'd been perfect for her, or so everyone had said—same background, same tastes, same dignified manner. But something important—something she couldn't even quite identify—had been missing, and a few weeks before the wedding, she'd called it off.

Now, as Paul stood beside her in the moonlight, she glimpsed the essence of that missing element. An invisible magnetism tugged at her, made her want to move closer. And the closer she got to him, the more intense the pull became.

"How nice to stand here and just gaze at the moon," she said, wanting to break this oh-so-intimate silence and ignore the basic physics of opposite poles attracting.

"Glad you're enjoying yourself. I suspect you don't get to do that very often."

"Do what?"

"Relax. Enjoy yourself."

Lauren turned to look at the moon again, reflecting a moment on Paul's words. "No, I suppose I don't. My life's been fairly demanding since Mother's illness. It hasn't left much time for fun."

"Couldn't you have hired someone to do day-to-day management, give yourself a little slack?"

"Well...no, not at the time." Lauren's mind drifted back to the week after her mother's stroke, when she'd taken the helm. "You see," she continued, "there was so much to straighten out when I first took over...." Momentarily she forgot herself, forgot where she was. All of what happened in those first days, every terrible second, nearly tumbled out in a rush.

Quickly, self-protectively, she changed the subject. "But, what about you? Surely you couldn't be as successful as you are and still take time to relax."

"Actually," Paul replied, "fun is my first priority. That's what it's all about. What's the use of making money—having money—if you don't enjoy it?"

"Why, for your family, of course," Lauren responded quickly. "For their future."

"I don't have any family." His blue eyes darkened, and the moonlight revealed lines of sadness around them that Lauren hadn't noticed before. She felt a sympathetic pang.

"My mother died last year." He turned his head toward the sea. "Cancer."

"Oh. I'm so sorry, Paul." She reached out her hand and placed it over his. It was cold, as was hers, and at the place where their skin met a sudden warmth stirred. How easily the meeting of two people could warm the cold places inside them both, she thought, as heat pervaded her hand.

"She was a great mother. I miss her." He turned her hand over, entwined his fingers with hers. His grip tightened for a moment, then relaxed. "But there are times when I think I was a bit much for her. After everything started happening she seemed befuddled most of the time.''

"Started happening?'' Lauren wasn't sure what he was talking about, but he seemed so sad, she wanted to draw him out. Inside, a bell went off. *You don't want to know about this man,* it warned. But she did, she really did, so she ignored it. "Did something bad happen?''

"Not unless you consider being a star contestant on 'Wizard Kids' bad.''

"You were on 'Wizard Kids'?''

"Yep,'' he responded, his mood lightening. "Some twenty years ago. I was not quite seven and the longest-running contestant in my age group. Ever.'' He didn't seem to be bragging. Quite the contrary, he spoke matter-of-factly, as though this happened to everyone.

"You were *that* Paul? That bratty little genius kid?'' Lauren remembered watching the show as a girl, being irritated by the cocky little boy who was always first with the answers and usually spouted some smart-aleck joke to boot.

"Goodness, Lauren, and here I thought you were always unfailingly polite.'' If Paul hadn't laughed, Lauren might have taken him seriously. Still, she couldn't help but wonder why she was being so outspoken.

"Sorry,'' she said, with a rueful grin. "You were kind of cute, but you also reminded me of my own bratty little brother. He hasn't changed much.''

"Have *I?*'' Disengaging his fingers from hers, he engulfed her hand between both of his. "Have I changed, Lauren?''

Lord, her hand felt good inside his! He'd almost jumped at the jolt her touch had caused. Even now, a delicious electricity coursed through him. Yet, he'd vowed to avoid this.

"Yes," she replied. "You've changed." Her voice was husky, throaty. Paul sensed an invitation there, wondered if he only imagined it, then realized he was hopelessly ensnared. He saw her sway slightly, step closer to him as, almost of their own volition, his feet also moved forward.

"For one thing," she whispered, "you did something about that scruffy hair." She reached up, smoothed his fluttering strands into place. Paul closed the final gap between them and lowered his mouth to hers.

Don't do this! Lauren's mind screamed. But at the first touch of Paul's lips, the scream drifted far away. Like his hands, his mouth was cool, but when it touched hers, warmth flowed, flooding her body. It seeped through her face, her scalp, her neck, down her torso into her toes. She shuddered from pleasure, sliding closer to Paul. When he dropped her hand and pulled her hard against his body, the explosive energy pulsating in her chest shattered her into pieces.

Sweet, so sweet, Paul thought. Like chocolate fudge or cotton candy. Compelled to taste more of her, he flicked his tongue against the narrow separation of her lips. She opened for him, meeting his tongue with her own in a maddening dance. She lifted her arms and placed her hands behind his neck, tangling her fingers in his hair, pressing aggressively against him. He felt that familiar stir between his legs and the exquisite pleasure the pressure of her hips created.

It was only a kiss, he reminded himself, taken off guard by the sudden physical reaction. But his body didn't care what his mind thought. He ran his hands down the full length of her back in frantic, possessive motions that he feared would offend this reserved woman even while he knew he couldn't stop.

When he pushed up her coat and clasped her buttocks, she moaned—a rich, deep sound that nearly drove him wild.

Then she pulled away with short jerky movements. A protesting groan escaped Paul's lips, which Lauren silenced with little feather kisses as she slithered out of the down coat. Dropping it unceremoniously on the deck, she nestled back into his arms.

Was this what he'd sensed behind her composed exterior? This immense, wild abandon? Lord, she had needs. Driving, powerful needs. As did he.

He drew her closer, lifted her, and with legs weak from desire, staggered toward the nearby deck chair. All the while, he rained kisses on her forehead, her closed eyes, her neck. Small whimperlike mews came with ever-increasing intensity from her throat. Her hands drew frenzied paths on his shoulders.

"Lord, you're beautiful," Paul whispered in her ear as he sank onto the chaise longue. He leaned back, holding her in his lap, nearly unhinged by the pressure of her weight against his full erection.

So, this was what had been missing, thought Lauren, deliberately squirming on top of Paul, glorying in the effect she was having. Chemistry. Elemental, volatile chemistry.

Even as she reclaimed Paul's lips, she told herself she shouldn't be doing this. Theirs was a business relationship. They were moving far beyond the bounds.

But the total mindless pleasure of his artful hands wiped out all reason.

She wanted him. She ached for what their union promised. As his tongue drove deep into her mouth, she claimed it, held it, then nipped it with gentle bites.

Boldly she turned, straddling him, feeling his hardness between her legs. With a strangled whimper, Paul slipped down the strap of her tank top, revealing her full breast. She gazed down at him, then. His eyes were closed, his lips parted with hunger. His breath came in ragged spurts. "You're beautiful too," she crooned.

At the sound of her voice he opened his eyes. Their gazes locked. Intimate, so intimate. And the power of that intimacy shook Lauren like an orgasm. All pretenses, all games, were stripped away. Tenderness, vulnerability, a capacity for love, were revealed in the blue depths of his eyes with a poignancy that was painful—and shattering.

With lightning speed, she swung her legs off Paul and swiveled to sit on the edge of the chaise longue. Her back to him, she pulled the straps of her top back onto her shoulders.

"What are we doing?" She spoke in a hoarse whisper, unable to find her real voice. She felt embarrassment. She felt guilt. She had nearly made love to Paul. Made love, despite her deceitful plans.

"What men and women often do," Paul responded with a choked laugh. "At least, I thought that's what we were doing."

Yet, despite his considerable physical discomfort, Paul felt relieved. Their locked gaze—mere moments earlier—had evoked a powerful emotional shock. Her silvery-blue eyes had glowed, seemed to draw him inside her to a core that threatened to swallow him.

It was scary, very scary. And behind it had come a niggle of guilt that Paul tried to ignore.

Lauren drew herself up and stood, turning to look at him. "Well, it wasn't very sensible," she said stiffly. "After all, this isn't appropriate behavior for potential business partners. We'll have to remember that in the future."

Now Paul laughed fully, unable to hold himself back even in the face of Lauren's offended expression. "Oh, Lauren, you're precious. We practically tore each other's clothes off. Now you're primly reminding me that we acted inappropriately. Darlin', we have a big problem. I don't think we can ignore it."

Woodenly, Lauren turned, walked over to pick up the coat she'd feverishly discarded earlier. Paul saw her shiver as she slipped back into it. She was cold, he realized. And probably hurt.

As usual, he'd been a big, insensitive lug. But damned, he was hurt too. The kind of sparks they'd ignited off each other didn't happen every day. Passing up this consummation was painful indeed. But he couldn't deny her logic. Considering their fledgling and deceptive business arrangements, making love did seem out of the question.

But, damn, she was one sexy woman!

He got up and moved toward her. She stood at the railing, staring out, her arms wrapped around her body.

"We're almost to the harbor," she said listlessly. A sheaf of hair, broken loose from its restraining pins, framed her face and shimmered with silvery reflections of the moon.

He grasped her shoulders and turned her toward him. She shuddered beneath his touch and Paul wondered if she had suddenly found him repulsive. He dropped his hands. "I'm sorry," he said. "You're right. Our relationship doesn't have room for this. I shouldn't have let it start."

Lauren forced a smile, wondering if Paul realized that even his sexless touch on her shoulders had sent a rush of desire through her. She tried to tell herself it was lust, but somehow wasn't quite convinced. His boyish apology, so protective and implying he was entirely to blame, touched a soft spot in her that she usually kept hidden.

"Thanks," she replied, honesty not allowing her to say otherwise. "But we both know this happened by mutual consent."

"So, by mutual consent, we'll make sure it doesn't happen again." Stepping back, he put out his hand. "Agreed?"

Keeping the forced smile firmly on her face, Lauren took his hand. "Agreed."

As a charged current passed between their joined hands, Lauren knew this was one promise she might not be able to keep. Chemistry often overwhelmed common sense. Nevertheless, no matter what might come about between her and Paul, she was committed to her deceptive course.

There simply was no alternative.

CHAPTER FIVE

"SIT DOWN, MOTHER. I'll get you coffee." Lauren gently steered her mother to a spacious love seat.

"Don't treat me like an invalid, dear," Cheri chided in a genteel Southern drawl. Nevertheless, she allowed Lauren to guide her.

Lauren ignored the comment. Even the thought of Cheri Lee being an invalid twisted her stomach. Cheri Lee didn't *look* disabled. Having diligently followed her rehabilitation regimen, she'd overcome the slight drooping of one side of her face several months earlier.

Today, her face, still firm and full of animation despite the inevitable wrinkles that age brought, was tastefully made up. Her herringbone silk suit fitted her slim figure becomingly. She held a cane in one hand.

Her cane wasn't the usual metal monstrosity. Its handle was silver, formed into a lion's head, and the staff was smooth, polished wood down to the four rubber-tipped feet. Only Lauren's mother could make the effects of a stroke seem classy.

Lauren moved to a narrow alcove that housed a microwave, a small refrigerator and a coffeepot, and lovingly prepared her mother's coffee. Artificial sweetener, no cream. Even at sixty-three, Cheri Lee counted calories.

"E.J. will be up in a few minutes. And Jessie is late. As usual." She handed her mother the cup and saucer. Cheri took them in both hands, her left one trembling slightly. Lauren looked away, trying to ignore what she'd seen, then sat in a chair opposite her mother. "I wish they'd get here so we can put this merger thing behind us."

"You're completely certain this wouldn't be good for us?" Cheri delicately took a swallow of coffee, then set the cup on a table beside the love seat.

"Completely. For the reasons we talked about on the phone. Of course, E.J. feels otherwise."

"I know. I've never seen him quite so worked up about the business end of things. But, personally, I'm glad they're late. There's something I want to discuss with you."

Lauren swallowed hard. Had E.J. somehow persuaded Cheri Lee to side with him. "About the merger?"

"No. About me. I want to come back to work." Cheri Lee's lovely jaw set in a firm line as she spoke, and Lauren recognized the stubborn gesture.

The announcement horrified Lauren. What if her mother fell? Had another stroke? And beyond the health concerns, what if she wanted to resume control? At one time Lauren had angrily wanted to confront her mother with a litany of her crimes, but Cheri Lee had been too ill to withstand it. Later, Lauren had understood that a confrontation would serve no purpose and had decided to never bring up the subject. Now she might have to. Yet, how could she tell her mother that in the three short years since Ellis, Sr. had died, she'd almost driven the company into bankruptcy?

"Do you think you're ready?"

"It worries me that you have to run the business all by yourself. It's a huge burden for you. Besides, I'm going crazy at home. My exercises take an hour, then all I do is ramble about."

"But Mrs. Barlow is there," Lauren protested, sidestepping the issue of the business.

"Mrs. Barlow has the house to take care of," her mother responded in an ever-thickening drawl. "And I know this may sound snobbish, but how long can I play gin rummy with a woman with whom I have nothing in common?"

Lauren murmured words of understanding and sympathy, then said, "I know you're bored, but don't forget that production on the Minx promotional videos starts in January. Between that and the sales convention, you're going to be chasing your tail. I'm afraid if you come back now, you'll wear yourself out. How could we launch the new line without you?"

"Very flattering, dear." Cheri patted Lauren's arm with an immaculate hand, her fingernails perfect pink ovals. "But we both know you could carry on."

"Could I?" Lauren ran a finger along her lower lip, preparing to express her doubts. "No, I don't think so. Oh, I could *do* it, but I don't have your flair for firing up an audience. We need you very much, Mother. So, relax for the next couple of months, indulge in long lunches with your friends, facials and stuff. We need you at that convention. Badly."

"Sensible," Cheri replied. "As usual. I suppose you're right. Boredom won't kill me. But it still concerns me that you have to run this place alone. It's too much for you."

Lauren smiled in relief as her office door burst open, cutting off her need to respond. She turned to see Jessie bustling through, carrying a large box and several small bags.

"Sorry I'm late." Jessie wore a brilliant purple top and a turquoise wrap skirt. Leather sandals covered her feet, the straps wrapping their way up her legs. Her big hazel eyes sparkled. "I passed a store while I was driving to the office and saw this wonderful Greco-Roman gown. It's *perfect* for the Christmas party. I just couldn't pass it by." She reached into one of the bags. "And look." Pulling out something that looked endless, she cooed, "Isn't it wonderful?"

Lauren didn't even try to suppress her laugh. Jessie held a coiled upper-arm bracelet. At the top was the head of a cobra with two jade stones for eyes and glittering diamond fangs. "It isn't a costume party, Jessie," Lauren said between laughs.

"Every day's a costume party," Jessie retorted.

"And what are you going to do with that awful hair?" Unlike Lauren, Cheri didn't appear amused. "Are you planning to humiliate me by coming dressed like Cleopatra and wearing milkmaid pigtails?"

"Oh, get with it, Mom," Jessie replied airily, as though the comment meant nothing. But the quick movement of Jessie's hand to her braids betrayed her true feelings.

Jessie flopped into a chair and slipped the bracelet on her arm, looking at her mother with a fixed gaze, while Cheri stared at the bracelet as though afraid it might come alive and bite her.

Jessie, who'd been working as a set designer on an off-Broadway play when Cheri suffered her stroke, had returned home immediately. Since then, she'd visibly struggled to ignore Cheri Lee's endless criticisms of her mode of dress, her friends, her life-style. Today, it seemed, Jessie's patience was wearing thin.

"Want something to drink, Jess?" Lauren asked, hoping E.J. would show up quickly.

"Something cold would be good," Jessie replied absently, holding out her arm to admire her new find.

The door opened and Lauren let out a sigh of relief.

"I hope I haven't held you up," E.J. said.

His white lab coat was unbuttoned and flapped around his hips as he entered the room. He wore a wrinkled dress shirt and a tie beneath the coat, which Lauren knew he'd donned in deference to their mother. It had always seemed to Lauren that E.J. and Jessie had been cut from the same mold. Her brother's green-flecked hazel eyes and thick red-brown hair were nearly identical to his sister's. Even more obviously, the square set of their jaws and the upward tilt of their noses showed their relationship.

Lauren alone had inherited Cheri's Nordic coloring and aristocratic bone structure. Her siblings took after their father. And like Ellis, Sr., both had a flawed sense of style. But while Jessie's choices were flashy and fun, E.J. simply had no style at all. Funny, Lauren thought, that her mother never harassed E.J. about his clothing—only Jessie—though each marched to their own drummer.

Lauren had noticed subtle changes in them since Cheri Lee's stroke. They'd both become more accommodating, even submissive. It struck her then that she had changed, too, but in the completely opposite direction.

"E.J., please tell Jessica she can't wear that disgusting bracelet to the annual Christmas party," Cheri Lee commanded autocratically.

E.J.'s eyes darted around the room as though he were looking for an escape route.

"What bracelet?" he asked warily. Then his eye caught the snake on Jessie's arm and he burst out laughing.

"It's great!" he exclaimed, but seeing the look of disapproval on Cheri Lee's face, he added, "Semi-great. Not too bad. Well, maybe a little out of place."

"Really, E.J., you can't encourage her like this. It's simply in bad taste." As her mother spoke, Lauren wondered if she resented this new deference—considered it another confirmation of her invalidism—for it seemed she'd pushed them harder lately, as if hoping they'd lash back and give her a lusty argument.

"Mother," Lauren interrupted. "We have a lot of business to discuss this morning. Can't we confer on Jessie's party clothes another time?"

"Cheri Lee Cosmetics represents good taste, Lauren. Jessica has to realize she has a position to maintain. She simply can't continue dressing like one of those Greenwich Village beatniks or, worse, those granola people. It's time she did something productive and stopped dabbling with being an *artiste*." The sarcastic emphasis Cheri Lee put on her final word was the last straw.

"Mom!" Jessie popped up from her seat, scrambling to get her packages as she stood. "I can't put up with this anymore. I'm twenty-six. Old enough to dress myself and decide what to do with my life, thank you. If you'll be ashamed of me, I just won't *go* to the Christmas party."

Cheri reached for her cane, clutching the handle like a lifeline. "Not go? You simply must. It's expected."

"It's expected, it's expected." Jessie mimicked. "What about what *I* expect? All I want is the right to be who I am." Arranging the bags so she could easily carry them, she glared at her mother. "Whatever the rest of you decide about the business is fine with me. I'm sick of it."

"Jessie!" Lauren called as her sister marched toward the door. Jessie couldn't leave now. She didn't even know what they were meeting about. "We need you."

"No, you don't." Jessie yanked the door open and stepped through. "No, you don't," she repeated, then slammed the door behind her.

But not before Lauren heard the sob in her voice.

Lauren sat back down and the trio stared at one another in stunned silence.

"She'll calm down," Cheri finally said, with a look that asked for confirmation.

"I guess so," E.J. replied vaguely.

"She always does," Lauren concurred, but then knew she couldn't play this game anymore. "Mother, you really need to ease up on her. Jessie is never going to be what you want her to be. I know you love her anyway, but I'm not sure she does."

The pain in her mother's eyes tore at Lauren's heart but she stood firm in her conviction, and after a long silence Cheri conceded, "Maybe you're right—at least about one thing. I do love and want the best for Jessica. It's... Well, we don't seem to agree on what that is."

Lauren and E.J. nodded. After another empty moment, Lauren brought the subject back to business.

She gave her mother the presentation portfolio. Cheri examined it for a long time, looking up occasionally to ask if some particular fact was true.

As much as she longed to deny it, Lauren truthfully replied yes, while E.J. launched into a litany of the advantages.

Finished with the portfolio, Cheri looked up. "This offer looks good, Lauren. I'm uncertain about why you object."

Lauren's only defense was that Paul had never firmly promised he wouldn't sell the company. In light of all the benefits E.J. had listed, that defense seemed weak indeed, so she presented an abbreviated version of her strategy, omitting the one important detail that Cheri Lee would certainly dislike: that if all went as planned, the merger itself would never take place.

"Essentially," Lauren concluded dispassionately, "I'm proposing to invite Paul into the firm for sixty days so we can investigate his offer more fully."

"What good would that do?" E.J. scowled suspiciously, and Lauren knew he sensed she was hiding something.

"Give us a chance to evaluate his sincerity. Then, if we're convinced he's not just looking for a way to take over the company and sell it, we can vote to accept his offer for a merger."

"I already believe he's sincere," E.J. insisted.

"I know, I know. But I don't," Lauren answered, growing weary of E.J.'s high emotion. The vote was in the bag. Why didn't he face it?

Jaw clenched, E.J. restated all they'd gain by completing the merger now, then hotly finished with the greatest reason of all: "Twenty-five million, Lor! With that kind of money, all our problems will be over. And without a controlling interest, he can't do us any harm.''

"No harm? Have you forgotten that man's history? Who knows what kind of maneuvers he's pulling behind the scenes?''

E.J. snorted, dismissing her question. "No harm. And I think he can do us a lot of good. I vote we accept his offer now.''

"I haven't called for the vote yet, E.J.''

"Mother's still chairman of the board," E.J. countered irritably. "She calls the vote. Or have you forgotten?''

Lauren turned, an apology in her eyes, but Cheri waved her hand in a calming gesture. "No. It's right for Lauren to be doing this. She's got all the responsibility, she should have the authority, too. Another thing," Cheri added. "In all the excitement, you've both forgotten that no one has made a motion on this.''

"Right," E.J. agreed hastily. "I move we accept Paul's offer, effective immediately.''

"Mother?" Lauren glanced at Cheri Lee, expecting her to table the motion.

After a long hesitation, Cheri spoke. "I second.''

Lauren felt as if she'd been slapped. Her mind raced.

With knee-jerk quickness, she blurted, "I amend the motion to make the acceptance effective January first.''

"No!" E.J. countered. "We need the capital now!''

"The amendment stands, E.J." Lauren wanted to smack him soundly and struggled to retain control of her voice. "Mother, do you second?''

"Yes." This time it came without hesitancy.

Lauren breathed a sigh of relief. "Okay. The motion on the floor is as follows: Cheri Lee Cosmetics will accept the merger offer proposed by Paul Sherwood, effective the first working day of the New Year."

She nodded toward her brother. "How do you vote?"

"Aye," said E.J. "I guess this is better than nothing."

"Nay," said Lauren. "It's worse than nothing."

They both stared at Cheri, waiting. Lauren's heart thudded painfully. Thank God, she'd at least made the amendment. But, of course, there was nothing to worry about. Cheri Lee would vote with her. Surely, she would. For, if not, Lauren would have a new set of difficulties. Between now and January, she'd have to find a way to reveal Paul for what he was.

Beneath the surface of these thoughts ran others, so subtle Lauren was barely aware of them. Which Paul? they asked. The heartless destroyer of livelihoods? The puzzling man-boy with an unusual childhood? Or the erotic, sensual man with whom she'd almost made love?

As Cheri's lips pursed in contemplation, Lauren fenced with her warring thoughts.

E.J. had said this merger would end their problems.

Lauren knew better. Hers would just begin.

LAUREN CLUTCHED THE telephone receiver, frustration mounting at her sister's absolute refusal to discuss business. It had been almost two weeks since Jessie had stormed out, and her feelings hadn't changed a bit.

"When are you going to get it, Lauren?" Jessie's voice sounded hard, unyielding, very un-Jessie-like. "I don't care about the company. I don't want anything to do with it."

"It's too late to request a new mother, you know." Wanting to lift Jessie's mood, Lauren attempted to stay light.

"No, I can't get a new mother, but it isn't too late to move to another place."

"I don't understand. You two argue all the time, so why not let this one blow over like the rest?"

"That's just like you, Lor. In all your thirty-one years, you've never crossed her. I've really been trying and you know it, but she acted like I planned on wearing a G-string and pasties to that party."

Jessie's voice grew thick. She hesitated a moment, then added, "I want to live my own life—without interference from her. Is that too much to ask?"

"I guess not. But you're still a shareholder and I need you. We voted on this offer—"

"I'm sorry, Lor, someone's knocking on the door. It's probably the realtor. He said he'd be right over to show me some listings."

The huskiness was still in Jessie's voice, and Lauren didn't believe someone was really at the door. But conceding that the time was wrong, she let Jessie go, telling her she'd phone back later.

After saying goodbye, Lauren sat at her desk, staring off at nothing, the receiver still in her hand. What was happening to their family? A routine squabble between her mother and Jessie now appeared to be an irreparable breach. She and E.J. were barely talking. He'd been furious about her amendment, and angry at Cheri Lee for agreeing to it.

Lauren wasn't pleased, either. When Cheri Lee's pursed lips had finally opened and the response had been "Aye," Lauren had left the room and stalked to the employee cafeteria to drown her disappointment in a lukewarm cup of vending-machine coffee.

Why had Cheri Lee sided with E.J.? Lauren had asked herself as she'd settled down at a table as far as possible from the few employees in the cafeteria. It had been Lauren who'd stepped in during that state of emergency and taken over, Lauren who'd unraveled the snaggled affairs of the company. Yet, at this crucial moment, Cheri Lee hadn't trusted her judgment.

As Lauren wrangled with these thoughts, a memory waltzed through her mind. Had she been five years old then? Six? It didn't really matter.

All that had mattered was that silly dress. Done in bright fuchsia organdy, its crisp fabric was gathered into billowing beauty. Pink bows dotted the ruffled neckline and hem, and a wide, matching sash encircled the waist.

Lauren had touched the dress, loving the scratchy feeling. In a dress like this, she'd known she'd look like a princess. She'd ached to put it on, to twirl in front of the mirror and see her mother's eyes light up at how pretty she looked. . . .

"Look, Mama. Isn't this bea-u-tiful?"

Cheri looked up from a rack she'd been inspecting. "Uh-huh," she replied idly, then continued her search.

Lauren stretched on her toes, lifting the dress from its rack. Clutching the hanger in her small hand, she toted it to her mother. Cheri, engrossed in her shopping, barely noticed.

"Mama, look." Lauren tugged her mother's hand. "Can I wear this to the party? Ple-ea-se? It's so pretty."

Cheri's eyebrows lifted ever so slightly, and Lauren knew her mother didn't like the dress. She never liked what Lauren liked. With a sinking heart, Lauren continued to wheedle. If Mama saw her, actually saw her, in the dress, she'd love it, too. "Can I try it on? You'll like it, you'll see. And you wouldn't have to buy me new shoes. It goes with my pink ones."

"But it's so...gaudy, dear. This one's much nicer." Cheri held up a pastel-blue dress. Velvet, with a white collar. A dopey Alice-in-Wonderland thing like the dresses she always made Lauren wear.

"No! I want a pretty dress. I want this one!"

Cheri stooped and stroked Lauren's hair. "It is pretty, honey, but it's not suitable.

"I don't want a suit'ble dress. I want this one." Lauren bit her quivering lip and fought back her fear. She usually did what her mother asked. But this dress ... She had dreamed of a dress like this.

"I know. But when you're older you'll understand." Then her mother smiled real wide, straightened, and took Lauren's hand. "Tell you what, we'll buy them both. When it's time for the party, we'll choose then."

Lauren sniffled. "'Kay," she said. But she wasn't fooled. She'd played this "We'll choose then" game before. She always lost.

And when the clerk packed her dress, oohing and aahing over the pretty organdy and telling her what a lucky girl she was, Lauren knew she'd never get to wear it....

Several years later, when the dress had been long outgrown, Lauren had come across it again, still packed in the original box. She'd laughed that she'd ever wanted to wear the tasteless thing. Without a second thought, she'd thrown it away.

"Lauren."

She looked up. Paul stood above her, looking every inch the successful executive. It annoyed her that he'd appeared in the cafeteria now to interrupt her brooding. She'd wanted to collect herself before telling him the results of the meeting. But even in her bitter mood she felt the electricity between them.

"E.J. told me where to find you," he explained, sitting down without waiting for her invitation.

Lauren scanned the cafeteria. It was empty now except for a few scurrying food handlers. Relieved to know they wouldn't be overheard, she asked what she knew was on Paul's mind.

"Did E.J. tell you about the shareholders' meeting?"

"Just that your mother voted to accept my offer." Paul leaned back in his plastic chair, tilting the front legs off the floor. "That our deal is on as I proposed it. He said you'd fill me in on the rest."

"I'm afraid it's not all you hoped for." She couldn't suppress her wry smile, didn't want to. Although Paul was clearly attempting not to gloat, Lauren saw straight through him. Yet sitting so near him made her breath quicken, her nervous system skitter. She stared at his hands, which were wrapped around the back of his chair, observed the fine sprinkling of hair and the narrow ridges of his veins—and remembered how they'd felt caressing her.

Her resolve for revenge weakened, but, reminding herself how much was at stake, she said with forced bravado, "The transfer of shares won't take place until the first working day after the New Year."

Paul's startled expression gratified her. "Why?"

"To give me time to be certain you're sincere." She leaned forward then, placing her elbows combatively on the table. "Let's get one thing straight, Paul. You may have E.J. fooled, but I still think you're hiding something. I have sixty days to make sure you don't get your hands on this company. If no ugly surprises pop up, then the sale will go through. If not, you're out."

"So this is war, huh?" Paul's smile was smooth, condescending.

"Yes, it's war," she agreed, not smiling in return.

Paul leaned forward, bringing his chair to the floor with ear-shattering force. He enclosed her wrists with his hands. Lauren's skin burned beneath them.

"Look, Lauren. This merger will be profitable for us all. If you persist in opposing me, I assure you it's you, not I, who will get hurt. But that's not what I want. I've been looking forward to working with you. I want...friendship between us. Maybe I want more than friendship."

Lauren angrily pulled her wrists from his grip. "That will never happen," she snapped.

With a sigh, Paul stood. "I'm afraid you're right."

Turning, he took a few steps, then looked back. "It'll take about a week to wrap up some other affairs, then I'll be here as much as possible. Have my office ready on Monday."

Before Lauren could object to his order, his broad back had moved rapidly away from her. He'd looked tall, formidable... and very, very male.

Now Lauren giggled mirthlessly, recalling that throughout the argument with Paul her biggest struggle had been to keep her hands off him. Her entire body had trembled from the effort.

She'd known then, knew now, that she was doing what was right. Right for the company. Right for the Aftons. This strife in her family would blow over once the merger was squelched, and she had the inner strength to make sure that it was. Her only doubts centered around the disturbing chemistry between her and Paul. Paul Sherwood, she reminded herself firmly, simply wasn't a *suitable* lover.

Then, with a pang of regret, she thought of the organdy dress again and how she'd never, ever, worn it.

Because it wasn't suitable.

JESSIE SLOWLY LOWERED the receiver onto its cradle and wiped the tears from her cheek. She needed to look upbeat because she hadn't fibbed to Lauren. Someone was knocking on the door, but it probably wasn't the realtor. Their appointment was for tomorrow.

She crossed the uneven plank flooring of her apartment, reaching the windowpaned door in long, easy strides. She parted the cheerful print curtains, then quickly let them close, surprised and outraged.

Bill Rosen!

The nerve of him. She'd cooked him a wonderful dinner, dressed as sexily as she knew how, kissed him heartily—and wow, what a kiss! But all he'd done was ask if she wanted to sell her stock. She never wanted to see him again.

She swung the door open.

"What a surprise," she said sweetly, trying to cook up some delicious revenge. But nothing came to mind. He was so darned cute.

And she couldn't quite figure out why. Truly he wasn't her type. She leaned toward tanned beach boys or tortured artists. What was so appealing about this formal-mannered man in his uniform of business and his wire-rimmed glasses?

He shifted his weight uneasily, his hands clasped behind his back, and suddenly she knew. He was so guileless. Most men would at least pretend they weren't uncomfortable. But not Bill Rosen. He didn't know how.

"I stopped to apologize for the other night," he said, carefully articulating each word. He gazed directly into her eyes for a moment, then looked away. "I would have done so sooner, but I wasn't sure how you would react."

"I should boot you out on your tush. But if you've brought me flowers or candy, I might just forgive you." Jessie could feel a glad smile cross her face, even though she wanted to remain cool. She thought about hating her traitorous mouth, but changed her mind as Bill withdrew his hands from behind his back.

"As a matter of fact, I did." He held an enormous box and thrust it toward her somewhat awkwardly. "Candy."

"Truffles!" Jessie squealed. "My favorites." How could she stay mad at a man who stood there like a schoolboy bringing an apple to the teacher?

She couldn't.

"I guess you can come in." She swung the door wide.

Bill squelched his sigh of relief. If Jessie had stubbornly refused to talk to him, he wouldn't have blamed her. What he'd done stank, and he knew it. But he'd been so damned uneasy, holding her in his arms. And he was still uneasy. His heart thudded unevenly as he crossed the threshold, but the thumping was exciting, made him feel alive, vital, in a way that he'd never known with anyone else.

What made Jessie so different? Undeniably, she *was* different—offbeat, even bizarre—especially when compared to the elegant women in his social circle. But so excitingly different.

She seemed like a little girl now as she enthusiastically ripped open the box of candy, popping one into her mouth and openly savoring the flavor.

"Want one?" Without waiting for a reply, she lifted a dark chocolate morsel and placed it against his lips.

Almost involuntarily his mouth opened, and as the sweet flavor of the chocolate pleasured his tongue, her fingers brushed his lower lip. Shocked, he realized he was fighting an impulse to lick those lovely fingers, and he turned away slightly, chewing religiously, unlike Jessie who was allowing her candy to melt in her mouth.

God, he wanted her.

"Would you care to have lunch with me?" Bill murmured, unable to understand why he could barely speak above a whisper.

"Love it," Jessie replied, turning to put the box down on a white-painted counter that separated the living area from a small kitchen. "I have to change first."

"No, you don't. You're perfect the way you are."
She was wearing something similar to what she'd had
on the first day they'd met. The sweatshirt was a dark
green this time, but otherwise nothing was changed.

"Not according to my mother," she shot back.
"But that's another story." She lifted a graceful hand
and patted his cheek. "Don't go anywhere. I won't be
long."

"I hope not," Bill whispered, still short of breath.
Jessie smiled, then disappeared through a door Bill
hadn't noticed before. He slumped into a comfortable lounger, totally forgetting his posture, hoping his
heart would stop beating so painfully in his chest.

What was he getting himself into?

An hour later they sat in a ramada on Point Loma,
looking out at the foamy sea, a box of tacos and bur-
ros between them. This had been Jessie's suggestion.
Eating fast food while sitting at a concrete picnic table, and chasing paper wrappers snatched up by the
wind, had never been Bill's idea of a good time. Now
he discovered he actually liked it. He was already becoming used to his surprise at what he liked when he
was with Jessie.

She had on a gauzy dress with voluminous sleeves
in a soft ivory color. As she took a healthy bite from
her taco, Bill held his breath, expecting the gooey filling to plop into her lap at any moment. But it didn't.
Bill suspected that things like that never happened to
Jessie. Or if they did, she didn't worry about it.

He bit into his own taco, enjoying looking at her. He
had decided to let his partner know he wouldn't pursue the stock purchase anymore. Sure, the guy would
be upset, but they'd work out something else. By now,
Bill had deduced that Jessie never intended to sell

anyway, that her interest in him had always been social. The knowledge warmed him, kind of pumped up his ego, in a way he found very pleasant.

"Bill?"

"Yes?" Jessie was looking at him now, her eyes half closed, and wearing a decidedly sultry expression. Bill hoped she was going to invite him to do something scandalous.

"About the stock." She plucked at a piece of lettuce on her taco wrapper, then popped it into her mouth. "I've decided to sell."

Whoosh! Bill's daydreams about Jessie went up in smoke. He felt a wrenching pain inside.

"We don't have to talk about it, Jessie. I didn't come about the stock."

"I know." Her smile told him how delightful she found that. "But it's time I got out of the company. Got away from my family. I really do want to sell, and there isn't anyone else I'd rather sell to."

Bill reached out and clutched a burro, studiously opening the wrapping, only to discover that he'd forced out the filling with his death grip. Taking a plastic fork from the colorful box on the table, he scooped up some beans and placed them in his mouth.

"I didn't realize you were so hungry, Bill. Too hungry to discuss business. That isn't like you." He didn't miss her veiled reference to the night he'd kissed her, and it suddenly made him angry. Everything about his timing had been off with Jessie. Then. And now.

He didn't want to discuss business with her today—or ever. Didn't want to face her reaction once she learned the total consequences of her sale. But this was his work; this was his job and his livelihood. He had to do what he had to do.

And she really wasn't his type, anyway.

"I'll send the papers over tomorrow," he said, then took another mouthful of beans. The day had lost its brightness.

CHAPTER SIX

"I'M READY WHENEVER you are."

Paul stood in the doorway of Lauren's office, tall and gorgeous. For a moment, as Lauren lifted her head from her work, her breath caught. She wondered if she'd ever stop feeling a throb of excitement every time she saw him. As he waited—hand placed casually on the doorjamb, suit coat and vest unbuttoned to reveal his lean torso—she acknowledged the attraction totally, yet remained determined not to submit to it. She briskly swept up the supplies on her desk, and got straight to business.

"I'd like to go over our presentation first." She folded her arms, knowing she and Paul were about to enter dangerous territory.

They were now thirty days into their uneasy partnership. Since their confrontation in the cafeteria, they'd carefully avoided clashing on any subject.

During the past weeks, Paul had kept predictable on-premise business hours—something Lauren hadn't anticipated. Nor had she anticipated his quick acceptance by her staff. In the short time he'd been there he'd already garnered tremendous loyalty; his opinions were well accepted, his influence was growing. Unfortunately he sometimes used that influence to block policies Lauren wanted, and today's subject was a pivotal issue.

Paul settled into one of Lauren's tiny mauve chairs, its contrast with his size making him appear even larger than he really was.

"I gather you still have reservations about the Minx program."

"Yes." Lauren pressed finger against her lower lip, searching for the right words. She'd planned on being less direct, but the truth came out almost without her volition. "The thirty-percent bonus level has too many holes."

"We've gone over this several times, Lauren. I thought we'd reached a meeting of the minds. Is there a new problem?"

The problem is us! her heart screamed. *I can't think straight when you're around.* Annoyed by these irrational feelings, Lauren answered more sharply than she intended.

"We could go broke paying those numbers, Paul!"

Paul shifted forward and let out a patient sigh. "True, we could, but we won't. The performance targets are so high, very few of the salespeople will make it."

"But that isn't honest." Paul's condescending sigh irritated Lauren further, and while she knew her tone remained sharp, she couldn't contain it. "It amounts to dangling a carrot!"

"Good grief, Lauren, when are you going to get some comfortable chairs in here?" Paul shifted position once, twice, then a third time.

Lauren uttered a small, impatient noise. "I'll order a La-Z-Boy chair just for you." She wanted to point out to Paul that he always changed the subject whenever ethical questions arose, but she wasn't completely comfortable with her growing outspokenness, so she decided against it. "For now, let's stick with my concern."

"Okay, Lauren, but I'm done beating around the bush." He pointed a finger at her challengingly, his patience obviously wearing thin. "It's called motivation, not carrot dangling. It's done all the time. You were worried about profit margins, and you can't have it both ways. The important thing is that we're together on this. If we send mixed signals to the staff, we'll lose their support. It's your decision, Lauren. I'll support whatever you decide. But unless you have a better idea, I suggest you go with what we've got."

"I'm glad you said that, because I do have an alternative." She lifted a file, pulled out a green ledger sheet and handed it to him. "I've done some figuring." The sheets showed that by lowering the bonus three percent, more people could reach it, yet costs would remain the same. Paul seemed unimpressed.

"What about the anniversary tie-in? The marketing people are ecstatic about celebrating the company's thirtieth year with this program. It makes great advertising copy."

"Ah, yes. Flash over substance," Lauren replied caustically. "Look at what I've got there. I think it will translate."

He hadn't even examined the sheet, and Lauren knew he didn't want to. Silence stretched, straining Lauren's nerves, yet she waited. When Paul bent his head to read, she knew she'd won this battle. The outcome of their cold war was anyone's guess.

Paul looked up, and whistled. "'Twenty-seven plus product plus customer equals twenty-nine. It takes you to make thirty!' This is good copy! It'll sell."

He directed his attention back to Lauren's work sheet and studied it for quite a while. Finished, he lifted his head and grimaced. "I've been hunting for glitches, but I can't find any." He stood and handed the sheet to Lauren. "Okay, I'll stand behind you on this. But be prepared for some flak when you present it to Marketing."

"Why should there be flak?"

"Just a suspicion I have," Paul answered evasively, glancing at his watch. "In any case, it's time for our meeting."

He gestured to Lauren's spreadsheet and suggested she take it with her. "In case of questions."

"I'd planned to." Lauren folded the sheet and placed it back in its folder.

The smugness—no, the confidence—in her tone irritated Paul. Should he tell her what he'd done? Probably. But he didn't quite know how. He'd overstepped, for sure, but between learning about the business and soothing the ruffled feathers of his investors, he'd been almost too busy to realize it.

As he and Lauren headed for the boardroom, he wondered how big the ensuing explosion would be.

Big. Very big.

Huge. Within minutes, the room became a scene from Paul's worst nightmare. Men and women sent flurries of simultaneous comments back and forth across the conference table. Some sided with Lauren's proposal, others ranted against it. Curtis Jordon, who directed the marketing department, glared down his wide nose at Paul, making it clear he blamed this whole fiasco on him.

When Lauren had first announced she wanted to reconsider the thirty-percent plan, Curtis had clearly struggled not to blow his top. One of his people, who'd obviously put considerable effort into an elaborate presentation using the three and zero, had barely contained an oath as she slammed the cover down on her flip chart.

Paul couldn't blame either one. They'd worked with the concept, believing wholeheartedly it would receive upper-management approval—a belief Paul had fostered.

He'd made a big mistake. He might know about the buying and selling of businesses, but he had a lot to learn about actually managing one. This was his first lesson. He should never forget that running a corporation took cooperation.

To Lauren's credit, she held her own. "Ladies, gentlemen," she quietly repeated until the group settled down. "I've never forced my opinions on you, and I'm not going to start now. What I'd like is the opportunity to convince you that my proposal will produce better results. Is that fair?"

Upon receiving a few grudging nods, Lauren rose and went to the easel where the chart rested. What had come over these people? She'd never faced such hostility before. Flipping the pages until they came up blank, she said a silent prayer that no one would notice her trembling fingers. Then she picked up a marker and began drawing the chart she'd shown Paul earlier.

She explained what the figures represented. "So, as you can see," she concluded, "based on performance history, the top production levels become more easily attainable, while the costs to Cheri Lee Cosmetics remain substantially the same. Perhaps, even lower.

"I would never wipe out your hard work without good reason. But you all know I've had grave doubts about the other program. I just didn't have anything better. Now, I do, but I'd like your input." Lauren surveyed the room, looking for belligerent faces. She wasn't disappointed. Since the biggest scowler was Curtis Jordan, she decided to handle him first.

"Curtis?"

"Your program's good, Lauren." Curtis's agitation was barely controlled. "But we've committed a lot to the first one. Hours of creative time, ads and flyers already in the works. Does it make sense to scrap it all?"

"I'm confused. Why did you go ahead before the final decision was made?"

"Sherwood said it was in the bag." Curtis turned to Paul, giving Lauren time to prevent the shock she felt from registering on her face.

Paul had told them to go ahead! He'd been so certain that his idea would be accepted, he'd started it without her approval! A dull throb erupted at the base of her neck, and her heart jumped in outrage. He'd been here only a few weeks and already was trying to push her out. But he'd now given her an opportunity to discredit him.

Before she could speak, Paul rose. "I owe you all an apology," he said, his voice soft and . . .

Humble, Lauren thought. Or he *appeared* humble. Good God, how could someone so arrogant feign that much humility?

"Sometimes a person gets carried away with an idea. That's what I did with the thirty-percent plan. Your ideas were brilliantly devised, your projected execution flawless and such an exciting departure from previous marketing strategies, that I was awed.

"I'm old enough to have learned the dangers of falling in love with an idea, but in my enthusiasm over your work, I forgot. When Lauren presented her modifications, I was dumbstruck. With a few simple changes, a possibly risky idea becomes fail-safe. I had no choice but to back her completely.... I'm sure, when all this emotion dies down, you'll see that this new proposal is dynamic."

Paul sat down. "Again, people, I apologize." Glancing at Lauren, he said deferentially, "Would you like to continue?"

"Certainly," Lauren replied stiffly. "And your gracious apology is accepted." She turned back to the chart and the remaining points of her presentation.

Glancing around, she observed people making quick calculations as she talked. Expressions relaxed, a few heads nodded, some faces smiled. Except for a couple of low murmurs the room was silent, waiting for her to finish.

She concluded by saying, "Do you think we can run with this?" The group agreed, almost in unison, and Lauren finally relaxed, allowing a big smile to cover her face. "Good. Now let's use this creative energy to turn the numbers back."

From then on the meeting ran smoothly. Soon they'd found a way to cut the losses on the old program and transfer some of the work to the new. The group adjourned amid a flurry of united purpose.

Closing in on Paul before he vanished, Lauren said in a soft, deadly voice, "I want to see you in my office. Right away."

"Certainly, ma'am." Paul didn't look concerned, and his nonchalance fueled Lauren's anger. She stalked to her office, heels clicking in outrage with every step.

When he appeared fifteen minutes later, Lauren was impatiently tapping her pencil against her desk, debating whether to page him like an errand boy.

"I know you're ticked, Lauren." He pulled up a side chair to Lauren's desk and sat down. Propping his elbows on her acrylic slab, he rested his head on his hands and gazed at her like a blue-eyed Galahad. "And I don't blame you."

Lauren sighed. Any moment now, she expected him to start panting and wagging his tail.

"What you did, Paul, could have had disastrous consequences." Lauren almost felt foolish. Paul still stared at her appealingly, interfering with her efforts to remain stern. She swiveled to face the wall. "I appreciate the way you handled things. You could have made me look like an overbearing ogre. But you can't ever do anything like that again."

"Look at me, Lauren." Paul's voice was a purring whisper. Lauren wanted to resist, yet the purr was so seductive. "What I said was true. Your plan is superb. The first program fired up my enthusiasm so much I didn't give it enough thought. I am sorry." Leaning forward, he touched her hand. "You have my word I won't do it again. Management is still new to me. I have a lot to learn...."

And you could teach me. Wasn't that implied in his hesitation? How easy it would be to believe those flattering words. How easy to forget to protect the company.

And the light touch of Paul's hand on hers made her feel almost dizzy. She hated the feeling. She loved the feeling. And she wanted Paul out of her office now.

She yanked her hand away and shot to her feet. "All right. You're forgiven."

A look of surprise shot across Paul's face, but he swiftly concealed it and got out of his chair. He appeared about to speak, when E.J. entered.

"Place your bets, folks! Place your bets!"

Lauren gaped at E.J. "What are you talking about?"

"The whole company's trading bets on how soon you'll boot Paul out on his ear." Laughing now, E.J. rubbed his hands together gleefully. "I put twenty in Paul's favor," he continued. "Course, I have inside information, so it's really not fair."

"And not very professional, either, E.J.," Lauren growled. "How could you encourage the employees to gamble?"

"Oh, lighten up, Lor. You guys need to do something to prove you're not ripping each other's throats out. This betting proves that our people notice your mutual hostility." E.J. flopped into one of Lauren's chairs, stuck out his legs, then shifted around. "When are you going to get rid of these hard chairs?"

Paul snickered at E.J.'s question. Lauren whirled, glared at them both, then crossed the room in agitated strides. As if she didn't have enough to deal with. Now the employees were betting on whether she and Paul would hit it off.

"Okay," she said, with feigned sweetness. "What should we do about it? I'm sure you two wise guys can cook up a brilliant idea."

"We could have lunch together every day in the employees' cafeteria," Paul offered. "It'll also serve another purpose. You said you wanted an open-door management policy. This is one way to do it."

"Hmm..." Lauren stalled. In her opinion, the charade wasn't necessary. The employees who'd bet against Paul would be counting their winnings in less than a month. If she had her druthers, Paul would be gone right now. But just that morning she'd gotten approval for a new line of credit based on Paul's presence in the firm. If word got out that the merger might collapse, the credit would be withdrawn before she could use it. She had to pretend to think that their perceived lack of unity was truly a problem. In that light, Paul's suggestion had merit....

But the idea of spending so much time with him sent her heart slamming against the walls of her chest. Why, oh, why was she yearning for the touch of a man who wanted to take what she'd devoted her life to? She wished she could believe in his sincerity. Wished it more than anything she'd ever wished before.

Except, of course, for the continued success of Cheri Lee Cosmetics.

"We could do that, I suppose."

Had to do that, she supposed.

"I like it," E.J. said."

"Great." Paul wore an amused grin. "We'll start today."

"Today," Lauren intoned, feeling as if she'd agreed to attend her own funeral.

"I'll see you around noon." Paul swept out of her office, looking very pleased with himself.

Lauren spun to confront her brother. Although they'd talked about their conflict over the merger, there was still tension between them. Yes, she understood that he wanted an active part in restoring the company to profitability. No, she didn't understand why he thought this was the only way. Now she wondered if E.J. didn't have another motive—one he was keeping to himself.

"Why are you always throwing us together?" she demanded to know.

She expected one of E.J.'s irreverent remarks, but he didn't even smile.

"You two are good together, Lor. Where he's brash, you're calm. Where he's all action, you like to think things out. I predict you'll make a hell of a team."

"This business doesn't need a team!"

"Who said I was talking about the business?" The expected smile appeared, and E.J. left Lauren's office before she could think of a comeback.

That night, as Lauren prepared for bed, she still couldn't think of a comeback. Indeed, she could think about nothing but the fact that she was being swept along on a journey that was not of her choosing.

She hadn't been exaggerating when she'd accused E.J. of continually throwing them together. Since Paul's arrival, her brother had called her to his lab with amazing regularity. Each time Lauren had responded, Paul had been there too. Then E.J. would manage to dream up some errand they just *had* to do together. Lauren was certain today's ploy had been another of the same ilk.

But now as she stood in front of her bathroom sink, brushing her teeth, Lauren accepted that her own feelings were sweeping her away. She'd wanted to bash Paul to a bloody pulp when she'd realized how he'd manipulated her people, but she'd been unable to hold on to that anger. And that lack of control terrified her.

Lord, how would she endure these next thirty days?

Whenever Paul was near, her resolve turned to quivering mush. She tried to be firm, wanted to be firm.... It just wasn't working.

The subterfuge was also killing her. At her family's direction, Lauren had ordered the sales contract drawn up, had delivered copies to the respective attorneys. She'd simply failed to sign the corporate minutes. Without that signature, the deal could be killed at any time by a reverse vote. With it, the sale was carved in stone.

She'd had several calls from Paul's attorney, had sweetly promised each time to send the signed papers over. By now the man probably thought she was a flaming dingbat, but Lauren was certain he suspected no ulterior motive.

Opening a bronze faucet and rinsing her toothbrush in the patterned sink, she turned her thoughts back to the meeting.

Paul was a flimflam man. Mercurial. Able to turn on a dime. Yet he was also a topflight negotiator. In all her years at Cheri Lee Cosmetics she'd never seen so many irate faces in one room—at the *start* of the meeting. Paul had been the cause, of course, but he'd also handled them brilliantly—validating their efforts while supporting Lauren's.

Padding naked from the bathroom, Lauren went to her bureau. As she opened the nightgown drawer she tried to resurrect her eagerness to pull the rug from beneath Paul's feet. But in retrospect, she realized that Paul had supported her. His charisma had already earned him many followers. He could have used that power to discredit her. Instead he'd given it back to her, multiplied it. E.J. had said they made a great team. Maybe he was right.

Business-wise, of course, Lauren thought, as her hand touched a black silk nightgown. The fabric, sensuously soft, had a soothing quality. She drew out the gown, forgetting her concerns for a moment. The gown had been purchased for her honeymoon, for the marriage that never came to be. After canceling the wedding, she'd put it in the drawer unworn.

She smiled, wondering why she'd bought it. It was unlike anything else she owned. Daring, scandalous even, the embroidered black on black garment featured spaghetti straps and a creamy transparent net inset from neckline to hipline.

Still smiling, she laid it on top of the bureau. What she wanted was something reminiscent of her childhood—something she could slip into and be comfortable in. Maybe she'd even suck her thumb before she went to sleep.

The bizarre image jerked her back to her problem. Yes, Paul had empowered her. Yes, E.J. liked him—as did Jessie and Cheri Lee, if their comments were to be believed. Yes, he had created excitement among the employees.

For one moment of conflict, Lauren completely believed in Paul—trusted that, indeed, he truly wanted to rebuild her company; trusted that, indeed, he truly wanted a relationship with her.

Skepticism returned quickly. No one could be a coldhearted businessman one moment, then a picture of boyish guilelessness the next. It had to be an act. Renewing her resolve to carry through her plans, Lauren carefully refolded the nightgowns she'd pulled out and started putting them back in the drawer. None met her needs.

Then, almost without realizing it, she picked up the black gown and slipped it over her naked body. As she climbed wearily into bed and turned out the lights, she wondered why she had done that. But she was too tired to change.

Nor did she want to.

"YOU'LL BE PROUD OF ME, Lauren." Jessie perched on the edge of Lauren's desk, swinging her bare, tanned legs, and chewing on the end of a pencil. "I phoned Mom a few days ago. We talked . . . and we worked things out."

Lauren arched a surprised eyebrow.

"You apologized?"

"Apologized!" Jessie scrunched her face, and put down the pencil. "No way. I simply told her I forgave her and we should stop being silly. I mean, she is my mother! We can't go the rest of our lives without talking." Jessie tilted her head and looked squarely at Lauren. "You think I was wrong, don't you?"

Lauren felt a familiar knot in her stomach. How did she always end up as mediator for these disagreements? She started to hedge, then decided against it.

"Not really, Jessie. Maybe you overreacted a little, but Mother, well, she does get on your case a bit."

"Oh, just a bit?"

The flash of offense crossing Jessie's face made Lauren think she might have opened a can of worms. What was getting into her lately? She'd become so direct, even when it made her uncomfortable. Well, it was done now, she might as well finish.

"Actually," she said with a sigh, "Mother rides you a lot. But what surprised me was I thought you meant that she'd apologized. As we both know, Mother *never* does that."

Jessie's responding laugh bounced off the walls and infected Lauren.

"For sure, Mom never does that. But I never thought I'd hear you admit it." Jessie slipped off the desk. Standing, she stared at Lauren. "What's with you these days?"

"What are you talking about?"

"First off, this unprecedented criticism of our virtuous mother." Jessie leaned down and ran her finger across the acrylic surface of Lauren's desk. "And what's this coffee ring doing on your so-spotless-I-could-puke desk?" Jessie pointed to an unmistakable brown mark half-covered by a file folder. "Is that another one I see over there?"

"I've been too busy to worry about coffee rings. Running a corporation takes a lot of time."

"You sure there isn't something else going on?"

"No, sister dear. Nothing." The expression on Jessie's face made Lauren laugh again. "Don't look at me like that. You're always reading things into what I say."

"I have to. You keep so much to yourself. Sometimes I worry about you." Jessie wasn't smiling now and Lauren realized she really was concerned. It had never occurred to Lauren that her family might worry about her. After all, she was the worrier. "But for the record, I approve of the changes," Jessie added.

"I'm so glad to hear that," Lauren replied drolly, then took the opportunity to switch topics. "And I'm also glad you changed your mind about the Christmas party.''

''Yeah.'' Jessie didn't resist the switch. It was one of the things Lauren appreciated about her sister. Unlike E.J., she knew when to back off. ''And I'm bringing that fab guy I told you about.''

''The business broker?''

''Uh-huh. He's a real cutie.''

''Boy,'' Lauren said. ''Talk about changing. I never thought I'd hear that you were dating a businessman.''

''Isn't it strange?'' A faraway look crossed Jessie's expressive face, then she brought her gaze back to Lauren. ''He really isn't my type. But he's just so cute.... I can't control myself with him.''

''Oh, you little harlot,'' Lauren teased.

''Yeah, ain't it great?'' Then Jessie's eyes darkened. ''Lauren, we need to have a heart-to-heart.''

''You got love troubles?''

''Not exactly... But they are related.''

A staccato rap on Lauren's door interrupted them. Paul stood at the threshold. ''Hello, Jessie,'' he said with a pleased smile, obviously glad to see her. ''I came to pick you up for lunch, Lauren, but since you two are visiting I'll come back later.''

''Not necessary,'' Jessie said. ''I'm meeting someone soon, anyway.'' She winked at Lauren. ''The cutie I told you about.''

''Could we do lunch?'' Lauren glanced at her calendar. Grimacing, she said, ''Next Friday?''

''That's okay, Lor,'' Jessie replied blithely. ''I'm going away for a week. I'll call you when I get back. Maybe I can work this out by myself. If not, I'll let you know.'' She picked up her handbag and headed for the door. Pausing for a moment, she smiled broadly at Paul. "I'm leaving her in good hands, aren't I?"

"Absolutely." Paul smiled, waving back, while Lauren fought the flush brought on by the suggestion in her sister's words. Not Jessie, too! Was the whole world trying to shove her into Paul's arms?

"I like your sister," Paul said, after Jessie was gone. "She's open and natural."

Unlike me, Lauren reflected, although Paul had said nothing of the sort. But men were always attracted to Jessie. Truth was, *people* were attracted to Jessie. She made them feel comfortable, made them laugh. *Unlike me,* Lauren thought again. Then, pushing away the thought, she responded in the only way she could. "Yes, my sister's a doll." And she meant it, of course; it was just that—

"But, of course, she isn't you." Paul grinned sincerely, then bent and picked up Lauren's purse.

Lauren felt a small shock at Paul's comment. Had he known what she was thinking? He couldn't have said anything more perfect. She smiled back, accepting her purse.

"Ready to do the cafeteria thing?" he asked.

"Guess so. Someday we may win an Academy Award for our act down there."

Paul's smiled vanished instantly and his eyes darkened. "Is it really so bad, Lauren?"

"Uh, no. It was just a bad joke. Sorry." Clutching her purse self-protectively, she turned and headed for the door.

"Sure," Paul said quietly, following her.

Lauren was glad to find the elevator full, which relieved her of the need to make conversation. As they rode to the basement, she noticed how eagerly people greeted Paul. One woman showed him a picture of her new grandchild. A man thanked him for getting a needed piece of equipment quickly. Clearly, he had a talent for winning people's affection. As he had so aptly done in her case, Lauren thought darkly.

Soon they were seated across from each other at a table, their food trays touching. Lauren glanced around awkwardly, trying to avoid Paul's eyes. Ever since they'd started these lunches, Paul had been unfailingly distant. Polite, almost formal. Each time she looked at him, she felt a pang of loss. Especially today. That offhand compliment had been his first move beyond the impersonal.

She'd thrown it back in his face, and wished she hadn't. His question echoed in her mind. *Is it really so bad?* No, it wasn't bad. Being with him every day, sitting across from him, yearning to take his hand, to get closer, was worse than bad. It was absolute hell.

A woman stopped at their table, holding the hand of a little girl who looked to be about four. A man stood by the woman's side. She introduced them both to Lauren and Paul—her husband and the daughter he'd brought by so they could all have lunch together.

"You're pretty," the little girl said. "And he's handsome." A plump little finger pointed at Paul. "Is he your husband?"

Lauren laughed nervously as the mother admonished her daughter. "It's all right," Lauren said, wanting to reassure them that this wasn't a terrible blunder. Then looking at the girl, she answered, "No, honey. He's not my husband. We both work here."

Paul had also blanched at the question, but when Lauren laughed, so did he. He picked up the child and placed her in his lap. "Are you going to work here when you grow up?"

"Oh, yes. I just lo-o-ve makeup. Don't I, Mommy?"

"Sure do. I have to keep mine under lock and key." The mother then told her daughter they had to hurry and get their lunch before time ran out. The child slipped off Paul's lap, gave them a small wave, and the trio moved on.

As she watched them leave, Lauren reflected that these lunches had been wonderful for morale. When her father was still alive, he and Cheri Lee had done this often, claiming it made the employees more comfortable. It now seemed a tradition had been revived. Maybe when Paul was gone, she and E.J. could continue it.

The thought made her uneasy. Paul had to go, of course, but it was becoming increasingly obvious that his absence would create a gaping hole. She cut into a portion of chicken, trying not to think about Paul's eventual departure and the emptiness she felt.

"You're good with kids," she said.

"It's easy. I like them a lot." Paul took a bite of pork chop.

"That's nice." Lauren lifted a piece of chicken to her mouth.

They both chewed, both gazed around the large, bustling cafeteria. And waved, nodded, smiled. They did almost anything but look at each other.

At the scrape of a chair, Lauren turned her head to see E.J. settling beside her.

"You two look like you're shackled together by invisible ankle chains," E.J. announced.

Paul chuckled, obviously getting E.J.'s point. Lauren got it, too, but she pretended she hadn't. She fixed E.J. with an imperious look, much like one her mother often wore.

"What are you talking about?"

"If one were watching—which one was—one would think you two would rather spend a lifetime in Hades than one hour here. You guys aren't fooling anyone, Lor. You've got to do better than this."

"Dammit, E.J. Sometimes you're a royal pain. We're doing the best we can." Lauren turned to Paul for confirmation. "Aren't we?"

Paul chuckled again, then burst into laughter. A few heads turned to stare in surprise. "What do you think, Lauren?" Paul asked, his eyes full of mischief. "Think we create a picture of harmony?"

"Okay, okay," Lauren responded irritably. She hadn't been aware their uneasiness with each other had been quite so transparent. "What do you suggest?"

"Something to cap it off," E.J. answered. "You'll like the idea, I'm sure."

"Oh?" Lauren said warily. These days, E.J.'s suggestions usually meant nothing but trouble for her, and his roguish expression assured her she wouldn't like this one at all.

"Oh?" Paul echoed, also sounding wary.

"Attend the Christmas party together!" E.J. stood, looking very pleased with himself. "Harmony during the holidays. Has a nice ring, don't you think?"

"Nice," Lauren replied dully, unable to conjure up a reasonable refusal.

"Great," said Paul, with little enthusiasm.

"Marvelous. Simply marvelous." E.J. walked away. To return, Lauren hoped, to the hole he had crawled out of.

She turned then and glanced at Paul. Their eyes met, lingered. A current of fear and excitement, tangible as a two-hundred-and-twenty-volt shock, passed between them.

"Do you think we can carry it off, Paul?" Lauren clenched her fists, willing away the unsteadiness in her voice. "Can we create the illusion that our goals are in harmony?"

"The illusion?" Paul lifted a thick brow.

"Do you honestly believe they are?" Anger replaced Lauren's unsteadiness. She was so tired of the pretense.

Then Paul smiled—a smile that told her he knew what she meant and agreed entirely. "Tell you what, Lauren. I'd be proud to escort you to the party. Maybe we can discuss this then."

Lauren felt a burden lift from her shoulders. While she certainly wouldn't confess all, at least she no longer had to pretend she had nothing up her sleeve.

"Maybe we will, Paul." A grin, wide and happy, spread across her face. "Then again, maybe we won't."

CHAPTER SEVEN

LAUREN HADN'T FELT SO lighthearted in a long, long time. The Christmas party was being held in the large ballroom of an old San Diego hotel and was a wonder of lavish decorations. Huge lavender bouquets hung from the ceiling. The largest one, directly in the center, trailed long flowered streamers that nearly brushed the tops of their heads as she and Paul wended their way through a forest of lavender-covered tables.

White runners, bordered by small trees covered in hundreds of sparkling lights, separated groups of tables into more intimate blocks. A huge Christmas tree, covered in lavender and white bows and loaded down with gifts, sat beside a low stage at the front of the room.

It reminded Lauren of a fairyland, and tonight she felt like a princess. She didn't know why she should feel so exceptionally good. All she knew was, every time she looked at Paul her heart expanded further.

After they'd agreed to attend the party together, something strange had happened during their daily lunches. They had begun to talk. Really talk. They discovered they saw things eye-to-eye when it came to management. Both believed in the open-door policy, and in actually observing people work. Paul called it MBWA—Management by Wandering Around. Both thought that employee stock-ownership programs created more loyalty in the work force.

Additionally each had a thing for seventies music, had loved *The Phantom of the Opera, Cats* and *Little Shop of Horrors*. Paul liked convertibles, Lauren preferred sedans. Lauren liked high tech, Paul preferred leather and burlap. Yet they'd laughed about these differences, each saying the other's taste was "in their mouth."

Mostly Lauren had discovered that she really liked Paul Sherwood. Judging by his response to her, he liked her, too. They also tacitly realized this mutual admiration could prove highly inconvenient sometime down the road. But tonight was three days before Christmas and Lauren didn't care to dwell on that inconvenience. She wanted to dance, to laugh, to enjoy herself. Being with Paul enhanced her enjoyment of the evening very much.

Coming back from her mental journey, she looked up to see Paul smiling down at her. A warm glow enveloped her and she smiled back. They had been covering the room together, greeting employees and their husbands, wives and significant others.

"Look." Paul nudged her ribs, then gestured in the direction of Curtis Jordon, who was discreetly slipping a folded fifty-dollar bill to one of his co-workers.

"Some bets are being paid off," he whispered, with a soft chuckle.

"Bet Curtis thought he had a sure thing." Lauren laughed out loud, not really caring if she was heard. She brushed down her beaded maroon camisole and fluffed the mauve folds of her full-length chiffon skirt, feeling free and happy. She'd worn her hair down for the evening, and it was full of bouncing curls that brushed her bare shoulders. She turned her head, tossing the curls back, as she searched for family members.

"There's Jessie." Lauren pointed to a table near the stage, then slipped an arm around Paul's as they headed in that direction.

Lauren hadn't talked to Jessie since she'd made her uncharacteristic visit to the office. She wondered what Jessie had been about to say when Paul had interrupted them, and felt a twinge of inadequacy when she realized that she'd forgotten about it until now. Never mind. They could spend the evening catching up. Maybe they'd take a trip to the ladies' room the way they used to when they were younger.

As she and Paul moved between tables, greeting more employees in the process, he asked, "Is your mother here yet?"

"No. She always arrives in a limousine about forty-five minutes late. She likes to make an *entrance*." In the past, Lauren had been uncomfortable with the whole idea of Cheri Lee's "entrances." But tonight it seemed completely natural, just part of who her mother was. Even when Paul raised a mildly amused eyebrow, she felt at ease.

"That's Cheri Lee." Lauren laughed indulgently. "After all, these years people expect it." When had she acquired this easy acceptance? Lauren wondered. Recently, it seemed, but she couldn't quite pinpoint when.

"Show biz," Paul said, as if he understood perfectly.

"Show biz," Lauren repeated, wondering how it was that Paul always seemed to understand.

At the family table now, Lauren hugged her sister, who welcomed her effusively. Taking Lauren's hand, Jessie turned to a man sitting next to her who was now rising.

"Lauren, I'd like you to meet Bill Rosen."

Jessie hadn't exaggerated when she said Bill wasn't her type. Jess wore the white single-shouldered gown she'd purchased the day of the shareholders' meeting. Her hair was French-braided and coiled on her head, set off by a single hibiscus. The serpent bracelet adorned her arm. She looked every inch an Egyptian princess, and one would expect a toga-wearing prince to accompany her.

At times like these, Lauren was glad she was good at concealing her reactions. Bill reminded her of a David Niven with glasses. Natty he was, in his oh-so-crisp navy suit, tasteful tie and matching pocket kerchief. But how unlike Jessie's usual leather-clad escorts with their ponytails or butch haircuts.

Still, if he made Jessie happy...

"So nice to meet you." Lauren greeted Bill with genuine warmth, then drew Paul forward for an introduction.

The two men shook hands. Quite formally, Lauren observed, like opponents squaring up for a match. Perhaps Paul was beginning to feel like a member of the family, feeling proprietary toward Jessie, and sizing Bill up to see if he would be good to her. Not that it mattered, Lauren thought with amusement. If Jessie liked Bill, she wouldn't care what anyone thought.

E.J. was there, too, obviously uncomfortable in his traditional Christmas-party tuxedo. He'd brought a quiet, pretty woman who, Lauren suspected, would fade into the background for the entire night, like all E.J.'s previous Christmas-party dates.

Introductions finished, Lauren and Paul took their seats at the round table. A waitress appeared to take their cocktail orders and Lauren ordered white wine. Turning back to face the group, she realized the outer layer of her skirt had twisted unpleasantly beneath her.

She shifted, smoothing down the wispy fabric. Comfortable again, she lifted her hand only to have it yanked back by a sudden tug.

"Uh-oh." The clasp of her diamond dinner watch had caught on a bead of the camisole, pinning her wrist halfway between waist and armpit. She struggled awkwardly to untangle the watch and was on the verge of jerking it loose when Paul intervened.

"Let me. You wouldn't want to rip that pretty top." Paul slipped his fingers over her wrist and felt for the spot where the bead had caught the watch guard. As he worked to disentangle the clasp from the beads, the top of his hand brushed the underside of Lauren's breast.

Until that moment, Lauren had been so focused on the people attending the gala, she'd been able to forget the powerful sexual pull between her and Paul.

No more.

Paul's touch generated an intense surge—a desire that swept back memories of their entwined bodies on the *Gypsy Rose*. Lauren stifled a gasp.

In the same instant, Paul freed the watchband.

"There," he said.

"There," Lauren echoed in a whisper, wondering if Paul had felt that surge, too.

His hand remained on her side and Lauren looked up at him. His expression was soft, containing boyish admiration and barely concealed awe. His eyes held promises . . . of wondrous moments, of glorious happiness . . . Promises of love.

Love?

Was that *love* she saw in his eyes?

"What *are* you two doing?" Jessie's delighted laugh sharply reminded Lauren where they were. A hot flush suffused her cheeks, and she gave an embarrassed little laugh.

"My—my watch got snagged. Paul was . . . was . . ."

"You caught us," Paul shot back smoothly. "It's not often a man can cop a gentlemanly feel in a place like this." He chuckled pleasantly, although Lauren noticed his laughter sounded a bit strained.

"But success is ours." He lifted Lauren's wrist high, making a V sign with his free hand.

Jessie clapped her hands in mock accolade. "Your hero," she teased her sister. "Still, you gave us an intriguing moment there. It could have been the best entertainment of the night. Oh, the possibilities. How boring the truth often is."

Not boring at all, thought Lauren. But Paul's witticism had allowed her to relax.

"You're so jaded, Jessie," she said teasingly, no longer feeling caught in a private moment.

"Since that's coming from someone who thinks going out for frozen yogurt is a big thrill, I'm not going to pay much attention to it," Jessie retorted.

"She's thinking about hitting the big time," Paul returned before Lauren did. He still held her hand, which she allowed to relax in his grip. It felt so right there. "Lauren's told me she'd love to try skydiving."

"Oh, sure." Jessie scoffed. "E.J.'s a jumper, but never Lauren. If anyone has her feet on the ground, it's my sister. Does she plan to wear a parachute, or will it be a kamikaze mission?''

Jessie turned to Lauren for confirmation, while E.J. complained of being hurt that Lauren hadn't asked him to take her.

''Actually,'' Lauren confessed, ''I did do ground school once, but I chickened out on the plane, which is why I'd never go up with you.'' Lauren stared at her brother archly. ''Paul was nice enough not to give me a bad time about it. He even offered to go with me if I ever wanted to try again.''

''Lauren!'' Jessie's eye's widened in genuine surprise. ''You never told me that.''

''You were in New York at the time, and I had almost forgotten about it until Paul told me he jumped.'' It had been so long since Lauren and Jessie had traded insults, and Lauren, greatly enjoying herself, felt expansive. She glanced at Paul and added, ''Maybe I'll take him up on it.''

''My, my, Lor. You're full of surprises tonight.'' Jessie was smiling in astonishment and curiosity, looking back and forth at Lauren and Paul. She said to Paul, ''Tell us about some of your experiences.''

''Sure,'' Paul agreed. ''But first, how about it, Lauren?'' He looked at her in anticipation, wearing a challenging smile.

''Wait,'' Lauren said, her eyes skipping from face to face, realizing everyone was waiting to see what she'd say. ''Are you asking me to jump?''

''Uh-huh.''

''She'll never do it, ' said E.J.

''Not in a million years,'' Jessie added.

"When and where?" Lauren tilted her jaw stubbornly, suddenly impatient with her siblings' image of her as a prim and proper scaredy-cat.

"I've made reservations for the day after Christmas. I can call one in for you, too. What do you say?" Paul's smile had vanished and his new expression told her that he'd understand if she refused.

Jessie and E.J. still fixed her with knowing gazes—gazes that told Lauren they thought they knew her inside and out. She wanted to prove them wrong.

"You're on," she proclaimed, and when her brother's and sister's expressions remained unchanged, Lauren realized she'd have to actually go through with the jump before they would become believers.

"Don't look at each other like that, you two," Lauren admonished. "You guys aren't so brave. Didn't you both cry when I took you to the haunted house?"

"What did you expect from a four-year-old?" Jessie retorted. E.J. interjected his own response, and the three of them launched into a new round of insulting banter, which had been their custom since childhood. The others in the party, amused and picking up on the mood, joined in. Even Bill, Lauren was pleasantly surprised to note, got caught up in the interchange. She'd pegged him as, well...stuffy, and was glad she'd been wrong.

"I'm going to rescue you before this gets out of hand." Paul, still laughing at one of Jessie's witty comebacks, stood up and took Lauren's hand. They walked onto the dance floor, and he took her expertly into his arms. "They're playing our song."

"I didn't know we had a song," Lauren said jauntily, still feeling reckless.

"What's the name of the song playing?"

"'The Wind Beneath My Wings.'"

"Our song," Paul replied. "From now on."

"Oh." Lauren's wit suddenly deserted her. Paul had been teasing. She wished he hadn't been. She wanted it to be true; wanted them to have a song, to build memories.

Paul brought her closer to him, and now her ear rested on his chest. She heard the soft movement of his breath, felt the beat of the music, sensed something swelling within her very core. The words began etching themselves into her mind, bringing a hazy recognition. The song spoke of an element in their relationship she'd overlooked. What was it?

"You don't have to do it," Paul said.

"Skydive?" She knew exactly what he meant. She always knew these days.

Through her eyelashes, she saw him nod.

"I know it frightens you."

Lauren drank in his wonderful, rugged face. His jawline was smooth, freshly shaven. The night on the *Gypsy Rose* he'd had a faint stubble, and she recalled the delicious tingle she'd felt as it brushed her face, her breasts. She had soared with him that night. It hurt to know she'd never do it again.

"Yes," she whispered. "It frightens me." *And so do you.* "But I want to do it anyway." Yes. Oh, yes, she did. But even as she spoke, Lauren didn't know what she really meant. Did she want to fall from a plane? Soar in the sky?

Or did she yearn to soar in Paul's arms?

"Cheri Lee's here!" someone shouted. A crescendo of voices repeated the announcement until it sounded like a chant. The band stopped playing, mid-song.

"Her highness's entrance." Lauren smiled up at Paul as he released her from his arms. The comment had been made without malice, lovingly in fact, and Paul recognized how easily she accepted the flaws of her loved ones—how easily she would accept his flaws.

Paul allowed Lauren to take his hand and pull him toward the door.

"She always comes in the front," she explained.

"Does she do this every year?" The sheer flashiness of this ritual reminded Paul vaguely of Cotton.

"Every year."

"With a straight face?"

Lauren laughed. "Oh, she takes it very seriously. As do the employees, so you'd better not say that too loud."

Paul noticed a bevy of disapproving glances directed at him, and decided to be prudent, keep his thoughts to himself.

Soon Cheri appeared. E.J. had somehow materialized by the door, holding a sheaf of lilacs and daisies, which he placed in the crook of his mother's arm.

Cheri, covered from head to toe in a stunning lavender sheath, smiled regally, her free hand resting on her queenly cane as she surveyed the room. The subdued lights reflected lushly off the rich fabric of her dress as Cheri walked—no, thought Paul, *glided*—down the velvet runway, her head turning from side to side as she smiled and greeted employees. They crushed against each other, eager to see her, commenting enthusiastically on her wonderful gown, her flawless hair.

Paul was dumbstruck. These people clearly adored the autocratic Cheri Lee, much as the British adored their queen.

How had she commanded such loyalty? He looked down at Lauren, who wore the same adoring expression. In that instant, Paul realized Lauren would someday inherit this loyalty, would earn it as her mother undoubtedly had. She would be less dramatic, more democratic, but the employees would adore her, as well. It was part of her heritage.

What right had he to take it from her?

The question haunted him throughout the evening. Dinner was served immediately after Cheri had taken her seat, but Paul could only pick at his meal, his appetite destroyed by what he'd seen. To his regret, once Cheri joined the table, the Afton children abandoned their banter and the conversation became decidedly mundane. He was trying to devise a mildly controversial topic so he could lose himself in the ensuing discussion when the music stopped.

Drums rolled, the reverberations ricocheting throughout the room. E.J. materialized on the platform, standing before the microphone, his shirtfront bowing over his lavender cummerbund, the matching bow tie slightly askew. Paul had been so distracted he hadn't noticed that E.J. had left the table.

"Ellis Sr. wore a tuxedo so well," Cheri murmured as E.J. began to introduce her. The woman's subtle put-down of E.J. enraged Paul for reasons he didn't understand.

"But E.J.'s a helluva man," he responded coldly. Both Lauren and Cheri looked at him sharply.

"Why, of course he is. Just like his father." Cheri stood then, smoothed her skirt, gripped her cane, and floated toward the stage.

"So, without further introduction, I give you Cheri Lee Afton!" E.J. announced.

The cheers drowned out Paul's thoughts as Cheri climbed onto the dais with E.J.'s assistance. Even after she mouthed numerous thank-yous and waved the crowd down, whistles and cheers still arose from the back of the room.

"This Christmas, as every Christmas, we gather to celebrate and give thanks for the abundance Cheri Lee Cosmetics has given us throughout the years. This year my family and I would especially like to give thanks to each and every one of you. For without you, dear friends, there would be no Cheri Lee Cosmetics."

Her voice was strong, clear and quite beautiful with its melodic Southern accent. Paul became caught up in her rhetoric, finally recognizing the source of the power of this woman he would have preferred to dislike.

With each word, each sentence, she gave credit for her success, their success, to the people cheering her.

"And I want... I want..." Cheri's voice wavered, faltered. She swayed toward E.J., placing a hand on his arm for support.

"What I want is..." She looked toward E.J., her eyes losing their clarity, confusion covering her aristocratic features.

A low murmur ran through the crowd.

"Oh, dear God!" Lauren exclaimed softly. She leaped to her feet, ready to rush to the stage, then stopped. What could she do? What would she say?

Her public-speaking abilities had never been good. This wasn't her arena.

She stared down at her sister who was gaping in dismay. Jessie—with her flamboyant way, her years of dramatic training—could turn this disaster into victory.

"Jessie!" Lauren cried. Jessie turned her head, her eyes wide with shock. "Help her. Help Mother."

"No... Oh, no, Lauren. What can I do?"

"What you always do. Turn it into a joke," Lauren answered sharply. "Just get her off the hook."

"But you, you always do this stuff.... I can't."

Waves of hushed whispers undulated through the room as Cheri Lee Afton stammered. "What I mean to say is... Oh, dear, E.J., what do I mean to say?"

"Now!" Lauren commanded, and, as if she'd been shot, Jessie leaped up and sprinted across the parquet dance floor, onto the stage.

"Mom..." Jessie said. "You know E.J. never remembers to bring your speech notes. But I have them." She plucked a facial tissue from the bosom of her dress, extended her arm, and waved it jauntily. Most of the employees had known Jessie since childhood and had enjoyed, even encouraged, her outrageous sense of humor. Their tension exploded into a thunderous burst of laughter.

The din gave Jessie time to cross the stage and place her arm around her mother. "It's okay, Mom. It's okay," she murmured. Hoping she could carry this off while fighting back her tears, she pasted an amused smile on her face. Apparently sensing what Jessie was doing, Cheri matched the smile with one of her own.

As the first burst of laughter died, Jessie delivered her next one-liner with perfect timing. "Written on a tissue, of course. But think how useful that is. When you're done with your speech, you can use it to remove your makeup." The crowd roared again.

E.J. moved to guide Cheri from the stage, but Jessie shook her head. When the second round of laughing subsided, Jessie raised her hand, asking for silence.

"As most of you know, Mom has had a few health challenges lately, and we decided that it would be easier on her if she didn't conduct the entire program. So...we concocted this little charade for your amusement. Didn't we, Mom?"

Jessie turned to Cheri, who nodded, still wearing a slightly cockeyed smile, which worried Jessie immensely. She leaned forward and kissed her mother's cheek, struggling against the choking fear in her chest, then straightened and said, "Say good night, Mom."

"Good night," Cheri replied in a small, hollow voice.

Jessie then gestured toward E.J., who helped Cheri off the stage as the crowd applauded enthusiastically.

Lauren's mixture of emotions—relief at Jessie's brilliant performance and a gripping fear that her mother had suffered another stoke—nearly paralyzed her. She remained in her chair, staring numbly at her clutched hands.

Paul touched her shoulder. "I'll help you get her to the hospital."

With his help, Lauren rose, suddenly aware that she was trembling. Paul rubbed her bare shoulder. "You're freezing cold."

With a mechanical nod of agreement, Lauren crossed her arms and massaged her icy skin, but the only warmth she felt came from Paul's gentle touch.

Shaking off her lethargy, she moved forward to assist E.J. Paul stayed by her side.

"Our first award tonight is for Employee of the Year," Jessie was saying from the stage. "Wonder who our hapless workhorse, er, that is, our devoted recipient . . ."

Thanks to Jessie's irreverent presentation, the employees were totally absorbed. No one was paying attention to what was going on behind the scenes. As Lauren reached her mother's side, she felt she was overlooking something highly significant about this moment. But her attention was focused on Cheri Lee, and she allowed that thought to drift away.

"Paul and I will take you to the hospital, Mother," Lauren said quietly.

"I'll go with you." E.J.'s brows drew together in worry.

Lauren almost agreed, but then noticed a few furtive glances coming their way. Cheri Lee was the company's figurehead, idol and motivator. It was one thing to speak of behind-the-scenes health problems, quite another to have it happen onstage. Besides, the Aftons had played down the previous stroke, implied it had been mild, and that Cheri Lee just wanted to take it easier after so many years of hard work.

"Stay and finish the program, E.J. Jessie needs your support," Lauren said decisively. "Also, if people suspect what really happened tonight... Well, it would be demoralizing."

"But, I—"

"Lauren is right." Although Cheri's voice quivered, Lauren gulped a relieved breath. At least her mother was lucid enough to recognize what was going on. "Come see me afterward, E.J. I'm fine. You'll see."

Cheri patted E.J. on the hand. Still looking uncertain, he returned to his table.

Paul and Lauren escorted Cheri out a side door where Paul thoughtfully draped his jacket over Lauren's bare shoulders before leaving to get her sedan.

A few moments later they were speeding down the highway to the nearest hospital, Paul in the driver's seat, Lauren in the back holding her mother.

"Jessie was brilliant, wasn't she?" Cheri said sadly.

In the rearview mirror, Paul could see Cheri's head resting on Lauren's shoulder while Lauren stroked her hair. A lone tear ran down the older woman's face, followed by a choked sob. The pathetic sound nearly tore Paul's heart out. He didn't belong here, wasn't needed except to drive the car, and felt like an eavesdropping intruder.

"My mind went blank," Cheri sobbed against Lauren's shoulder. "I don't...know what... happened."

Lauren didn't say what Paul knew she must be thinking. Cheri had just suffered another stroke—undoubtedly small, but still a stroke.

"The doctors will tell us," Lauren soothed her. "You'll be okay, Mother."

"I won't be able to do the sales meeting, Lauren. This can't happen again." The sobs had subsided and Cheri's voice had grown stronger.

Paul felt, rather than saw, Cheri abruptly righting herself and pulling out of Lauren's arms. "Damnation," she whispered. "It's hell, getting old."

"You're not old," Lauren replied reassuringly, and Paul was almost convinced that she believed it. "This is an illness, not old age."

"An old person's illness," Cheri retorted. She sounded like her usual self. "I feel fine now. I don't want to go to the hospital. Take me home, Lauren."

"Mother," Lauren answered firmly, "we're going. I don't want to upset you, so don't argue. You will see a doctor tonight to make sure nothing else happens."

"Very well. If it makes you feel better." There was genuine love and appreciation in Cheri's voice.

A longing inside Paul grew to an overpowering ache. His father had vanished before Paul had learned to walk, leaving his mother to raise him alone. His two-year reign on "Wizard Kids" had separated them for long periods of time, during which he'd been cared for by impersonal network chaperons. Shortly before his thirteenth birthday, he'd left home for good.

First there had been college, where he'd obtained a master's degree in finance at nineteen. He'd then headed for Chicago to earn his enfant-terrible reputation on the Mercantile Exchange. Then, he'd gone on to New York and Cotton. When he and Cotton had quarreled and parted, he had returned to California where his only family—his mother—lived. Then she, too, had left him.

The hospital was coming up and Paul followed the signs to the emergency entrance, wishing this ache in his gut would vanish. Stopping at the entrance, he turned to Lauren and Cheri.

"I'll find someone to bring a wheelchair." He sprinted out of the car, running inside, feeling as if he were running for his life. He prayed, with sudden urgency, that Cheri would defeat her affliction. Even more, he prayed that Lauren's family would survive.

He'd never had one. He didn't want Lauren to lose hers.

CHAPTER EIGHT

"I DON'T KNOW WHY I need all these tubes and wires," Cheri grumbled in her deep drawl.

"We need to monitor your vital signs. And the oxygen will do you good." Cheri's family doctor, who'd accompanied them from the emergency room to the intensive-care unit, smiled compassionately as he supervised the nurses' activities.

He'd been calm, reassuring, as he'd explained to both Lauren and Cheri that she'd had what he termed a ministroke. There appeared to be no permanent damage, but it bore watching, and some further testing was in order. Cheri needed to stay in the hospital for the next twenty-four hours.

"At least you don't have to wear one of those awful gowns, Mother," Lauren said, leaning against the doorway. She'd phoned the housekeeper and asked her to bring some night things and, of course, the ever-essential makeup kit, so her mother would be more comfortable. "It's not all that bad."

"There's so much left to do for Christmas," Cheri objected as a nurse slipped an oxygen tube into her nose.

"It will wait." Fatigue had seeped through every pore of Lauren's body, even the curls of her hair. She could feel them wilt as she spoke.

"It'll have to wait," the doctor said firmly, checking all the connections to Cheri's body. Lauren noticed one of the nurses giving him an unappreciative glance, but for her part she was glad the doctor was being so meticulous. Satisfied, he took Cheri's hand, patted it, and told her he'd see her on morning rounds. He left and the nurses followed.

The minute he was gone, Cheri removed the oxygen tube.

"Mother!" Lauren rushed to the bed.

"I'll put it back." She patted for Lauren to sit. "But I want to talk to you first."

"We can talk later." But Lauren complied and perched on the edge of the bed, expecting a nurse to come in any moment to shoo her out.

"No." Cheri's gray eyes grew solemn and Lauren noted a tear in one corner. "If I should die—"

"Don't even say that!" Suddenly the tears Lauren had been fighting all night rushed to her eyes. She blinked them back, swallowing the sob that wanted to follow. "You won't die, Mother."

Cheri smiled. "Probably not, especially if you have any say about it. But I need to explain something. I know you were hurt when I sided with E.J. on the merger, Lauren. It's been troubling me ever since that I never told you why."

Lauren took her mother's hand and stroked her skin. It felt dry, parched, and made her suspect that Cheri was very fragile right now. "We don't have to talk about it at all. Really, we don't."

"Yes. Yes, we do. You see, although I know you're capable of it, I don't think you should run Cheri Lee Cosmetics by yourself. And after you refused my offer to come back and help, I knew that's exactly what you would do." Cheri freed her hand and brushed Lauren's cheek. "It will consume your whole life, dear. You'll find yourself focusing on it day and night. I want more for you—a husband, children, a fulfilling social life...."

"But I love the company." How was it, Lauren wondered, that she'd never known her mother felt this way?

"I know. That's why I worry about you. You're so dutiful. Always have been. But sometimes I think a little of Jessie's rebelliousness, a little of E.J.'s easygoing ways, would do you good."

She understood them so well, Lauren realized. Almost better than they understood themselves. And none of them knew it.

"All I want to say," Cheri continued, obviously getting tired now, "is give Paul a chance. Together, I think you can build something beautiful. Apart, you risk fragmented lives...."

Cheri's voice trailed off and her eyelids drooped. Lauren stood and insisted that her mother go back on the oxygen. A nurse appeared at the door, frowned slightly and told Lauren her time was up. Lauren nodded and bent to kiss Cheri Lee's forehead.

"I'll give it a lot of thought, Mother."

Beneath the tubes, Lauren could see Cheri Lee's mouth turn up. Lauren smiled in return. "I'll see you in the morning," she said, then picked up her evening bag and went into the hallway where Paul was waiting. The nurse dimmed the lights as she left.

Paul was seated in a chair flipping through a magazine with obvious inattention. He looked up as she approached.

"How is she?"

"The doctors are optimistic," Lauren replied.

"Good!"

Sincerity rang in that single word, and she saw that Paul cared very much—more than she'd ever suspected. She thought about her mother's message, the one hidden between the lines. Cheri Lee hadn't been talking just about the firm. First E.J., then Jessie, now Cheri Lee. Was her entire family determined to pair her with Paul?

Paul got up and placed a supporting arm around her shoulder. "Ready to go home?" he asked, gazing down at her with concern.

Lauren nodded, and as he led her to the elevator, she wondered what *was* standing in the way of their relationship. She saw nothing but caring and open support in Paul's stormy-blue eyes, and could tell from his gaze that he, too, wanted them to be together. The answer to her question became crystal clear.

The only one standing in their way was herself.

BILL WAS LIKE HER shadow that night. Always by her side, quiet, strong, and *there*. Most of the men Jessie had dated in the past had been walking egos, consumed by their own interests or their bodybuilding, and typically during a crisis like tonight's, would have made a hasty exit with mumbled excuses about "hating hospitals," and not interfering with "family stuff."

Jessie had never been disturbed by this. She wouldn't have wanted those men with her, anyway. But Bill was different. There was warmth and sensitivity beneath his stiff exterior, and she craved the solace it gave her.

She'd been a little irritable with him at first, surprised by his steady presence, and annoyed that she'd actually wanted it. He hadn't seemed to mind. Now, as they stood outside her mother's intensive-care room, he touched her shoulder lightly in an effort to comfort her. A flood of gratitude washed through her and she leaned against him. It was late—after midnight—and the hospital had allowed them to come up only because she was a family member.

"I'll wait here," Bill said, removing the hibiscus from her hair. "And remember, it's not as bad as it looks. The doctors said she should be fine. Out in time to enjoy Christmas."

Jessie nodded, looking down at the wilted flower in Bill's hand. The antiseptic smell and hushed sounds in the softly lit hallways filled her with dread. Her father had died in a hospital, amid the same somber silence and acrid odors.

She couldn't bear it if her mother died, too, especially with all these bad feelings between them. Now she wanted to go in, kneel beside her mother's bed, and confess everything. Confess that all she'd ever wanted was her approval; confess that she'd sold out Cheri Lee Cosmetics. But her mother needed love and support tonight, not hurtful confessions, and Jessie was determined to provide it. Bill's presence made it easier.

"Thanks for being here." She straightened, reluctant to leave him outside, then stepped into the black rectangle leading to her mother's bed.

"You were spectacular tonight," Bill said to her retreating back. "A natural star. Your mother would have been proud."

She looked over her shoulder and smiled wanly, thinking she should hate the sight of him since he was the one who'd persuaded her to sell.

But she didn't.

Bill Rosen was wonderfully different. He made her feel unique, capable, likable, in a way she hadn't felt since her father's death.

Bill watched Jessie's shadowy form move toward the figure in the bed. He didn't have to be there to know what she was seeing. "Resting comfortably in progressive care," the doctors had said, but Bill wondered how anyone could "rest comfortably" with tubes in their noses, tubes in their arms, and wires connected to all parts of their body.

Recalling how he'd felt when his father had suffered a heart attack, he could imagine the emotions racing through Jessie. Especially in light of the stock she'd sold to him. Guilt punished cruelly, and although Jessie had never said so, Bill knew she'd severed her heritage with the sale.

He'd often wondered what had occurred to make her want to cut family ties, but after meeting Cheri Afton he knew instantly. Those two viewed life from entirely different perspectives. It would be miraculous if they found even one thing to agree upon.

When Jessie had accepted his offer to buy, he'd decided to abandon any personal interest he had in her, knowing their relationship would end the day she discovered his true intent. He saw no purpose in starting something that would inevitably end badly.

But Jessie had openly pursued him. Invited him to a lunch at Rosarita Beach in a rustic little restaurant where they'd eaten shrimp, flour tortillas and salsa. She'd delighted him with tales of her year in the circus, about glittering costumes tacked together with safety pins, about the morning the Tattooed Man had been caught in a rainstorm and she'd spent the rest of the day repairing the damage.

"You mean those guys aren't really tattooed?" Bill had asked in mock shock. "You've just shattered one of my most cherished childhood beliefs."

She laughed, took a healthy swallow of Mexican beer, and replied, "Our circus couldn't afford a real one."

Bill thought then that he'd never met a woman more vital, more glowing than Jessie Afton. The pain of anticipated loss had been overwhelming and he'd promised himself never to see her again.

But she phoned again, this time with spare tickets to the opera. Bill hadn't been able to find—hadn't wanted to find—an appropriate refusal.

How different she looked when he'd picked her up that night. He wouldn't have been surprised if she'd greeted him wearing hiking boots and a formal gown. But she'd looked almost ethereal, in an ankle-length challis skirt and a glittering sweater, her hair French-braided and crowned with a single live flower.

Throughout the performance, he'd glanced at her, thinking she was mercurial, unpredictable, exciting. And his pain nearly tore him apart.

He hadn't planned to kiss her that night at her door. He had planned to shake her hand and send her inside. Alone. But she was so lovely, so tempting, her glossed lips parted, her eyelids half shut . . . Before he knew it, he was lowering his head.

Lord, he could feel her in his arms even now—alive, fragrant, passionate. He'd deepened the kiss, thrust his tongue into her mouth to taste the exquisite sweetness of her, and she'd welcomed him, encouraged him, teased him with her response.

"Come inside," she'd whispered in his ear, her breath like a spring breeze. "Stay."

"Yes," he'd answered, despite all his good intentions.

Then Jessie had led him to her bed. And, ignoring his stab of guilt, Bill had followed, knowing he'd stay with her until the inevitable happened.

"Is Jess with Mom?" The voice, accompanied by rapid footsteps, interrupted his thoughts, and Bill turned to see E.J. rushing toward him.

"Yes." Bill looked at his watch. "She's been in there about ten minutes."

"Wish they'd let us all in at once. This waiting is hell."

"The doctors said it was just a ministroke," Bill offered, reminding E.J. of what he was sure he already knew. "Said she should recover well. They just want to monitor her for the next twenty-four hours."

"Yeah...I know. Should recover well." E.J. sounded bleak. "That's what they said about Dad."

"I hear you," Bill answered, running out of assurances.

"Jessie did a helluva job tonight," E.J. said, and Bill felt relieved at the change of subject.

"She sure did." Bill had been awestruck by Jessie's stage presence, her timing and quick wit. He'd seen this side of her before, and she'd told him she'd studied acting in New York for nearly two years, had even performed in a few Shakespearean productions. Yet it had never occurred to Bill that she could transfer this skill to a public arena.

"Jessie's a very special woman," he said almost dreamily, not caring if he sounded like a lovesick calf.

"Yes, she is. Too bad she doesn't know it."

"She will," Bill replied, suddenly knowing that no matter the cost, he would not allow Jessie Afton to slip from his life. This woman was too special to ever let go.

"She will," he repeated emphatically.

He looked down then, and saw the flower still clutched in his hand. Its pristine petals had grown crumpled and limp, were edged with brown.

The flower was dying. Bill wished he knew how to bring it back to life.

PAUL'S JACKET WAS STILL draped over Lauren's shoulders when they reached the door of her home. They stood beneath the soft lights that flanked her front entrance and he waited while she scrambled through her silver bag, looking for keys.

"They don't seem to be here," she said wearily, as though this one extra problem was just too much for her. Tear tracks streaked her face. She looked so tired Paul ached for her. She'd been strong and in control through the entire affair of checking her mother into the hospital; later, though, after leaving Cheri Lee in the darkened hospital room, tears had streamed down Lauren's face. She'd cried without a sound, and Paul had wanted to pull her to him, comfort her. But he hadn't.

Now he did. "The keys are around," he assured her, relieved that she didn't pull away. "We'll find them."

Lauren rested her head on Paul's chest, allowing herself to draw comfort from his strength.

"Thank you, Paul."

He smiled quizzically. "What for?"

"For being here tonight."

Without really meaning to, she tilted her head and placed a soft kiss on Paul's lips.

It was meant as a gesture of gratitude, not passion, but the minute her mouth touched his, something primitive exploded inside her. *Paul must feel it, too,* she thought, as he deepened the kiss with a fierce pressure that swept every ounce of breath from her body. She parted her lips, allowing his probing tongue to graze her teeth, capture her tongue, and begin a dance that whispered of tandem rhythms, steaming bodies and tangled sheets.

She slipped her arms around his neck and pulled him closer to her, losing her grief in the wondrous pressure of his mouth; in the feel of his chest against her breasts, hips against hips, thighs against thighs.

He released her mouth, raining tiny frantic kisses along her cheekbones. He lifted his hands and tangled them in her curls, then trailed his lips along the curve of her neck. She arched her head back, drinking in the glorious sensations, the newfound joy that eclipsed her pain.

Suddenly he stopped, and dropped his arms to clasp her to him fiercely, his breath heavy against the top of her head. She sank against him, her cheek resting on the luxurious fabric of his jacket. She could hear the rapid thudding of his heart.

As he held her there, so possessively, so tenderly, she knew she could never carry out her plan, and she thought about what her mother had said.

The words of "their" song played through her head. *Wind beneath my wings.* That was exactly what Paul had been tonight—had been for a long, long while. Ever since that fateful marketing meeting, when he had stepped into the shadows and let her shine, drawing power away from himself and bestowing it on her. He'd allowed her to soar.

His efforts had enhanced the firm, enhanced her. She saw now that he'd been telling the truth. He did want to change. She'd been wrong about Paul, terribly wrong. He wasn't her enemy, he was her friend. And she wanted him to be more. Much, much more.

With a burst of joy, she lifted her head to drink in his wonderful face. His breath felt warm and sensual, erotic as a soul kiss, and she looked at him, knowing all the happiness she felt was reflected in her expression.

Guilt stabbed Paul like a rusty knife, the pain so intense it seemed physical. Her face told him everything. She loved him. Trusted him.

And he would betray her.

"You're wonderful," she murmured.

"That's nice of you to say," he replied stiffly.

The knife twisted as he saw her glow fade. *Someone please help me.* He loved her, but his career—his whole life—was on the line. How had this happened? How had he become so hopelessly involved?

"Did I say something wrong?" Her voice was soft, puzzled.

"No, Lauren. Nothing you ever say is wrong." He choked slightly, and the words came out huskily. He tightened his embrace, hoping she'd accept what he'd said and not press.

"Good," she whispered against his chest, relaxing in his hold. She smelled so sweet tonight; her usual lilac scent had been replaced by something more exotic—a spicy, heady blend that made his blood rush.

Her body seemed boneless beneath his touch and he ached to pull her even closer, to lose himself and his painful thoughts in the sparks he knew they'd ignite off each other.

But he couldn't. His guilt—intense, tormenting—tore him apart. He wanted Lauren Afton, wanted her forever as his wife. And the minute his carefully conceived plans came to fruition, they would destroy any chance of that.

He needed to think. Given time, he could come up with a solution—a way to have it all. And when he did, he'd make love to Lauren with all the passion and tenderness she deserved. But not tonight, even though he knew Lauren expected it, wanted it.

No, not tonight. His impending betrayal loomed too large.

He searched for a convenient avoidance technique. Obediently, as always, his quick mind recalled what he'd forgotten earlier.

He forced a chuckle.

"What?" Lauren asked, still smiling.

"I just remembered where your keys are."

He released her, stepped back, reached into his pocket and pulled out some keys. Hers. He dangled them and feigned a sheepish grin. "Sorry. I put them in my pocket. Guess it was automatic."

"Sir Sherwood to the rescue." Lauren turned, unlocked and opened the door, then looked over her shoulder, an unmistakable invitation on her face. "How 'bout some coffee?"

Wrapping his arms around her, he leaned against her back and placed a kiss on her head. "You've had a hard day and night. What you need right now is sleep."

Turning, she started to protest, but Paul placed a finger over her mouth. "Shh... Listen to me. Sleep, that's what you need. I'll see you the day after Christmas with your present."

"Present?"

"Skydiving, remember? You and me, darlin', we're going to fall through the sky."

"Oh, my Lord, I forgot!" The stark terror on her face almost made Paul forget his guilt. He laughed.

"Not going to back out on me, are you?"

Lifting her chin in that proud gesture Paul had come to love, she replied, "Certainly not." Then her expression changed. "Unless Mother's condition changes."

Paul nodded in understanding. "I'll be at my ranch." He pulled out a wallet and gave her a card with the number. "Call me if anything happens. But I'm sure it won't."

"No... The doctor said..." But she still looked uncertain.

He planted a kiss on her forehead. "He knows what he's doing. So believe it." He gave her a little pat on the back and sent her inside. "Now scoot and get some rest. The big event will be here soon."

Turning, he headed for the driveway and his car. As he walked, her whispered reply caressed his ears.

"Yes. Soon."

She wasn't talking about skydiving.

Neither was he.

PAUL SPENT CHRISTMAS EVE alone. He'd released his staff and refused the many business invitations he'd received. The silence nearly deafened him; he hadn't been prepared for that.

He opened the sliding doors of a concealed wet bar, reached beneath for some ice cubes, and dropped them individually into his glass.

Plunk, plunk, plunk. The sound echoed his feelings. Picking up a bottle of Scotch he poured a healthy shot, then crossed an Oriental rug and resumed his seat in a glove-leather recliner.

Leaning back and taking a sip of his drink, Paul recalled how the interior designer had argued with him about the recliner, telling him it wasn't stylish. But Paul had convinced the man he was after comfort, and if style was sacrificed, so be it. Well, he had his comfort, all right. He looked around the beamed, high-ceiling room with its rough-hewn walls, Spanish tile, and patterned rugs that had cost a small fortune, surveying the luxurious enclave he'd created for himself.

Now it all seemed hollow. He'd built this place for his mother, but she'd been so absorbed in the little company she'd built while Paul was growing up that she'd only found odd weekends to visit it. She'd seemed happy enough during those times, although she'd occasionally commented that it was awfully big. Since her death, Paul, too, had found it awfully big. And empty.

Lauren, he knew, would be spending the holiday with her family. He could imagine the warmth and affection there, as they exchanged carefully selected gifts. Smells of pine needles and baked goods would probably fill the rooms and they would hug one other with an abundance of love that was only a dim memory for Paul.

He glanced at his Christmas tree, which had been decorated by his housekeeper in stunning shades of rose and turquoise. It was beautiful, breathtaking, all his. But there were no presents beneath it. Gifts had arrived, of course. Stylish boxes, impersonally and elegantly wrapped for givers who'd never even seen the contents. Gifts similar to the ones Paul had sent out. The only gift that mattered to him was a small soap carving of Galahad that his housekeeper's son had given him. Everywhere Paul looked in his huge room, he saw loneliness.

Galahad stirred beside him, then stood and laid his head on Paul's knees. Paul scratched him behind his ears. The collie wagged his tail, and Paul leaned over, placing his head against the dog's soft coat, thinking about his new strategy.

Lauren would be upset at first, but everything would work out in the end. Not that she was the only one who would react badly to this surprise move, but holiday junkets had put everyone out of reach and there wasn't time for notification. Not that Paul would have contacted them under any circumstances. The element of surprise would work in his favor, giving no one time to stop him.

With a humorless chuckle he imagined the horrified expression on his partner's face when he learned the news. His backers, too, would sputter in outrage. They'd all put a lot of work into this, and a change of this magnitude would alarm them. But he could pull it off. *Had* to pull it off. If he failed, Lauren would hate him, would walk out of his life. The consequences were greater than any he'd ever faced before.

"So, what do you think, Galahad? Think it will work?" Paul wrapped his arms around Galahad's bulky body and stared into the fireplace that mirrored his own emptiness.

How had this happened? He'd never thought being alone meant being lonely. He was a man on his own path, unencumbered by baggage. The knowledge that he'd come this far by himself used to make him feel good. For a moment he wondered when he first became aware of his loneliness. The answer came immediately. It was the day he met Lauren Afton.

"It has to work, Galahad," he said, his voice echoing through the cavernous room. "It just has to."

CHAPTER NINE

"MERRY CHRISTMAS! Merry Christmas!"

Wearing a silky white robe, Lauren swept into the spacious living area of the house where she'd spent most of her childhood. The fragrance of sugar and cinnamon drifted into the room, adding to the euphoria she'd awakened to.

Life was wonderful! Her mother had been discharged from the hospital as promised, and her prognosis was very good. Today was Christmas morning. And, tomorrow... Oh, on the glorious morrow she would see Paul again. Wonderful, beautiful Paul.

"Morning, Lor," Jessie and E.J. replied in tandem.

E.J., in a hole-ridden bathrobe, lay on one of the antique sofas, while Jessie sprawled on the green velvetlike carpet.

"Where's Mother?" Lauren asked.

"Baking cinnamon rolls and making hot chocolate." E.J. wore a pleased grin. "What else would she be doing on Christmas morning?"

"She was already up when I came down at seven," Jessie piped up. "I was kind of disappointed. I wanted to surprise her by doing it myself." Jessie rolled onto her stomach, tangling her bright print caftan in the process. She rearranged it as she added, "But it's a real relief to see the doctors were right."

"Like I said," Lauren replied, "Merry Christmas!"

Cheri entered, carrying a tray, and all three Aftons leaped up.

"Let me, Mom."

"That's too heavy."

"Where's your cane, Mother?"

"I can do without that wretched cane for one day," Cheri said, her drawl thickening. Brushing off their offers to help, she placed the tray on a Queen Anne coffee table. "I'm certainly capable of carrying a half-pound tray."

"But you shouldn't, Mom." Jessie scurried to fluff a silk pillow for Cheri. "You mustn't exert yourself."

"Rubbish." But Cheri sat in the place Jessie had prepared. "Surely I can fix a morning repast for my children. Now stop worrying and help yourself before everything gets cold."

Cheri had been unusually quiet since her release from the hospital. Lauren had suspected she was depressed about this new stroke, or worse, was hiding terrible news. But now, listening to her mother's usual gentle scoldings, she released that worry for good. Finally assured of her mother's well-being, she took a steaming roll that fairly dripped hot icing and ate it with pleasure.

The last three days had been magical. Since Cheri's release, they'd all been staying in the big house, under one roof for the first time in years. Somehow Jessie and Cheri had avoided even minor disagreements, and Lauren's resentment of E.J. had mysteriously disappeared.

Now, as Jessie began handing out presents, they giggled and teased each other as they had when they were children. Only their father's absence kept this day from being perfect, and even that couldn't dim Lauren's spirits as she took a box that Jessie handed her.

As was their custom, no one opened their gifts until all were distributed. Once that had been done, all opened their presents with abandon, ripping off the shiny wrappings and carelessly discarding exquisite bows.

Jessie's gift to Lauren was a fragile bone clasp for her hair, which Jessie swore came from Africa and was carved from the thighbone of a headhunter's victim.

"Ugh," Lauren said, but she pulled her hair back with it anyway.

There was a new, plush robe for E.J.—a gift from Cheri that everyone knew he'd never wear. But he surprised them, made them turn their heads as he doffed his old one and snuggled into the new. "It's warmer," he said when they all gaped at him in surprise.

Jessie opened a box from Cheri. "How wonderful!" she lied. It was a pink, tailored suit much like the ones Lauren wore. Lauren expected Jessie to lay it aside, but instead she insisted on modeling it and left the room to change.

When she reentered, swathed in pink, she looked like a wilted pansy. Her braids hung over the collar, orange against pink, and the saucy peplum detracted from her slim waist.

"Take it back, dear," Cheri said. "That's what I get for forcing my taste on you. You look much lovelier in your own clothes."

Jessie burst into tears. Frowning in dismay, Cheri rose. "I didn't mean to hurt your feelings. It's just . . . the dress doesn't do you justice."

"Oh, no, Mom. I'm not hurt." Jessie wrapped her arms around Cheri, inhaling the baby-fresh fragrance she'd always associated with her mother. "I'm... I'm... Well, it's... You've never said I was lovely before."

Cheri hugged Jessie tightly, kissed her cheek, then pushed her back to arm's length. "Haven't I? Well, I guess we'll have to correct that. You *are* lovely, dear, and never more so than you were at the Christmas party." Slipping an arm around Jessie's waist, she looked at them all and said, "I've got one more special surprise for each of you, then there's something I want to discuss."

Soundlessly, she crossed the carpet and left the room. Jessie moved to the marble mantel, rested an elbow on its cool surface and felt the warmth of the traditional Christmas fire against her ankles. E.J. and Lauren stared at her, waiting for her to speak. She ignored them, gazing instead at the massive Christmas tree in front of a gabled window.

A clumsy papier-mâché Dino the Dinosaur hung from one branch. Her mother had helped her make it when she was six. An imitation Barbie doll hung from another. That was Lauren's contribution. Then there was E.J.'s space capsule. The tree was cluttered with their awkward ornaments, made year after year with Cheri's guidance.

Still sniffling, she blew out a breath and looked at her siblings, her friends since birth.

"I've been a jerk," she said.

"No more than usual," E.J. shot back.

"Mother hasn't always been easy on you," Lauren defended her.

"No," Jessie said emphatically. "You don't understand. I sold my shares of Cheri Lee Cosmetics. Mom will never forgive me."

Lauren's excited gasp and E.J.'s look of total shock confirmed her opinion. "You guys don't think she'll forgive me either, do you?"

E.J. ran his fingers through his hair in a gesture of total futility. "It's not just that."

"No, it's not just that," Lauren echoed, then sighed. "Please, tell us who bought them—quick, before Mother gets back. She mustn't know yet. Not so soon after the stroke."

Jessie nodded, horrified. Clearly something was going on that she didn't know about. "Why, Lor? Why can't I tell her?"

"We're transferring a large block of shares to Paul Sherwood on the day after New Year's." Lauren got up abruptly and began pacing the room in agitation.

Jessie knew Lor only paced when she was badly upset. "So? What's that got to do with it?"

"The family no longer owns controlling interest in the company, Jess." E.J.'s tone implied she was a total idiot.

"We'll just have to buy my shares back." It was the only solution. Bill wouldn't mind. She was sure of it.

"Not without capital," Lauren stated flatly, clearly weary of Jessie's lack of understanding. "We're nearly broke. That's why we're letting Paul buy in."

"Oh, God!" Jessie's hand flew to her mouth as she realized the enormity of what she'd done. She'd never considered who owned what or why, never really listened when Lauren talked about the business. Of course, she still had most of the money, but Bill had associates. Wouldn't they expect a profit? As she stood there, her hand over her mouth, her eyes saucers of horror, Cheri came back in carrying three large rectangular packages wrapped in brown paper.

"Mom!" Jessie exclaimed.

E.J. and Lauren turned to look at Cheri. Lauren quickly masked her expression and E.J. turned away to compose himself.

"We were wondering what your surprises were," Lauren said quickly, walking toward Cheri. "We're dying from suspense, aren't we?"

"Dying," Jessie intoned.

"Good." Cheri beamed. "I want you to open these at the same time."

She handed a package to Lauren, placed another in front of E.J., then set the last beside Jessie. In silence, they complied. Lauren was the first to sigh in wonder.

"Oh, Mother, it's beautiful."

"Oh, Mom!" Jessie exclaimed.

"It's great, Mom," E.J. murmured huskily.

"I found this wonderful artist and gave him a pile of old snapshots. I wanted something that would remind you each of special moments with your father." Cheri's voice was soft, and thick with emotion. "I hope I've succeeded."

"You have," Jessie replied, gazing at her painting. Done in a Rockwellian style, it showed her and her father bent over a go-cart as he helped her fix a broken wheel. That day was still a vivid recollection for her and one she referred to often when they talked of him.

E.J.'s painting showed them with fishing poles, headed for a stream, while Lauren's portrayed her father pushing her high in a swing. These were memories both had spoken of many times.

As Jessie gazed in wonderment, a less pleasant memory came to mind. She saw herself at eight years of age, clutching a hand-sewn costume, excitedly thanking her mother who was bent over the kitchen table filling cosmetics orders. . . .

"You made it perfect, Mommy," Jessie said. "It's so cool. I just can't wait for you to see me in it tonight. You'll be so proud."

Cheri looked up, her flawless face dismayed. "Tonight? Your play isn't tonight, is it?"

"Don't be silly. You know it is." But, even as Jessie reassured herself, her little heart sank. Her mother had forgotten. Just like all the other times. The only thing that ever mattered to Mommy was that makeup stuff.

"Oh, darling," Cheri exclaimed, kneeling to wrap her arms around Jessie. "I thought it was tomorrow. Your daddy and I have a meeting tonight."

"You can't!" Jessie wailed, pulling back from her mother's embrace. The smell of face powder permeated the room, the fragrance nauseating her. "I'm the star. I wanted to make you proud. You promised me." She broke into huge, gulping sobs. "After you missed the last one. You pro-o-omm-ised."

Cheri straightened, looking down at Jessie sternly. Jessie saw the sternness, but missed the guilty tears brimming in her mother's eyes. "Don't take that tone with me, Jessica. Your father and I work very hard to give you all a nice life. Didn't I stay up nights making that costume for you? You never appreciate anything. Now straighten up, help me put these packages together, and I'll try to think of something."

Jessie swallowed her tears. Mommy didn't love her when she was bad. She'd try to be good. She turned to pick up a box of powder. But her disappointment was too great. She was a star tonight. She wanted Mommy and Daddy there.

"No!" she screeched. "You won't! You never do!"

Picking up the powder box, she threw it at the wall, spewing talcum through the room. The sickening scent filled her nostrils, and she spun away, her stomach lurching in repulsion. Sobbing, she ran from the kitchen—the kitchen filled with those awful smells.

"I hate stupid makeup! I hate it! Hate it! Hate it!"

"Jessica!" Cheri called, but she ignored the voice and ran up the curving staircase to her room. Slamming the door behind her, she plunged into the Cinderella comforter and heap of coordinating pillows her mother had sewn for her and sobbed out her disappointment.

Later, her father had come up, and tried to explain how sorry they were, but business had to come first. Jessie turned away, barely listening, and still later, when she heard her mother whispering to her father about how hard it was to do right by them all, she didn't care. She was going to be a star, and her parents didn't even want to be there.

When she performed that night—with only Lauren and her girlfriends to cheer her on—she realized with a sudden burst of childish insight that if it weren't for the dumb company, Mommy and Daddy would have been there.

It was the company's fault. And she never wanted anything to do with it. Ever. She'd never wear makeup. She hated Cheri Lee Cosmetics and she hated what it made. . . .

"Are you all right, Jess?" She looked up to see Lauren staring at her with concern.

"Yeah!" she whispered, seeing the portrait clearly again. But that wasn't all she saw clearly. She glanced once more at the Christmas tree, with its carefully preserved memories. She stared at the painted go-cart, remembered the Cinderella bedspread. All symbols of her parents' love.

She saw also that Cheri Lee Cosmetics was simply another manifestation of that love. Her mom and dad had done this—built the company, performed labors of love, given them comforts and luxuries Jessie now took for granted. They'd done it for their children— for E.J, for Lauren.

And for her.

Why had she always believed her mother didn't love her?

Tears again flooded her eyes, but she blinked them back, not wanting her remorse to interfere with this day, with her mother's delight in giving them these special gifts.

Ignoring the reality that divergent viewpoints would, in all probability, always make her relationship with Cheri Lee difficult, Jessie vowed to hereafter treat her mother with kindness and respect.

Lauren didn't try to hide her tears, and even E.J. appeared to be losing the struggle. They all gathered around Cheri Lee, hugging her, expressing their thanks.

Cheri pulled a tissue from somewhere, dabbed all their eyes, then her own, before saying, "Now, on to our discussion."

She returned to the place Jessie had prepared for her earlier. "I've given a great deal of thought to what I'm

about to say, ever since the party. My...stroke—
coming at such an unfortunate moment—made it clear
to me that I can no longer function as Cheri Lee Cosmetics's spokesperson.''

As mouths opened to protest, to reassure her, Cheri
shook her head. ''No, no. Don't try to be kind. It's
true. We can never allow that to happen again.'' She
tilted her head, fixing her full gaze on Jessie. ''Jessie,
I want you to take my place, to conduct the April
convention.''

''Me?'' Jessie's ears rang from the announcement.
She, a spokesperson for the company? No! What
could Mom be thinking of? But as she started to out-
line all her objections, the full weight of her betrayal
came back to her, along with the promise she'd made
just a few minutes earlier. She held her tongue, deciding to hear Cheri Lee out.

''You,'' Cheri repeated quietly, with a proud,
beaming smile on her face. ''I wasn't so disoriented
the other night that I failed to notice your brilliance.
Lauren and I have discussed this dilemma. It's been
inevitable that I'd have to step down someday. Lauren believes she doesn't have the charisma to take my
place—''

''I *know* I don't, Mother,'' Lauren interrupted.
''And I think this is a wonderful idea.''

''So do I,'' E.J. added.

''What if I'm not accepted?'' Cold fear clutched
Jessie's chest. It was one thing to clown and ad-lib for
an impromptu audience, quite another to be a visible
symbol for an entire company. ''I'm so different from
you, Mom.''

''True, you don't do things the way *I* would, but
people loved you the other night. So will the sales

force. It's your differences that will make it work. You'll be your own special self, not just an imitation of me. I believe in my heart it will work.'' Cheri's smile was now fairly bursting her face and Jessie couldn't help but melt beneath its power. How many years had she wanted to make her mother proud of her? Here was her chance.

''But I understand your reservations,'' Cheri continued before Jessie could say, *I'll do it, I'll do it.* ''So I'm suggesting we start out in a smaller way. I was scheduled to do a promotional video to launch the Minx cosmetic line. Instead, you do it. If you really hate all the hoopla, we can reconsider.'' Cheri paused a moment. ''I think you'll be a smash. You're more in tune with the times. I'm not such a fossil that I've failed to notice the world has changed.''

''I'll do it, Mom,'' Jessie cried, no longer able to hide her tears. They streamed down her face as she scrambled to her feet, then went to sit by her mother and sink into her open arms. ''You're not a fossil,'' she choked out between her sobs. ''You're beautiful.''

''Thank you, dear.'' Cheri smoothed Jessie's hair lovingly. ''There is one thing, though.''

''What?'' Jessie asked through a sniffle.

''You'll have to start wearing makeup.''

The tone of her mother's pronouncement struck a hilarious chord in Jessie's mind. In the midst of a sob, she broke out laughing.

''Makeup? Oh, no, Mom!'' Drawing away, she raised her arms in mock horror.

''After all, dear, that's what we sell.'' Cheri smiled with droll humor.

Yes, they sold makeup. The very thing Jessie had always hated. But not anymore. Not anymore. Cosmetics had driven them apart. Now they would bring them together.

"One must suffer for beauty." Jessie's repetition of Cheri's often-used phrase made everyone laugh. And as Jessie looked at her family's smiling faces, only one question ran through her mind.

How—oh, how, would she tell her mother the awful truth of what she'd done?

LAUREN AWOKE THE NEXT day filled with excitement—and apprehension. It had been an enchanted Christmas, full of love and healing. But after spending the past three days in the enormous house where she'd grown up, all the while feeling like a little girl again, she was glad to be waking up in her own bed.

She'd hung her gift on the wall facing the foot of her bed, and as she gazed at the portrait of her father pushing her high into the sky as her legs bent under the swing, she was filled with the same sense of wonder she'd felt the day before.

It had been three years, but she still sorely felt the loss of her father. An often-preoccupied, lumbering giant of a man, he'd been gentle, kind, giving. Sometimes his absence felt like a gaping wound in her life; at other times, it was a barely perceptible twinge. Yet the loss was always felt. The portrait made it easier in some undefinable way.

After stretching languidly beneath her handmade Amish quilt and breathing in the lilac scent emanating from room fresheners that her housekeeper always spread through her rooms, Lauren shook off the last vestiges of that little-girl-at-Christmas feeling.

Today she felt like a woman. Bold. Free. Courageous. A woman who wanted a marvelous man with a healthy lust that she knew would make her mother's eyebrows rise in disapproval.

Although, perhaps not, she reflected with a smile. After all, her parents had produced three children and had seemed to love each other very much. She giggled at the thought, and rose, happy to be alive, happy to be an Afton, happy about the way she would be spending the day... and the night.

For this very night, without doubt, she would take Paul Sherwood to her bed and finish what they'd begun nearly two months ago on the *Gypsy Rose*.

Everything she saw while going through her morning routine seemed more vivid—from the arrangement of carnations and daisies on the kitchen table to the brilliant pink handle of the spatula she used to scramble her eggs. Not even the frightening prospect of parachuting from a plane interfered with her happiness. Indeed, the idea almost exhilarated her, and she shoved away the memory of the gut-wrenching, limb-paralyzing fear she'd experienced the last time she tried.

Today she would succeed. For once in her life, she would grab what she wanted. She'd make that jump. She'd take Paul Sherwood as her lover. The thought of both events occurring in the same day made her skin fairly tingle.

Her breakfast finished, she rushed to her bedroom to dress. She slipped on a light sweater. The brush of fabric against her skin felt like a caress. Paul's caress. But then, as she stepped into soft, white jeans, a recollection of the only blot on the previous day flitted into her mind.

Jessie. Wow, what a switch! Lauren still found it hard to believe that her stubborn, independent sister had agreed to take the spokesperson's role. Not that Lauren doubted Jessie could do it. Indeed, the exact thought had occurred to her right in the midst of Cheri Lee's crisis. But she was also certain of what had brought about her sister's ready agreement.

Still, the problem wasn't insurmountable. So Jessie had sold her shares. She probably had most of the money left. As flighty as Jessie seemed, she lived modestly and was always sensible about investments, employing good counselors and heeding their advice.

They'd keep this news from Mother for a while. Maybe they could repurchase the stock before she ever found out. Profits were already on an upswing. Maybe... She'd discuss it with Paul.

Because on the very first working day of a brand-new year, Lauren would abandon her original plan. The day after the Christmas party, she had signed and filed the withheld minutes, and sent copies to both lawyers by courier.

There was no turning back now, but Lauren didn't care. Paul had earned her trust. Together, they'd take Cheri Lee Cosmetics into a new era.

The doorbell rang. Lauren checked her hair and makeup one last time, then rushed to answer the door. When she opened it, her heart skipped in anticipation.

Just seeing Paul filled her with joy. He wore a khaki jumpsuit that strained at his broad shoulders, then tapered to his narrow waist. A breeze fluttered through his golden hair. But it was his glad smile that filled Lauren's heart, and she stepped forward to allow his arms to enclose her.

As she basked in his hug, she felt something flopping against her back. "What's that?" she asked, reaching behind her.

"I brought you a jumpsuit." Paul stepped away and held up a suit nearly identical to his. "You just slip it on over your clothes."

Lauren grinned up at him. "How is it you always have clothes that fit me?" A jealous imp inside her wondered about Paul's former girlfriends.

"My mother was about your size." His eyes sparkled as if he didn't expect her to believe him.

"Oh, sure." But she took his hand and led him inside. "Have you eaten? Would you like coffee?"

"No time. We're expected in half an hour."

Lauren slipped into the jumpsuit, picked up her purse, and then she and Paul went to his car. As she got in, she saw that the back seat was empty.

"Where's Galahad?" she asked as Paul climbed in.

"My trainer's got him on a special diet, so I left him at the ranch for a week." Paul started the car and pulled away from the curb.

"Is he ill?" Lauren asked, frowning.

"No," he answered forcefully. Then, in a quieter voice, he added, "But he's getting on in years. Needs special attention now and then."

Before Lauren could comment, Paul said, "Are you still sure you want to parachute?"

"Sure? No." Lauren stretched her arms, her fingers brushing the fabric rooftop of Paul's car. A restless energy bounced inside her body, wanting release. "But I'm going to do it anyway."

"Good girl." Paul chucked her under the chin. "I'll be waiting for you."

"Aren't you going with me?" Fear gripped Lauren's chest.

"Of course, I am." Paul laughed and Lauren feigned a pout.

"It's not funny. Don't scare me like that."

"Don't worry, darlin'." He lifted one hand from the steering wheel, drew her against his shoulder, and whispered into her hair. "I'll never desert you."

HER EYES WIDE, Lauren stared at him through her goggles, her trembling hand holding the guy wire in a death grip. Then her lips formed a smile. A broad, bright smile—frozen into place.

As Paul looked at her, observed the thin white rim around her mouth, he realized how terrified she was. Why had he talked her into this? Regardless of his assurances, skydiving was dangerous. What if she forgot her instructions? Got her lines tangled? Forgot how to activate the emergency chute if hers didn't open?

"Lauren, you don't—"

"Banzai!" she cried, crossing her arms to grip her shoulders and falling backward off her narrow foothold beneath the wing of the plane.

For an instant, Paul's fear for Lauren paralyzed him. Telling himself the jump master had quizzed her beforehand, that she knew what she was doing, didn't quell his anxiety. He plummeted over the edge, intent on catching up with her.

What if ... ?

One, one thousand, Lauren counted, the absolute clarity of her mind astounding her. She knew she was terrified beyond being terrified. Her ears roared. She felt as if she'd left her stomach up in the plane; the sensation was much like riding on a swift elevator. The plane, white against white in the colorless sky, grew smaller and smaller. Nothing—not the classroom instructions, not the ground simulations—had prepared her for the pure emptiness around her.

Two, one thousand. Three, one thousand. Nor, when she'd clung to the icy guy wire, ignoring her screaming instincts, had she been prepared for the frigid cold that bit her cheeks and stole her air so she couldn't breathe. But breath was in her now, as were the numbers that would guard her fragile hold on life.

Never before had she realized just how fragile a hold it was. She remembered the release form she'd signed: *Skydiving could cause your death,* it had said.

Four, one thousand. Five, one thousand. Whump! As promised, her tether to the plane held, opened her chute, and halted her fall with flesh-shattering force. *Like a cosmic brake,* she thought, as her body shuddered from the impact. Almost automatically, she moved to her next step. Slipping her wrists through leather straps, she grasped the parachute's lines, looking up and breathing a giant sigh as she saw that the chute had popped open into its perfect irregular rectangle. Every cord in that complex web of lines fell into alignment.

Beautiful. She'd never seen anything more beautiful.

It was so silent now, so peaceful. She gazed downward, fighting the spin of terror in her stomach, and searched among the green and brown patches. High. She was so high. And the ground was very far away.

But when she spotted the giant *X* drawn on the landing field, laughter erupted from her tumbling gut.

Enormous gratitude for her life filled her entire being.

She'd done it! She'd faced her own mortality—overcome fear. She knew now that there was nothing she couldn't do. She also knew her smile was covering her entire face. She looked up, saw Paul above her, and her smile widened.

More expert at free-falling than she, he had caught up with her just as her tether activated. With relief, he saw that her chute had opened, that she'd gone through her safety routine without a single hitch. He'd smiled at her startled expression, watched it change from relief to astonished wonder, then to hysterical glee.

Paul's chute opened and as he went through his own routine, he remembered his first jump, his own giddy laughter. Assured his chute was operational and having spotted the landing field, he turned his head toward Lauren and made an okay sign with his fingers.

Her luminous face sparkled. She returned his signal, opened her mouth and shouted something, but the wind blew her words away.

Paul pointed to his mouth, then to the ground, indicating they would talk then. She nodded. Still grinning ear-to-ear, she pulled the rigging, guiding the parachute toward the landing spot.

Admiration for her filled Paul's heart. She hadn't forgotten a thing, hadn't allowed fear to rob her mind. This woman could do anything. Even make him love her.

Yet that was no longer a frightening prospect. After his crippling moments of doubt, he'd come to the realization that his new strategy would work. Sure,

Lauren would be angry, but she'd come around. He could have it all. They could have it all.

Relaxing, Paul deftly performed the same maneuvers he'd watched Lauren perform, then enjoyed the peaceful ride. It was quiet up here. A man could almost believe in Olympus, almost hear the gods speaking. Everything on the ground seemed to move slowly, to have a grand order about it.

Up here in heaven, life seemed very simple.

But now the earth was rapidly approaching. Again Paul worried about Lauren. He prayed she hadn't forgotten the landing instructions, and he reviewed the procedures in his own mind as though he could telepathically communicate them to her.

He landed first—toes and then heels, knees bent—then ran behind his chute to catch it. He heard the thud of Lauren landing directly behind him, saw her stumble, catch her balance, then run to her own chute.

Then her laughter filled his ears, followed by a whoop. As he gathered up his crumpled chute, he saw Lauren doing the same, her efforts hampered by bursts of laughter.

"I did it, Paul. I did it. I did it!" She whooped again, rolling up her chute as her words bubbled out. "I actually jumped. I can't believe it. Did I do everything right, Paul? Did I?"

She whirled, hugging herself through the ball of nylon in her arms. "I can't believe I really did it."

Paul sprinted to her side. "You were perfect," he said, caught up in the wonder of her triumphant babble. "Perfect."

He dropped his bundle, took hers and did the same, then enclosed her in a congratulatory hug. She wrapped her arms around his neck, saying, more softly now, "I really did it."

"I never doubted you, darlin'," Paul replied. "When do you want to schedule your next jump?"

"Next jump? Oh, no." She jerked back and stared at him, her eyes pools of terror. "I don't think I could do it again."

Laughter burst from Paul's throat before he could stop it. At Lauren's offended reaction, he pulled her back into his arms.

"I love you, Lauren."

The words spilled from his mouth without thought but as he saw Lauren's face soften, he didn't regret a single one.

"I love you, too." She lifted her face, her eyes closed, her lips slightly parted, waiting for his kiss.

Hers was the sweetest kiss Paul had ever known.

CHAPTER TEN

PRESSING LAUREN'S BODY impossibly close, Paul fumbled with the lock. Impatiently, Lauren grasped his buttocks, grinding her hips against him. A blazing heat, low in her belly, intensified, radiating outward in ever-widening circles. It traveled to her knees, her toes, making her legs weak and rubbery. It burst upward to her head, burning out all thought. She moaned deep in her throat and nipped at the tender lobe of Paul's ear.

Dimly, she gave thanks that the alcove of her entryway protected them from view. How scandalous, to be stroking each other like this in broad daylight—deliciously, wantonly scandalous!

He loved her. His words still sang in her ears—sweet, soft, tinkling with melody.

She threw an arm around Paul's neck, wanting to bring his eager mouth against hers, to savor the glorious feel, the delectable taste, of his sculptured, masculine lips.

"Wait," he whispered against her mouth. "This damned door. It won't open."

With an impatient groan, Lauren pivoted. She grabbed the doorknob, gave it a vicious push, and turned the key. All the while, Paul nuzzled against her back, running hungry hands up and down her curves.

The door gave, swinging fully open from the pressure of their bodies. Together, they stumbled over the threshold, losing their balance.

With a soft laugh, Paul caught himself and supported Lauren before she crashed to the floor. But then his knees collapsed and they sank together onto the plush carpeting.

Paul wrapped his arms and legs around Lauren. With frantic whimpers, she molded herself to him, fitting curve against curve, hardness against softness, as though they were parts of a whole finally coming together again.

"So soft, so beautiful," he murmured. Loosening his embrace, Paul lifted Lauren's sweater, brushing her sensitized skin as the sweater moved upward. "I want you, darlin'. I want you."

She ran her tongue along the tantalizing curve of his lower lip. His words rushed into her parted mouth, filling her with joy, torrential desire, overwhelming love. "Yes, yes, yes," she replied, in breathy little whispers.

Paul pulled back, drawing Lauren's sweater over her head. He saw her reluctance to part in her eyes—eyes now dark with need. Casting the sweater aside, he clutched her to his chest, feeling the skittering beat of her heart merge with his.

She loved him. He had thought she did. Yet, when she'd revealed it, he realized he had only hoped so, had longed for a confirmation, but had feared it would never come.

Swiftly he dispatched her brassiere. With a gentle push he forced her to the floor, his legs still pinning hers. He gazed at her then, her eyes closed, her lashes fluttering. He stroked a breast—a firm, perfect breast—then traced ever-larger figure eights, wanting to explore every part of her, know every inch of that beautiful skin.

He could feel her tiny shudders beneath his feathery touch, and the vibrations sent waves of desire throughout his body. His own need was swelling, growing. "Oh, Lord," he moaned, lowering his hands to the buttons on her jeans.

She moved her own hand down, touched one of his, and began to unbutton the jeans herself.

"No," Paul said, his voice rich and husky. "Let me. I want to undress you; look at you."

Look at me, thought Lauren, her eyes opening in alarm. What if he didn't think her beautiful enough? But Paul caught her gaze, and smiled—the most perfect smile Lauren had ever seen. Adoration, even awe, filled his face, and Lauren knew then that his love for her was so great that all he'd ever see was beauty.

As was her love for him.

But Paul wore way too many clothes. Shyly, Lauren lifted her hands and began unzipping his flight suit, trailing her fingers down his exposed skin, much as he had done to her. The crisp sprinkling of hair tickled her fingertips, sending trembling vibrations through her nervous system.

Desire—hungry, mindless desire—consumed her body, her mind. She gasped in need, no longer able to simply savor these delightful sensations, and yanked down Paul's zipper.

As Lauren arched beneath his hand, Paul's weakly harnessed hunger broke loose. In a torrid flurry of jerks and tugs, they finished undressing, then reunited their heated, trembling bodies. Meeting Lauren's bare skin with his own almost undid Paul. Lord, her skin was soft. And warm...so warm. As he touched that wondrous place between her thighs, the fiery heat caused him to cry out. Lauren touched him then, guiding him to the glory he knew awaited.

"Now!" she pleaded, opening herself to him.

Paul moved over her, entering that welcoming place, knowing that he was stepping through a door from which there was no return.

"I love you," he cried.

"I love you," Lauren cried, taking him fully inside, wrapping her legs around him, holding him, wanting him, rocking him, loving him. Until...

The tremors shook Paul's body so forcibly he knew he was shattering into millions of pieces. He didn't care. He submitted, sank into the endless waves of pleasure that racked his body. Beneath him, he heard Lauren scream, and he knew she had joined him at the glorious place where the mind vanished and only love existed.

"I love you," they pledged in unison. Paul held Lauren to him, wanting this moment to last forever.

Later, afraid of crushing Lauren with his weight, he slipped onto the floor and brought her tenderly against his chest, stroking her tangled hair. She snuggled closer, folding one leg over his.

The heating system clicked on, humming, echoing the sound of their ragged breath. "You're wonderful," he murmured, kissing the top of her head.

"So, *so* are you!" She wrapped an arm around his neck, nipped his ear. "Lord, what a release of tension."

Paul laughed. "Is that all it was?" But his voice was teasing. He knew what she meant. There simply weren't words to describe it.

She laughed, too. "Oh, Paul I love you. How lucky we are."

"Very lucky. I might never have found you. What an awful thought." This time he kissed her nose. He wanted to kiss each pore of her creamy skin.

But *were* they lucky? The day after New Year's loomed large in Paul's mind, consuming him with fear and doubt. *Better to have loved and lost than never to have loved at all.* Wasn't that how the saying went? *What bull,* Paul thought. To have found something this magnificent and lose it had to be the worst hell possible.

Reassuring himself that he had everything under control, Paul kissed Lauren's chin. "How 'bout a shower? Unless, of course, you just want to roll around on the carpet forever."

"Tempting." But Lauren rose, extended Paul a hand, and helped him to his feet. "A shower sounds good. I have lots of fluffy towels. Want to join me?"

Paul smiled wickedly, and chased a giggling Lauren into the bathroom. Under a steaming rush of water, they teased each other, laughed, had a water fight, and touched each other as much as possible. All the while, Paul's thoughts drifted to the impending share-transfer meeting. He wanted that day to never come. He wanted that day to be over.

What he didn't want was the fear of not knowing.

Later they dressed, went out for Chinese food, then returned to snuggle on the couch and watch mindless situation comedies. Even before the evening news came on, they'd gone into the bedroom and crawled beneath Lauren's Amish quilt to continue exploring each other's bodies. When Paul entered Lauren for the second time that day—this time holding her astride while he viewed her sublime body—he again cried out. And this time when he yielded to those mind-numbing shock waves, he knew his cry wasn't only from passion.

He lay awake well into the morning, cradling the sleeping Lauren in his arms, listening to the sweet sound of her even breathing, inhaling her lilac scent.

Like a mantra, he mentally repeated, over and over, what he hoped was true and feared was not.

They *could* have it all. They could *have* it all. They could have it *all*.

BILL'S EYES SHOT OPEN to see Jessie, her arms propped beneath her head, looking at him. It usually warmed him to awaken to that appreciative gaze, but this morning he saw a pensiveness in her expression that he'd never seen before.

Morning? He glanced sleepily at the clock. It was nearly one in the afternoon. He and Jessie had spent New Year's Eve celebrating with champagne, funny hats, and noisemakers. He'd always preferred spending the holiday quietly at home, but Jessie loved a party. In the end, a portion of the evening had been spent his way. After sharing their midnight kiss, they'd driven to the shore, where they'd walked hand in hand on the beach, then made love on the sand, hidden from passersby by a sheltered rock cluster.

The evening had been fun, exhilarating, and passionate. Passionate beyond his wildest dreams. Lord, he loved this woman—also beyond his wildest dreams.

"Bill?"

He turned at the question in Jessie's voice. They'd had a wonderful evening, were planning to share a wonderful day. Why did she look so sad?

"Is something wrong?" He lifted a strand of her hair. Mussed, freed from its braids, it rippled over her shoulders in sensual profusion. Desire surged through his body.

"Would you sell me back my shares?"

Bands of hard crushing steel clenched Bill's chest. He'd always known this moment would come. Perhaps not quite this way, given Jessie's lack of interest in her family's firm. But he'd known it would arrive somehow.

He'd thought he was prepared, wasn't expecting this deathly, suffocating force that squeezed the very breath from him. He let her strand of hair drift down, clasped his hands behind his head and stared at the ceiling.

"I can't, Jessie. They're already in the hands of my clients."

Jessie's one hope evaporated. Bill's voice had the dull drone of an undertaker explaining funeral arrangements to a grieving family. Yet she didn't give up. "Can't we offer to buy them back? I still have the money."

"You'll lose a fortune. Penalties, lost interest."

"I don't care about the money, Bill." Jessie shot up, assumed a cross-legged position beneath the crumpled silk sheet, and continued hotly, "I've got to get those shares back before my mother finds out!"

His sigh sounded exasperated, and Jessie stared at him. Bill stared back, not speaking, and she saw those soft eyes, chocolate brown and dreamy, turn hard and focused.

"They'll expect to make a profit."

"That means we can do it. Lauren knows now, so I can ask her for the difference."

Jessie smiled, running a hand gently across Bill's furrowed forehead. She'd expected Bill to smile, too. She knew he wanted to do this for her. But the smile never crossed his lips.

"One of my partners is verging on bankruptcy. This deal is his only hope. He'll need double what he paid, at least, just to keep even. Maybe more."

"Double? Oh, Bill! This will kill Mom if she ever finds out." As if of their own volition, Jessie's hands flew to her face. She pressed them against her lips, stifling an anguished sound. Quiet tears spilled from her eyes. Bill sat up, his chest splitting with pain over the agony he'd caused her.

"Oh, baby," he crooned, leaning back on the bed and pulling her with him. "Jessie, baby. I'm so sorry I did this to you. But it's too late. Too late."

"I never knew until now how much I love my mother," she whispered so softly Bill could barely hear. "How can I ever face her after what I've done?"

She sobbed on his shoulder in gentle, soundless heaves. Having no answers, Bill just held her, stroked her, allowed her to cry. His own tears of guilt and remorse burned his eyes. He wanted to tell Jessie the truth—all of it. But he had other loyalties that clashed with his love for her.

Beneath his hand, lightly resting on Jessie's shoulder, he could feel her heaving subside. Although she sniffled occasionally, she no longer cried. She lay still, her head resting on his shoulder, her hair brushing against his face. Torturous minutes ticked by during which Bill flagellated himself for doing this to Jessie, for allowing himself to get involved, for loving her.

Then she shot straight up, resuming her former position. Although tears streaked her face, she no longer looked forlorn. "I've got it. I'll buy half now, the rest later." She touched Bill excitedly on the arm. "Call them tomorrow. Tell them. Please, Bill."

Her pleading eyes were the last straw. Bill's throat closed. Turning abruptly away, he swung his feet to the floor. "I'll do what I can."

He stood and headed for the bathroom, afraid to breathe. He should have stopped this thing sooner because there was no going back now. Too many people, too many purposes, were involved at this point. Bill had already pledged the shares. There was nothing left but to ride the deal out.

Closing the bathroom door behind him, Bill slumped against the wall. Sliding slowly to the floor, he covered his mouth, trying to quash the angry roar erupting deep in his gut.

"BILL SAID HE'D TRY." Jessie toyed with a silver napkin ring, inspecting the inlaid design as though it held untold secrets. "He didn't sound very optimistic."

Lauren took a sip of coffee from a bone-china cup, then placed it on its saucer as a waiter bent forward to refill it. She looked at Jessie, who was despondent and remorseful, then at E.J., who seemed bereft of solutions.

They'd been in the restaurant for nearly an hour, hashing over the details of Jessie's sale of the shares. Nothing had been resolved. Even if they combined Jessie's assets with funds from Cheri Lee Cosmetics, there was no way to come up with double the amount Jessie had sold for.

Jessie had merely nibbled at her omelet, and even E.J. had left half his breakfast on the plate. But Lauren's plate was clean, her appetite unimpaired.

She knew she should be worried, even distraught, over this situation. But she wasn't. In less than an hour, she'd be handing more than a third of the company to Paul...placing it in good hands. "I'll talk this over with Paul after the meeting," Lauren said. "With his contacts, he might find a way to get us out of this."

"He's our only hope," E.J. agreed.

"And maybe Bill'll get a better price," Jessie suggested, a wan smile on her face. "He feels real bad about this."

Lauren nodded, signaled for the check, then said, "We'd better get back, E.J. The meeting will start soon. Remember, no matter what, don't tell Mother about Jessie's sale."

"Not me, sis." E.J. lifted his hands and made a hex sign. "No way."

"I'll come with you," Jessie offered.

"You hate meetings, Jess," E.J. reminded. "You don't have to be there today, since you're not—"

A shareholder anymore. Lauren wanted to bite E.J.'s tongue for him, but Jessie just grinned ruefully.

"I know," Jessie replied. "But I promised Mom I'd take over her role. Guess I'd better start learning what's going on."

The waiter had brought the check, and Lauren had signed it. Now they stood, preparing to leave. Jessie picked up her shoulder bag and slipped the strap over her arm, adding, "If I'd known more before, we wouldn't be in this mess."

Lauren patted her arm, gave her a sympathetic nod, and thought it strange that today Jessie was worrying about the company. Lauren hadn't been able to get worked up over anything since she'd faced her fears and jumped out of a plane, then into Paul's arms.

Love must do that to people, she thought. Turn them into blithering optimists, convinced they could conquer the world.

The trio remained relatively silent during the trip back. Jessie chewed on her thumb. E.J. drummed a tuneless rhythm against his armrest. And Lauren dreamed of all the wonderful sensations she'd share with Paul that night.

The meeting was a mere formality. She'd be plotting no intrigue today, anticipating no victory. No. She'd simply be sealing a partnership that would enrich her, as she hoped to enrich Paul.

When they entered Lauren's office, Cheri was already there, seated on the cushioned love seat. She looked up from a magazine she'd been skimming and smiled at her family.

"Today's the big day." Cheri looked over at Jessie who was solicitously preparing her mother a cup of coffee. "Jessica," she said. "I spoke with the video company. They suggested you contact them to go over the script. You might want to make some changes."

"Okay, Mom." Jessie took the cup to Cheri, then sat in a chair.

Just then, the door opened and Lauren's assistant stuck in her head, a perturbed look on her face. "Paul's here," the young woman said. "But—"

"But what?" Lauren asked, puzzled by the girl's demeanor.

The door swung open. Paul stepped through, followed by another man.

"Bill!" Jessie's heart leaped with joy. Maybe he and Paul had found a way to get back her stocks. Then she frowned in confusion. If so, why did Bill look like a man being dragged to his execution?

"Folks," Paul said blithely, "you all know my partner, Bill Rosen."

The verbal punch nearly drove Jessie's stomach through her backbone. *That lying, deceiving—*

For a moment, Lauren was stunned, unable to comprehend what was happening. Realization dawned slowly, bringing an agony so sharp she wanted to drop to the floor and curl into a tight, defensive ball.

How could she have allowed herself to be so deceived?

"What the hell is going on?" E.J. demanded, while Lauren dimly noticed that her mother's hand had flown to her heart.

Paul held up a piece of paper—Jessie's share certificate. "This is Bill's twenty-two percent of Cheri Lee Cosmetics."

"I don't think you need to draw us a map, Paul!" Lauren wondered if she had shouted; her voice seemed so far away.

"Don't get mad, Lauren. It's not that bad."

"You two-bit hustler," she hissed.

Paul looked shocked, even hurt. "No, Lauren. You don't understand. Let me explain. Even though Bill and I have controlling interest, I'm not—"

"Oh, I understand. You're ripping off our company." Although Paul had spoken gently, it seemed to Lauren that he was enjoying this triumph. He *had* to be enjoying it. Why else would he be doing it this way? She had joined with this man, made hot, sweet love with him...had given him all she had to share. Her icy pain began to melt, and was replaced by a low, dull heat. Her heart pounded now, sending blood roaring to her temples. Tears—salty blazing tears, too hot to flow—stung Lauren's eyes.

"You used me." She whirled, pointing an accusing finger at Bill. "And used my sister!"

At that, Jessie shot up from her chair, stormed across the room, and stood nose-to-nose with Bill.

Oh, no! Bill thought. Jessie was even angrier than he'd feared. As he saw her lift her arm, her palm flat, aimed at him, he didn't even attempt to duck.

"You bastard!" Jessie's hand connected with the side of his face with more force than he'd thought possible, but the hurt was nothing compared to his internal pain.

Jessie glared at Bill, watched the red welts from her fingers rise on his cheek. She felt no satisfaction. Spinning, she grabbed her purse, then bolted from the room.

No one moved. No one spoke. A phone rang somewhere in another room. A tree branch, disturbed by a coastal breeze, scraped the office window.

Lauren stared at Paul, saw his face with amazing clarity, watched as his expression changed from confusion to comprehension to pain. His lips compressed into a thin, hard line. His eyes grew cold. Turning to Bill, he said, "Make the motion. We'll handle this later."

"I move that Paul Sherwood be named chief executive officer of Cheri Lee Cosmetics," Bill said, in a clipped, even tone. The imprint of Jessie's hand stood out in sharp relief against his now pale skin.

"I second, and the motion carries," Paul responded, matter-of-factly.

"Oh, my God," Lauren whispered. She crossed the room and came back, her arms folded over her chest.

Finally she looked at Paul, unable to hide her tears any longer. "When are you going to sell off the company?" she asked dully. "I want to give our employees enough notice."

"That's what I was trying to tell you, Lauren." Paul moved forward and touched her shoulder. Lauren brushed his hand away and stepped back. "I'm not going to sell. The only reason I'm even taking the CEO spot is because my investors would have conniptions otherwise. But *we're* going to run this place. You and me, darlin'. Together."

"What!" Bill's voice soared in pitch. "You put me through all this, and you're planning to run the company?"

"You expect me to *believe* that?" Lauren asked.

"Lauren was right. You *are* a jerk," E.J. said.

Cheri alone remained silent.

Paul swiveled his head to see Bill's enraged face jutting forward from his nattily dressed body. Lauren eyed him as though he were some giant disease-infested rodent. E.J. clenched and unclenched his fist, and Paul expected one of them to land on his jaw at any time. Cheri gripped her cane with white-knuckled fingers. *Lord, what if she had another stroke?*

This wasn't going at all as he'd pictured.

He'd expected the bad moment that occurred right after he and Bill had entered. But the horror, the disbelief that had followed, felt like a bushwhack. Why wasn't anyone listening to him?

"I only went through with this, you jerk," Bill sputtered, "because we'd already gone so far you'd go broke if I pulled out. Now you come up with this harebrained idea that's going to bankrupt you. Didn't you think I had a right to know?"

"It didn't seem ... I didn't think—"

"That's your problem, Sherwood. When it comes to people, you just don't think." But Bill's anger seemed to have vanished. He squared his shoulders with a sad little gesture, then headed for the door. "You've cost me the only thing that ever mattered."

As the door closed behind Bill, Paul gazed around the room. The hate in Lauren's spacious office was palpable, hitting him in waves like an angry surf. He went to Lauren's desk and sat in her chair.

"The deal is done, Lauren," he said wearily. "Let's sign the papers and I'll get out of here. Maybe tomorrow, when everyone has calmed down, we can talk this over."

"We've nothing to talk about. It seems you pulled the wool over lots of people's eyes. I hope your investors eat you alive," Lauren said listlessly, no longer feeling anything.

"They probably will, which is your best reason for believing me. Why else would I risk that, if not for us?"

"Do me a favor, Paul, and stop insulting my intelligence."

She turned away, afraid the pleading in his eyes would make her want to believe him. It was just an act, she told herself as she picked up the contract folder. She handed the papers to Paul.

He took a lavender pen from its holder, signed his name, then gave the pen to Lauren. As she took it, her hand brushed his, and she noted that even after his betrayal, this slightest touch sent a thrill through her. She hated her body, she thought, as she wrote her signature.

"Now that you're CEO, I suppose you want this office."

"No." Paul fixed her with a hard stare, no longer trying to be conciliatory. "I'll fix up that rathole you gave me when I first got here."

"Good," Lauren replied, returning his glare. "Then, get out of *my* office."

Paul took his copy of the agreement, stood, then looked at her for a long moment. "Certainly. But I'll be back at noon for our usual lunch."

"You expect me to have lunch with you?" Lauren's eyes narrowed as she nearly snarled the question.

"People have come to expect it." Paul spoke quite coldly as he carefully folded his copy of the contract. "If, by any chance, you're thinking of ducking out on me, I want to make it clear that I'm giving you a direct order."

"And what gives you that right?"

"The motion that just passed. I'm in charge now, Lauren. Remember that."

With a curt nod, Lauren walked to her desk and sat down. In a deadly whisper, she said, "Get out, Paul. Just get out."

He inserted the contract in an inside suit pocket, then started for the door, his expression unchanged. As he pulled the door open, he turned toward Cheri.

"I'm sorry things happened this way, Mrs. Afton," he said. "I hope we can work it out."

The soft click of the door latch closing behind him sounded like a gunshot blast. Lauren lowered her head onto her arms and took a deep breath.

"We have to do something, sis." E.J. now sat in one of her tiny chairs, his head bowed, his hands clutching his neck.

For a moment Lauren wondered why it had to be her—always her—who had to do something.

"Do you have any ideas?"

"No."

"We'll find a way." Cheri's soft drawl came from the couch, and Lauren lifted her head.

"How, Mother?" It occurred to Lauren that, unlike herself and E.J., Cheri Lee appeared calm.

"I'm not certain. But I expected something like this might happen."

What? Had Cheri Lee known about Jessie's sale all along?

"How did . . . ? Why didn't you try to stop it?"

"Jessie used the family attorney. He called me right away, of course, attorney-client privilege be damned. Gerald and I are old friends." Cheri adjusted the brooch on her shoulder, giving it grave attention. Sorrow passed over her features. "Glory be, she must have been so angry at me to want to cast us off that way. I didn't want to make things worse between us. We were barely speaking to each other as it was. So I kept the knowledge to myself."

"But, Mother," Lauren said, too drained to be angry—or even shocked, "didn't you realize we could lose our company?"

Cheri responded with a knowing smile. "There's great love between you and Paul," she said. "And between Jessie and Bill. Reminds me a lot of your father and I when we were young." Her eyes grew misty. "This will all turn out for the best."

Lauren got up and went to sit beside Cheri. Draping an arm over her mother's shoulders, she pulled her close. "Oh, Mother," she said sadly, "you're such a romantic."

CHAPTER ELEVEN

I'M IN CHARGE NOW, Lauren. The phrase bounced through Paul's mind as he rode the elevator to Lauren's office. *Stupid, stupid, stupid!* What had possessed him to say something so heavy-handed? Particularly in light of what had happened.

Nothing had gone as he'd hoped. Before the meeting, he had reviewed all possible scenarios several times. He'd thought he'd covered all the bases. In his vision, Lauren had first reacted with shock and anger, but as he went through his explanation she became calm, reassured—then finally happy. She had welcomed him eagerly into the firm and into her arms.

Instead, his vision had turned into a nightmare, which he'd compounded with his statement.

Stepping off the elevator, he saw Lauren's assistant busily typing. She looked up as he approached, and smiled politely.

"Is Lauren around?" Not waiting for an answer, Paul brushed by the woman and peered into Lauren's office. It was empty. He turned back to the assistant. "It's time for lunch. Do you know where she's gone?"

"She left about ten minutes ago. Said she was going for a walk. Was she expecting you?" Icicles dripped from her voice.

"Uh, it was probably just a mix-up about the time," Paul responded.

"Probably."

"Yeah, just a mix-up." Feeling uncomfortable, Paul backed up, wanting to bolt for the elevator. "I'll hunt around. I'm sure she's here someplace."

"Good luck." But her tone said something entirely different.

He considered paging Lauren, then dismissed the idea. It would only make her angrier.

Paul searched the floor, checked both the marketing and art departments. No Lauren. Taking the stairs, he made a quick round of the main floor. Still no Lauren. Finally he trudged down the steps to the basement. She wasn't in the cafeteria. The lab was the only place left.

When he entered the lab, E.J. was sitting at a table, peering into a microscope.

"Seen Lauren?" Paul asked.

"No." E.J. didn't even look up, and Paul paused for a moment, wanting to talk to E.J. and explain this all away. But Lauren was his primary concern.

He decided to check the parking lot to see if her car was still there. When he stepped out into the sunny day, he took a deep breath. The animosity inside the building was palpable, was almost suffocating him. Glancing around, he saw Lauren's car in its assigned space.

Maybe she really had taken a walk. She used to do that a lot before they'd started eating together. He'd take a chance, wander around, see if he could find her somewhere in the parklike complex where the company was housed.

Birds chirped cheerfully as he walked. The California sun blazed brightly and wispy clouds floated across the sky. The day was bright and happy. Paul was miserable.

A few blocks along, he passed a coffee shop and glanced idly in the window, not expecting Lauren to be there. But she was, sitting at a counter, looking breathtakingly beautiful. And sad. Very, very sad. Paul went inside.

When he slipped onto the stool beside her, Lauren turned her head and looked at him. Saying nothing, she returned her gaze to a salad in front of her and began plucking at a lettuce leaf with her fork.

"We need to talk, Lauren."

"Oh?"

Just then, a waitress, wearing a crisp brown uniform and plaid-trimmed apron, approached and asked for Paul's order. He quickly gave it and when she was gone, turned to Lauren.

"Tomorrow morning," she began, before he could speak, "I'll call a general meeting and introduce you as the new chief. Other than that, I have nothing to say."

"Not about that. We need to talk about us. About why I did what I did."

"You've won, Paul. You have our company. What more is there to talk about?" Still not looking at him, she turned the lettuce leaf over.

Paul paused as the waitress returned with his order. He lifted his coffee cup, took a sip, and waited until his place was set.

"I have business problems, Lauren. Big problems. What I've done with Cheri Lee Cosmetics is a huge departure from anything I've ever done before. It's put me out on a limb, and—"

"Do I care?" Lauren lifted her chin and fixed him with a dark stare.

Paul blew out a breath. "Probably not. But I'm going to tell you anyway. Will you at least listen?"

"All right." Lauren bent her head and rubbed the back of her neck. "But I don't think it'll change anything."

Her acquiescence gave Paul hope and this time his breath carried a sigh of relief. But Lauren's stony face informed him his hopes could be premature, so he tried to garner all his persuasive skills.

"I won't try to kid you. My original intention was to buy and dismantle Cheri Lee Cosmetics. It's what I do. Except for a little company I have in Mexico, I've never attempted to run a business. I know about assets and balance sheets, not product and personnel."

"Obviously. Tell me something new."

Paul was treading on unproven ground, and Lauren wasn't giving an inch. For a moment he was tempted to give up, but reminding himself that, from her perspective, he'd done a terrible thing, he controlled his annoyance. Realizing that, he found himself wanting to reach out and stroke her cheek, to absorb the sadness he saw there. The sadness he had caused.

"As you know, Lauren, I used to work for J. Mitchell Cotton. What you don't know is that we parted under very unfavorable circumstances. Cotton wanted to issue some securities that I thought were unsound. We argued about it.... Anyway, after I left, I filed an opinion paper with the Securities Exchange Commission, which Cotton was pretty irate about. Since then, he's been messing with my acquisitions, creating some major financial losses for me. Cheri Lee Cosmetics is my last chance to keep what I've made."

"Was he doing something illegal?" She spoke impassively, and Paul tried to read her thoughts but came up with a blank.

"Uh, well, there are lots of ways to look at it. I just thought it was, uh, like I said, unsound."

"Nevertheless, you did what you thought was right, Paul. Cotton should understand that."

Paul laughed drolly. "Finance is like a big fraternity. You just don't do what I did and remain a member."

"So you used me as your ticket back into the club?" Her features hardened again and now Paul knew exactly what she was thinking. He leaned forward earnestly.

"No, Lauren. That's what I'm trying to tell you. I didn't intend to fall in love with you. And that's the only reason I changed my plans. There's nothing I'd like more than to hand you back your company on a silver platter. But I can't afford to do that. It would wipe me out." He ached to reach out and touch her, soften the edges of her expression, but he restrained himself. "We can rebuild Cheri Lee Cosmetics, make it wildly profitable. If we work together, it will still be there for the next generation. For E.J.'s kids, Jessie's kids. For *our* kids, Lauren." He gave in to his impulse then, and trailed his fingers over the curve of Lauren's cheek. "I love you."

Lauren jerked her face away as if he'd slapped her and looked directly forward, her mouth a grim line.

"In time..." She hesitated, still avoiding Paul's gaze. She'd understood Paul's implication, and had been startled by the burst of joy it had caused. But she'd quickly stifled it. "Maybe in time. I trusted you, Paul, even though I knew I shouldn't. Now... Now, I don't know what to do."

"Then there's hope for us?" He brushed her cheek again. This time she didn't pull away. "Please say there's hope, Lauren."

"*Hope* may be too strong a word." Lauren picked up her check, flicked the edge with a fingernail, then added, "We'll wait. See what happens."

She stood, ready to leave.

"Wait," Paul said, signaling the waitress. "I'll walk back with you."

"Was something wrong with the food, sir?" The waitress frowned down at his untouched plate.

"No." Paul took the check from her hand. "I wasn't very hungry."

He hurried to catch up with Lauren, who was already at the cashier's stand, paying for her meal.

"You could have let me buy you lunch," he said, as he handed his money to the cashier.

"Guess I'm just a cheap date." A small grin played around her lips and Paul relaxed a little. Things were already getting better.

As they walked back, Lauren began telling Paul about the general meeting planned for the next morning. "I'll try to act enthusiastic when I make the announcement. But the word is out, Paul, so expect a lot of unhappy faces."

"I know." Paul grimaced. "I've been getting the ice treatment all morning."

"What did you expect?" She asked the question pleasantly enough and without emphasis, but Paul found he had no real answer.

"I don't know. Not so much loyalty to your family, I suppose. I think I've always thought of employees as another asset, not as real people."

"Ah, then you've learned a lesson." Now a grin spread full-force across her face, lifting Paul's spirits.

He laughed. "Yes, the hard way." And her smile made him feel so good that he grabbed her hand and pulled her under a towering eucalyptus tree. Gently pressing her against the trunk, he said, "I love you," and placed a soft kiss on her lips.

Her mouth trembled beneath his, tightened, then parted oh-so-slightly in acceptance. Paul's heart soared sky-high. He moved forward, preparing for an embrace, when Lauren turned her head and splayed her hands on his chest.

"No," she said in a strained voice. "Not now."

"Don't you love me?" Paul hated the plaintive tone in his voice, but her rejection had torn him to pieces.

She didn't answer immediately. She inched along the tree trunk until she was no longer in front of Paul. Leaning back, she put her hands on the trunk and ran one finger over a heart carved in the bark. Paul's eyes followed the movement of her hand, then shifted back to her troubled face.

"Well, don't you, Lauren?" he demanded, terrified of hearing the wrong answer.

"That isn't the issue. The issue is trust."

"I know I've given you reason not to trust me, but I'll try to earn it back."

"It's not a matter of me trusting you."

"Then, what are you talking about?"

"Me." She thumped her chest, jutted out her chin. "It's you who can't trust me. Because from this day on, I'll be searching for a way to get back my family's firm." She whirled from under the tree and began walking in long, brisk strides. Stopping, she turned. "So, watch yourself."

Paul burst out laughing, a variation of the she's-so-cute-when-she's-mad theme running through his mind. Lauren wasn't amused. Her hands on her hips, she glared.

"I'm not kidding, Paul. One of these days I'll find a way."

Still somewhat amused, he didn't follow her. There was plenty of time to mend their relationship. Overall, their encounter had gone quite well, held promise for a future. But as he stood there, bathed in brilliant California sunlight, his amusement faded. He glanced at Lauren's receding back, then at the tree trunk, to the spot Lauren had toyed with. Inside the heart were two sets of initials: E.A. plus C.A.

Ellis Afton plus Cheri Afton?

Paul peered at the etching. It had been there so long that shredded bark filled in part of the carving.

So he thought this encounter with Lauren had gone well, did he? *Like hell,* those initials told him. *Like hell.*

He was in a battle with her heritage.

"THERE'S THIS LOVELY little isolated beach. Course we'll have to climb down to it." Jessie's voice purred in Bill Rosen's ear. Soft, it was; inviting. For over three weeks now, he'd called her daily, only to be greeted each time by a growling curse and the bang of a slammed receiver. What had brought about this change?

"But it's only a little hill," she continued. "Are you up for it?"

"Uh, sure," Bill mumbled into the phone. "What time?" A weight lifted from him and his spirits soared. No use bringing up sore subjects. Obviously she'd forgiven him; he didn't need to know why.

"Is eleven good?"

"Sure," Bill said again, not bothering to check his calendar. If he'd scheduled something, he'd cancel it.

Jessie was back in his life! Hallelujah!

"Bye then. See you in a little while."

He held the receiver a long time, ignoring the persistent hum, and stared dreamily into space. As the operator's warning came through the wire, he shot up from his chair and sped out of his office.

"I'll be back in a while," he called to Carol on his way out. Reaching the door, he stopped, looked back. "Have you heard from Paul?"

"No, not today." Carol looked worried. Maybe it was her husband again, Bill thought. He knew the man hadn't been well. "Do you want to see him for anything special?"

"No, just asking."

But as Bill raced to his car and sped off to his home, he thought about Paul. They'd patched up their quarrel, although the patchwork still showed. Bill had delivered a stern lecture to Paul about sudden, undiscussed turns in direction, and had listened patiently to Paul's explanation. As Bill pulled into the driveway of his sprawling adobe home, the garage door lifting in front of him, he felt a stab of compassion for this giant kid who happened to be his partner. But fortunately for Bill, Paul's problems weren't his.

He whistled a little tune as he went to his bedroom. The room, spotless as always, looked empty, unlived-in. For the zillionth time, Bill wondered why he lived in this sprawling mansion all alone.

Unlike Paul, Bill didn't truly enjoy the trappings of his wealth. He figured they just came with the territory. Paul always went for the brass ring. Of course, Bill had never achieved Paul's monumental success, but then he didn't have Paul's problems, either.

In fact, as of now, he had no problems at all.

Opening a dresser drawer to get out some swimming trunks, he laughed, realizing he was pondering which ones Jessie would like best. Resuming his tuneless whistle, he then went to the closet, unearthed a duffel bag, and busied himself packing for his day at the beach.

No siree, today he had no problems. None at all.

But, later, back in his office, Bill was a bundle of nerves as he glanced once more at a digital clock. Jessie was late—again. When he heard the front-door buzzer he jumped up like a jack-in-the-box, grabbed his bag, and headed for the lobby.

She was talking to Carol, looking like a goddess. Her red braids brushed the shoulders of her denim shift. Long, tanned legs, exposed from the knee down, ended in perfect feet, clad in leather sandals. He drank her in, as if seeing her beauty for the first time. Speechless—he felt speechless.

"Hi," he said softly, afraid of shattering the moment.

"Hi," she answered, her smile bright, almost too bright. "Ready?"

"You bet." He took her arm and started for the door. "I'll be unavailable for the rest of the day," he told the smiling Carol.

"Optimist," Jessie teased, patting his cheek in that familiar way, and Bill was elated. Yet through his elation ran an uneasy current. Didn't Jessie's voice sound a trifle hollow? Lack its usual zest?

But as they cruised up Highway 1, Jessie chatted freely—about an opera she'd attended, a boring party, her new sculpture. Talked about anything but the one thing on Bill's mind—Cheri Lee Cosmetics and the disastrous takeover. The few times he tried to bring it up, Jessie started on a new topic. The minutes passed quickly, and soon they were at the beach.

"Hill?" Bill exclaimed incredulously. Carrying Jessie's picnic basket and his duffel bag, Bill stared over the edge at the ocean below. "This is a cliff, Jessie. A blooming cliff."

She laughed, the color in her face high.

"I hope you have a case of champagne in this basket," Bill said. "It weighs a ton. How are we going to get down there with all this stuff?"

"A cinch." Jessie turned and peered provocatively over her shoulder. "Follow me."

She led him to a narrow path that curved its way to the bottom. Skidding a little as she started down, she looked back at Bill with invitation in her eyes. "Well, come on. If this was easy to get to, we wouldn't have privacy."

Privacy. Ah, yes. What wonderful things they could do with a little privacy on a sunlit, surfy beach.

"You sure get me doing crazy things, honey," he said. "But you're worth it."

Her responding smile looked more natural than before. She hesitated, then said, "Damn right."

With that, she continued down the path. Bill followed, cursing himself for not changing shoes as he slipped and slid downhill. More than once he had to scramble for support, nearly dropping his parcels in the process.

Finally at the bottom, he dropped his burdens, went over to Jessie and took her in his arms.

"Wait," she said, pulling gracefully away. "Let's get settled first." She took a blanket out of the basket and quickly shut the lid afterward.

"What do you have in there?" Bill peered over her shoulder, smiling. Jessie, always full of surprises, had probably packed a gourmet meal. "Let me see."

"Patience," she said, winking. "You'll see in good time."

"I hate surprises." And he hated waiting. Three weeks without Jessie! He wanted to hold her close, touch her, smell her, taste her.

"I know." She moved into his arms then, wrapping her arms around his waist. A hollow place inside Bill that he'd hardly known was there began filling up as the heat of her body warmed him. The cool ocean air enveloped them. Except for the sound of waves lapping against the shore, all was silent. Jessie snuggled closer and whispered throatily into his shirt, "Why don't you take off your clothes? We'll go skinny-dipping."

"The water's bound to be cold." Bill tipped back his head to give her a quizzical look. "Besides, it's broad daylight."

"No one can see us." She pointed up, and Bill saw it was true. They'd taken a winding path down the tree-covered cliff and were totally shielded from the highway. Even the sounds of passing cars had been left above. Smiling broadly, she added, "And I'll keep you warm."

Bill smiled at that wonderful thought. She stepped out of his arms and began shaking the blanket. It fluttered near his head, and he grabbed one end, helped her lay it flat, then plopped down.

"Well, aren't you going to undress?" Her hands on her hips, she stared at him.

Bill drank her in. The ocean framed her head, auburn against azure. His breath caught in his throat. He nodded and began with his shoes.

He'd left his coat and tie at the office, and now he quickly stripped off the rest of his clothing, neatly folding and piling it—undershirt on top of shirt, shorts on top of slacks, socks carefully tucked into shoes.

Jessie smiled indulgently. "Ah. Sweet, tidy Bill."

"Now you." Bill grasped her hand, tugged her down beside him and reached for her shift.

Jessie scooped up his clothes, then sprang to her feet. "First let me put your things in the basket. I know you hate sand in your clothes."

This reference to their heated lovemaking on New Year's Eve made Bill laugh, both from embarrassment and from the memory of that intense pleasure. He ran his hand slowly up her leg and felt her tremble beneath his touch. She wanted him. The tremble told him so. She wanted him as much as he wanted her. Then she stepped back abruptly, looking down at him with a bright smile.

"I'm also going to put the wine in the ocean. There's an inlet that's perfect for it just a little way down the beach."

"I'll come with you." Bill started to rise, but Jessie stopped him with a touch on the shoulder.

"No, no. Stay here and enjoy the rays."

"Okay, but don't take long," he warned her, falling back onto the blanket, savoring the sun's heat on his naked body.

"Why should I take long?" She turned, went to the basket and took something out. Then she started off, soon disappearing behind a curve in the coastline.

As Bill soaked up the warmth, he thought how lucky he was she'd forgiven him. To think he might have lost her. Then his smile turned into a worried frown. They still needed to talk about what had transpired with Cheri Lee Cosmetics. He had to tell her what he'd felt, how he hadn't wanted to betray her, how he'd been unable to resist her.

She'd believe him, of course. Would throw herself tearfully into his arms, declare her forgiveness. Wouldn't she?

The unexpected doubt shook Bill from his dreamy state. He looked about, expecting to see Jessie come around the bend.

Where was she? He glanced at his watch, but it wasn't there, either. Jessie had put it away with his clothes. How long had she been gone? The silence, so enchanting before, now seem ominous.... He felt nervous now, restless.

Also hungry. He got up from the blanket. Surely he could find a little snack somewhere in Jessie's heavy basket. He lifted the lid and reached inside, his hand striking a hard, irregular object. He drew his brows together, puzzled, and opened the lid fully.

Rocks!

Piles and piles of rocks, and... What the—?

Pop! Bill's elation, his certainty that all was well with Jessie and him, burst like a balloon pricked by a pin. Crumpled on top of the rocks was a note written in Jessie's large, loose scrawl.

Dear Bill—
Enjoy your lunch. Go for a swim.
May you sink to the depths of the ocean.
May the sharks gnaw at your bones for eternity.
Yours never,
Jessie

"WOULDN'T YOU LOVE TO have seen his face when he read the note?" Jessie sat on a stool, doubling over with laughter on top of Lauren's marble counter.

Lauren giggled, too, as a picture of a naked Bill trying to get home flashed in her head. Lauren admired her sister's nerve. Jessie hadn't sat idle, mourning her lover's betrayal. She'd gotten sweet, sweet revenge.

But was it so sweet? Somehow Jessie's hilarity seemed a little too fevered, her voice too rapid and high, her eyes too bright.

She wondered what it would feel like, doing the same to Paul? Would gloating over his extreme embarrassment fill her emptiness? She thought not, and her amusement faded. Reaching out, she touched her sister's arm. "He really hurt you, didn't he, Jessie?"

Her smile still wide, Jessie blinked several times in rapid succession as her laughing tears turned to sorrow and flooded over her lower lashes.

"I'm sorry," Lauren said. "I didn't mean to make you cry."

"'Kay. It's okay...." Jessie waved Lauren's hand away, then wrapped her fingers around her coffee mug, obscuring the wording. It read: World's Greatest Sister. The cup had been a long-ago birthday gift from Jessie.

But at this moment, Lauren didn't feel like a great sister at all. She had no words of comfort. Her own heart ached and she couldn't shake it off. How could she mutter some platitude like, "Forgive him," when she couldn't do the same?

"He's doing the stupidest things, Lor." Jessie looked up then, her face heavy with sadness. "The day after I stranded him, a man showed up at my door with a bunch of balloons that said, 'I love you.' The next day a singing telegram arrived. The guy sang this dumb little ditty that he said Bill wrote. Then yesterday a blimp floated over my house. It had Forgive Me, Jessie, written on the side."

Bill Rosen did these things? Lauren's eyes widened. She couldn't believe it. "He must really love you, Jess."

"That's what he says. He keeps calling every night, asking me to marry him. I hang up right away, but—Oh, Lor, I'm afraid to go home! Today he'll probably have a battleship in Mom's front yard. And...and it's getting harder to hang up."

"Do you love Bill?" Lauren touched Jessie's arm again. This time it wasn't brushed away. Jessie needed her sister's comfort now. These conflicting desires were tearing her apart. She'd finally restored harmony with her mother, finally felt like a member of the family. How could she let Bill back in her life when he'd betrayed her, devastated the ones she loved?

"Do you love him?" Lauren repeated.

"Yes, I do." Jessie's tears burst forth again, coming in racking sobs. "What—am I—going to do?"

Lauren got up, rounded the corner, and embraced Jessie, as she'd so often done when Jessie was small. Only this time her sister's tears came from something much, much worse than a broken doll.

"Hush, hush..." Lauren soothed her. She began telling Jessie what Cheri Lee had said the day of that wretched meeting. As Lauren went on, Jessie's tears abated. She listened carefully.

"You think Mom wants me to be with Bill?"

"That's sure how it seems to me."

Wiping her eyes hard with her knuckles, Jessie shook her head in disbelief. "After everything that went on?"

"Why don't you ask her yourself? You deserve to be happy, Jessie. If this is what you want, don't let it get away."

Picking up a teaspoon, Jessie tapped it on the counter. Maybe she would listen to Bill when he called tonight, let him explain. Her misery easing, she looked up at Lauren and realized she was now seeing—really seeing—her for the first time since she'd arrived there that morning. Lauren did not look well.

Feeling like a selfish jerk, Jessie touched her sister's cheek. She wanted to erase the blue-gray cast running from Lauren's lower lashes to her cheekbones, to plump out the deep lines of weariness stretching from her nose to the corners of her mouth.

Good, steady Lauren, Jessie thought, urging her to grab happiness while turning her back on her own.

"From what you said, it sounds like Mom approves of you and Paul, too," Jessie said pointedly. "Why aren't you taking your own advice?"

"Bill and Paul are two different people. Paul chose his course of action, Bill didn't."

"People change. Never in my wildest dreams would I have expected Bill Rosen to send me a blimp!"

Lauren grinned. "No. And I suppose Paul *could* change too." She took Jessie's arms and pulled her to her feet. "I'll think about it. But right now, go home and wait for Bill's next surprise."

Jessie recognized that further discussion would be fruitless. Deciding to give Lauren time before broaching the subject again, she smiled, kissed her sister on the cheek and went out the kitchen door.

On the way home, Jessie wondered what new entertainment Bill had planned. Maybe an airplane skywriting above her roof. Or maybe a clown would bang on her door, cartwheel across her living room, and hand her a love note. She laughed delightedly.

Racing up the stairs to her apartment, she felt a pang of disappointment when she found nothing waiting for her outside the door. Although maybe it was for the best. Now she had time to call Mom, confirm what Lauren had said.

Their conversation was brief. Cheri Lee had been on her way out the door for a luncheon with friends when Jessie rang. The explanation Jessie received after rushing through the details of her conversation with Lauren, erased all her doubts.

"All I've ever wanted is your happiness," Cheri said.

Jessie fought another rush of tears. Lord, she'd cried more in the past few weeks than she'd cried during her entire stormy adolescence.

"Go for it, dear. Isn't that what you young people say nowadays?"

"Oh, Mom. I love you."

"Of course you do. And I love you." Then, with a quick apology, Cheri ended the conversation. Jessie lowered the phone, not knowing what to do next. She hated waiting—it drove her nuts.

Walking to a sculpturer's pedestal, she lifted a damp cloth from her current project and began working the clay. Every hour she looked up to check the clock, yet only ten minutes had passed. Why was time moving so slowly? Where was Bill's surprise?

They'd always come by early afternoon.

Two o'clock came. Then three. Soon it was three-thirty. At three forty-five, Jessie slammed the cloth back on her sculpture, nearly overturning the pedestal with her force. Righting it quickly, she thrust clay-damp hands into her hair.

Bill had given up. No one was coming today. The yo-yo! Why had he quit so soon?

She crossed her small living room to the kitchen in long, agitated strides, turned and crossed back to the pedestal. She'd counted on Bill's phone call, had already worked out the way she'd allow him to beg for forgiveness—and for her hand in marriage. Since it was now clear he wouldn't call, she needed a new plan.

She could let him squirm a few days, then go to his office and see him; sweetly let him know she *might* be willing to hear his apology.

Or she could pick up the phone right now and call him.

Ridiculous. She could never sacrifice her dignity that way.

And that's exactly what she told herself, over and over, as she walked to the telephone and dialed Bill's office number.

Just as Carol's crisp voice answered Bill's phone, a knock sounded on Jessie's door. "Can you hold a sec," she said. "I'll be right back."

Could it be Bill's messenger? She didn't think so. Not this late. She opened the door. A deliveryman held a flat package and a clipboard.

"Sign here, ma'am."

Jessie complied, took the package inside, and stared at it curiously. No return address, no clue where it came from.

Bill!

She ripped the package apart eagerly. A white envelope, thick with documents, fell to the floor. She picked it up, wondering what it was. She'd been all wrong to expect skywriting or a clown. Today's present was decidedly more sedate.

Opening the envelope, she pulled out a sheaf of pages and slowly unfolded them. A stick-on note covered the top half of the first sheet. The words written there jumped out at her.

Now will you marry me?

Now? Why *now?* Then Jessie looked hard at the page beneath the note. Her gasp came so forcibly it was nearly a scream. The documents fluttered to the floor as Jessie raced back to the phone.

Carol had disconnected the line, obviously giving up on Jessie's return. Preparing to redial, Jessie held down the appropriate button. Before she'd released it, the phone rang.

"Hello," she said, planning to cut the caller short.

"Jessie?" The familiar voice, the oh-so-wonderful voice, was like music to her ears.

"Yes, Bill," she said on the catch of her breath. "Yes, yes. Oh, yes."

CHAPTER TWELVE

PAUL STIRRED RESTLESSLY in his gigantic bed, unable to sleep. His hands propped behind his head, his eyes focused on the ceiling, he watched the lazy revolutions of a gold-trimmed fan.

Three weeks had passed and nothing had changed. Oh, Lauren had introduced him as the CEO, all right—had even behaved as though it were welcome news—and they still shared daily lunches in the cafeteria. But beyond that, Lauren remained aloof, unreachable. She'd never brought up his implied offer of marriage, nor would she allow any conversation to become personal.

Once, when the effects of their estrangement became too great, Paul had leaned over during lunch, taken her hand, and asked to see her that night.

She'd smiled humorlessly and replied, "No sleeping with the enemy."

So it had come to that. They were now enemies. Or so Lauren saw it. His hopes, his dreams, had gone up in smoke.

Paul had known bad times in his life. Had known disapproval, loss. But only once before had he experienced this numbing despair: when his mother had died.

Her face appeared in his inner eye. He'd loved her and always knew she'd loved him. When Paul was less than a year old, his father had left—never to return, never to send money. Somehow Sharon had carried on. She'd worked nights as a waitress, had clothed him as well as she could afford to, and kept their shabby little home in East L.A. neat and tidy. But she'd always seemed slightly bewildered that life had done this to her.

Paul began demonstrating his amazing precocity early—learning to read by the age of three. At four and a half he took apart her clock radio, then put it back together in perfect order. He'd told her he wanted to fix the "buzz"—and he'd done just that. Sharon's bewilderment had turned to panic.

What should she do with this child? she'd asked her friends. They had no other family. Sharon had grown up in foster homes. How could she educate him properly on her meager income?

Paul had overheard these hushed conversations, recognized with his quick little mind that somehow he was a problem. When he started school, he soon found out why.

Boring! The teachers wanted him to sit in a circle with the other kids and read books with one-syllable words, wanted him to learn what two and two made. Paul had been doing long division for over a year.

Boring, boring, boring. He had made his teachers' lives a living hell; he'd built elaborate models from pencils, erasers and paper clips when he was supposed to be listening; he'd raised his hand every ten minutes to go to the bathroom, just so he could escape the monotonous lectures. Soon came the parent-teacher conferences that Sharon had feared. They put Paul in second grade. Still boring. Third grade. Dull,

dull, dull. All this before he'd reached seven years of age.

"We can't place him any higher," the school had said. "He'll lose out in social development."

As he ate breakfast one school-day morning, passing his time with the morning newspaper, Paul had seen an interesting article. . . .

"Read this, Mom." Sharon glanced up from the comics page and smiled with her usual bemused expression. Paul thought she feared this was another article on some advancement in astronomy or the like, and he smiled back affectionately. He had long ago abandoned talking to his mom about those things. She always got flustered.

Sharon glanced at the headline. "'Wizard Kids'? Oh, I love that show. Those kids are so cute." She read the article slowly, or so it seemed to Paul. He dug into his Fruit Loops cereal, waiting.

"Interesting," she commented when finished, apparently finding nothing pertinent.

"They're looking for new contestants, Mom, and tryouts are next week. You're always telling me I'm smarter than those kids. They win lots of money. If I could get on—win—we wouldn't be poor anymore."

"You *are* smarter, Paul." Sharon rolled her eyes upward, as if searching for an inspiration. "No." She shook her head. "Real people don't get on those shows. They're a setup."

"Are you sure?"

"No-o-o. Not positive."

"Then let's try." Paul smiled, supremely confident. He could get on. Could get his mom out of that greasy, smelly, coffee shop where she slaved every night. He'd be a champ, a top-notch champ. They'd be rich.

"All right, Paul, we'll try." Sharon bent over and kissed his nose. "After all, you are my little genius boy...."

So they'd gone to the audition. The show's producers had been dazzled by Paul's knowledge, his quick wit, and his funny "old-man" observations.

Paul smiled bleakly, thinking of Lauren's comment about his terrible haircut. Sharon had cut it herself to save money, and the producers had argued hotly over whether to properly trim the flyaway strands or leave them alone.

They'd left them alone, deciding the hair added to Paul's appeal. But Paul soon learned that the other kids—older kids who thought he was a pain to have around—thought he looked nerdy. He'd come to hate that hair, come to hate "Wizard Kids." Although his six-year-old mind hadn't recognized what he was doing, it was then that he had learned to change his personality to suit the people he was with.

He'd remained the precocious kid for the show's producers, feigned interest in baseball cards and dirt-bike racing with the other boys and talked about dolls and television shows with the girls. Only when he was with his mother did he feel comfortable being himself.

He'd stayed on "Wizard Kids" for two years, setting a record that remained unbroken. Scholarships came. He enrolled in a school for accelerated learners, completed grammar school by ten, high school at twelve. He and Sharon moved from their run-down house to a nice suburb. Sharon quit her job, returned to school and later opened a typing service. They hadn't gotten rich, but Sharon hadn't seemed to care.

After Paul had gained his master's degree and gone to work with Cotton, he'd built the ranch. He had asked his mother to sell her business and retire there, take it easy, but she enjoyed her work, she said. It kept her busy. Sometimes she told Paul she wished he'd come back to California, that she missed him a lot. Occasionally she suggested a vacation together that never came about. But otherwise she rarely complained.

After Paul had fought with Cotton and moved to San Diego, Paul had offered to build Sharon a house on the beach and again asked her to retire. No, she'd said. She had her work, her friends.

Realizing his mother would never become the lady of leisure he'd envisioned, Paul had ordered a new house built for her in Beverly Hills. Three days after the ground had been broken, Sharon had collapsed in her office and been rushed to the hospital. Paul had caught the first flight to Los Angeles.

Liver cancer. Deadly, but mercifully quick. Half delirious, Sharon had babbled in her hospital bed. "I've...missed you." She'd patted his head weakly. "I never...understood you.... I tried.... I've missed you."

When Paul sat at a funeral service filled with the strangers who'd been Sharon's friends, he'd thought he might die with her. Half mad with grief, he'd been consumed with remorse about his neglect, forgetting, for the time, how often she'd refused his invitations. All he could think about was how, in recent years, he'd focused all his energy on building his wealth.

That had been just a little over a year ago, and he'd survived, recovered. He'd purchased the *Gypsy Rose,* taken a cruise, and started using his wealth to enjoy life.

Paul sat up abruptly, trying to shake off his smothering depression. His clock glared at him with an accusing red eye. Five fifty-six. He'd been awake all night. Picking up his pillow, he pounded it into shape, anger bubbling inside him. Anger at himself. He thought he'd learned. But he hadn't. Otherwise, he wouldn't have alienated the only person who ever understood him.

Lauren.

Her face replaced Sharon's. He saw her rage, her streaked face—and the image tore at his stomach. Once again his driving ambition had come between him and a loved one. He'd failed Lauren, too.

And his mind, his facile mind that had been his greatest asset, could find no way to make amends.

The telephone rang, the sound bouncing through Paul's body like a ricocheting bullet. He jumped painfully, reached out to pick up the receiver.

"Paul, my boy!" Cotton's voice boomed on the other end. "Hope I didn't wake you."

The tone sounded less than apologetic.

"Actually, no," Paul answered. *Thanks to what you taught me, I've been awake all night.* "I've been waiting for your call."

"You have?" The genuine surprise in Cotton's voice amused Paul; he'd always loved playing with the very literal-minded.

"Of course not," Paul said, no longer amused. "What do you want?"

"I've heard this distressing rumor that some pretty blonde's put a ring through your nose. Thought maybe you needed out of a tight situation."

"Are you offering to help?"

"Your old job's yours for the asking." Then Cotton's tone lost its geniality. "It won't work, kid. That foxy little lady can't protect you. You can't hide among powder and face paint."

"I'm not hiding!" Paul's response sounded defensive, even to his own ears. Attempting to recover, he said, "I'm not interested in the job. Just stay out of my business and I'll stay out of yours."

"Did you really think I'd forgive and forget, Paul? Fortunately, that little paper of yours didn't cause me any problems. But that doesn't mean I won't cause you some. Unless, of course, you come back to work and bring those Cheri Lee Cosmetics shares with you."

"When hell freezes over. And I'm not taking this lying down, Cotton. So don't count your victory yet."

"Is that some kind of threat?"

"It can be anything you want." Paul swung his legs over the edge of the bed. "Now, if you don't mind, I've got a busy schedule. You're holding me up."

Resisting the urge to slam down the phone, Paul slowly lowered it. Cotton's response was audible all the way down. Calmer now, Paul focused on the most disturbing aspect of the unpleasant interchange.

Who was giving Cotton this information? There weren't many people who knew about him and Lauren. Few of his staff members even knew exactly where he lived. Paul reviewed the names of those who did. Bill, of course. And Mike Armstrong. Then there was Carol Walgren and two or three of Paul's top analysts. Not one of them had reason to help Cotton.

And why was Cotton so anxious for him to come back? Was it simply because of the cosmetic stock? Paul doubted that. Cotton had investments worth ten times the value of Cheri Lee Cosmetics. For a brief moment, Paul wondered if Cotton was obliquely trying to repair their breach. The thought carried a brief spurt of glad hope, then he squashed it. He had to go with the facts, and the facts indicated that Cotton was out to ruin him.

This had to end. For three weeks—twenty-one long, long days—he'd done nothing but trudge through his work by day and wallow in self-pity by night. It was time he took corrective measures.

Paul climbed out of bed and headed for his shower with more energy than he'd felt in days. He turned it on full force, then considered all his problems, examining his options. As the needlelike streams peppered his aching, sleep-deprived body, he developed a strategy. He'd knock his problems out of the ballpark one at a time. Eventually it would all work out. Nothing was ever as bad as it seemed, and even Lauren would be his one day.

"WHERE'S BILL?" Now in his Coronado Island office, Paul stood at Carol's desk, sorting through the mail. Usually Carol did that, but he'd hoped to find at least a postcard from his partner. Finding nothing, he looked up. "I've asked you that before, haven't I?"

"Oh, ten, twelve times, maybe," Carol answered pleasantly, reaching down to pat Galahad. "All I know is he said he'd be away about ten days. I promise I'll let you know if he calls."

"Yeah." Paul took his portion of the mail and went down the long hall to his office, Galahad close on his heels. As he passed the bull pen, Mike Armstrong called out his name.

"I need to talk to you. Right away." Mike got up from his terminal, picked up a stack of computer printouts and came into the hall. "Privately."

A ball knotted in Paul's stomach as they walked into his office, where Mike plopped the printouts on the desk. He sat down and waited for Paul to do the same. "Look at this."

Paul did, and didn't like what he saw. One of his largest stock holdings had tumbled more than fifteen points that day. He lifted his head to Mike. "Did you get me out?"

"Sort of."

"What do you mean, 'Sort of'?" Paul heard the hysteria in his voice and tried to quell it.

"Go through the rest of the reports." Mike looked serious, deadly serious.

Paul's nausea steadily grew as he scanned each page. Twenty points lost here, seven there; four, eleven, sixteen. Every stock he owned was down. "But the stock market's up."

Lame comment. The market went up, yet individual stocks went down. The market went down, still individual stocks went up.

But all at once?

Mike remained silent, shuffling and rearranging the reports Paul had scattered on his desk. The rustling sound grated on Paul's nerves.

"How much?" Paul wasn't sure he wanted to know.

"Probably a quarter million. You could ride this out, because at these lows the stocks are bound to go back up. But your broker is screaming for his margin call. We've got three days to come up with a hundred thousand. Otherwise you'll have to sell and eat your losses." Mike hesitated, appeared uncertain for a moment, then went on. "Paul, you're seriously overextended. This Cheri Lee Cosmetics deal's taken most of your resources."

"Yeah, I know." Paul picked up the market-summary printout. "Any clue as to how this happened?"

"*How,* yes, but not *why.* I ran an activity history on all these companies." Mike swept the length of Paul's summary sheet with his hand, then pulled a report from the bottom of the pile. "Take this one, for instance. There were small buys on this date, that date, then here. The buys go back more than nine months. When I add them all together, they amount to nearly ninety percent of what was dumped today.

"You've got trouble, Paul. Because this holds true for every stock on the list. Someone's trying to bring you down, trying big-time."

"Cotton," Paul said, then put his hand to his mouth, realizing he'd just bitten the eraser off his pencil. He spit it out in his hand and threw it into his wastebasket.

"Cotton," Mike echoed.

"Hunt around, Mike. See if you can find someone to bail me out. I'll do the same."

"Have you considered selling your Cheri Lee Cosmetics shares? Word on the street is there're lots of interested buyers." As soon as the question left Mike's mouth, Paul saw him flinch. Obviously Paul's flash of rage had registered on his face. He struggled to control his expression, his voice, before answering.

"Not yet, Mike. Not yet."

"Okay, Paul. It's your money." Mike got up, started to take his reports, then reconsidered. "I'll leave these here. I can print out more."

"Sure," Paul replied in a toneless voice as Mike went out the door.

Paul wished once more that Bill were here, that their easy camaraderie was restored. He needed his partner's steady, sensible advice. Although he wasn't sure why. He knew what Bill would say. Paul had been seduced by the game, had lived on the edge and should have seen this coming.

He remembered Bill's anger after the disastrous meeting. What, he'd asked, did Paul think he was doing by deciding to manage Cheri Lee Cosmetics? That wasn't Paul's area of expertise; he'd make mistakes—costly mistakes—which Bill had reminded him he could ill afford.

Paul, never one to reveal his true intentions, much less his feelings, had haltingly tried to cover up. Six months, a year, tops, Cheri Lee Cosmetics would be worth three times what it was that day.

"But can you afford the time?" Bill had wanted to know, as he'd explained with clenched fists that he loved Jessie Afton, wanted to marry her. "Your games have destroyed our relationship," he flatly accused.

"Then why didn't you cut bait?" Paul had angrily asked, growing impatient with Bill's diatribe.

Bill had stared at him in pure amazement. "Don't you realize that you would have been ruined if I'd pulled out?" Then he'd spun on his heel and stalked out of Paul's office.

At the time, Paul had been hurt and puzzled. After all, he hadn't known the depths of Bill's feelings for Jessie. Now he clearly saw how much his partner had sacrificed for friendship. And how it now seemed for nothing.

He wanted to explain this to Bill. They could work together, find a way to win Jessie back. He shook his head wryly, realizing he didn't even know how to win Lauren.

Hearing a noise at the door, Paul looked up and saw Bill. A glad smile crossed his face and he felt a sense of solace. "The wandering minstrel has returned," he said.

"Reluctantly." Bill settled into a well-padded armchair. Wearing a pair of chino slacks and a pullover, he looked tanned and relaxed.

"Where've you been?"

Bill's face lit up like a neon sign. "Reno. Jessie and I got married last Sunday."

"You what?" Paul stood and extended his hand, a myriad of emotions flooding his body. "Congratulations, buddy."

Paul meant it, yet envy and hope battled inside him.

"Thanks." Bill shook Paul's hand vigorously. "I'm one lucky guy."

"How did you do it? It couldn't have been easy, considering . . ."

Bill laughed, and Paul noticed that his laugh sounded like Jessie's—uninhibited, full of exuberance. Bill launched into the story of his brief courtship. He told Paul how Jessie had abandoned him on the beach, and that he would have been forced to hitchhike home naked if not for the swimming trunks in his duffel bag. Then he spoke of balloons, blimps and singing telegrams.

Paul tried to hide his amazement as he listened. When Bill finished, he said, "That girl's really loosening you up, Rosen."

"I know. It feels great." Bill stood. "I can't stay. Jessie's home, changing. She's scheduled to do the first session on the Minx video in an hour and I'm going with her."

Paul also stood, ready to bring up the subject of their disagreement to finally repair it. He hesitated, searching for the right words, when his partner's face became serious.

"I left one part out, Paul. And I think you need to know."

This obviously wasn't another amusing story. Paul had learned to dread expressions like the one Bill wore.

"I gave Jessie a wedding gift," Bill continued. "Her shares of Cheri Lee Cosmetics."

Had a boulder just struck Paul in the chest? Something had. He couldn't talk, couldn't breathe. Dimly, he wondered if this was how Lauren had felt the day he'd marched into her office with Bill.

He gulped air. "You can't do that, Bill. You pledged those shares to me. They weren't yours to give—not without my permission." It seemed to Paul that his voice came out of a deep hole in the earth. "Now I don't have control."

"I'm sorry, man. I know I breached our agreement, but... I had to do it. Jessie's the most important thing in my life." Bill put a hand on Paul's shoulder. "This could be best in the long run. You've never said, but I suspect you and Lauren have a thing going. Work things out with her. You don't need control. You need to learn teamwork."

"Thanks for the platitudes, friend. Maybe you should write them down, publish them someday." Paul turned, went to his desk and sat down heavily.

"Paul..."

"Forget it, Rosen. Go fetch your bride, enjoy your honeymoon. Right now, though, I'd appreciate it if you'd get out of my face."

With a sigh, Paul pushed back his fifteen-hundred-dollar ergonomically designed chair, propped his Bally shoes on his eight-thousand-dollar slate-topped desk, and stared at the fifty-thousand-dollar Muro lithograph on the wall of his office.

He heard Bill leave, heard his sandals flop against the carpeted hallway floor, heard the buzz of his voice as he spoke to Carol.

His friend? What a laugh. As he'd reminded himself many times before, Paul Sherwood had no friends, only associates.

A soft nudge against his knee disturbed his thoughts. Paul lowered his hand and scratched his collie's head, then gazed down into adoring, golden eyes. Nope, he reflected, Paul Sherwood had no friends except for Galahad.

Or did he? Was there a message for him in Bill's success with Jessie? Could he and Lauren still find happiness together?

But how could he go to her now? Bill had had something to offer Jessie; Paul's world was collapsing.

Still, the idea of marriage remained like a ray of light.

Paul opened a drawer and pulled out a leather-bound address book. He might not have friends, but he had a lot of contacts and they were all in that book.

He'd buckle down, hunt around, and soon the financial nightmare would be behind him. After that, he'd ask Bill where he'd ordered the blimp.

After that?

Why wait? The longer he let this estrangement with Lauren go on, the worse it would become.

No. Waiting wasn't a good idea at all.

LAUREN STOOD AT HER window, peering down at the parking lot. Paul held open the door of his Mercedes, waiting for Galahad to lumber out. She watched as he bent and stroked the dog's coat. His lips moved as he murmured something.

His voice would be soft, rhythmic, caressing, and Lauren remembered the delight she'd felt when those sweet, sexy murmurs had rushed to her ears.

How had she come to love this giant boy? *Why* had she come to love him? From the beginning her instincts had screamed that while he seemed mature and reflective, underneath lurked the heart of a careless adolescent.

Paul was like a Great Dane puppy. With every wag of his tail, every wriggle of his overgrown frame, he knocked over some cherished knickknack, sent it crashing to the floor. Lovable, yes. Dangerous, destructive? Yes, that too. He'd chewed a hole right through her heart.

Lauren continued window-gazing even after Paul had gone inside. He would be touring the plant now, Galahad in tow, disarming the employees. They had already forgotten their original animosity toward Paul's takeover because they liked him, trusted him.

As she had trusted. Oh, how she wanted to warn them. Stay clear of that flopping tail, those adorable puppy teeth. They hurt.

Returning to her desk, she finally acknowledged the ache in her heart. She wanted to forgive him. But his deception, his clumsy presentation of his controlling ownership, had wounded her deeply. Paul could still be hiding something that could pop up unexpectedly and cause great harm. It was her duty to make sure that didn't happen.

She picked up a product analysis on the Minx makeup and began studying it. For over an hour, she leafed through it, and at the end, realized she hadn't absorbed any of it.

Lauren stumbled through the rest of her day the same way. During lunch with Paul, she was withdrawn, only vaguely aware of his unusual cheerfulness. At quitting time, she rushed out, eager to get away.

At home, too distracted to cook, she got out a frozen dinner. After microwaving it, she ate with little enthusiasm. Then she stood, paced, and wandered into the bedroom where she changed into a roomy sweat suit. What she needed was something to fill her evenings. Her life had consisted of nothing but Cheri Lee Cosmetics for a long time. But she had been happy. Until now.

Until Paul.

She hated that thought, tried to push it from her mind, but it kept coming back as she meandered through the home that now seemed large and empty. There was nothing interesting on TV. She couldn't find anything good to read. Maybe a walk would do her good. Deciding it would, she got her keys and headed for the door.

As she stepped outside, she saw someone coming toward her.

"Paul!" For a ridiculous moment she felt he'd been reading her thoughts.

"Lauren!" he responded, with a crooked grin.

She wanted to stroke his face, run her finger across the cockeyed line of his mouth, but she forced back the urge. "Is there something you want to discuss?"

"Many things." He tilted his head toward her front door. "May I come in?"

Lauren hesitated. Inside? Away from prying eyes? She didn't know if her control was great enough.

"Please, Lauren." The open need in Paul's voice turned the tide.

"All right." She moved through the door with Paul behind her, then closed it. Panic careened through her body as she turned to face him. "What is it you want?"

"Us..." Paul looked down at the tiled floor and suddenly found himself fascinated by its intricate pattern. Why was he stammering? He had thought this would be easier. "I . . . I want us."

Lauren's weary outpouring of breath undid him. He stepped forward, barely a foot from her now, and placed his hands on her arms. She shuddered beneath his touch.

"Don't you know how much you mean to me?" he asked.

Lauren tensed. Paul felt her muscles contract as she prepared to pull away. Just touching her filled him with joy. Before she could move, he brought her close, trapping her in his arms. Her struggle was brief, ending when his mouth captured hers.

His kiss felt like cool water on a parched desert. All of Lauren's will vanished. A tremor of need vibrated through her and she returned his kiss with total abandon.

Their kiss went on and on for what seemed a blissful eternity, not ending even when Paul lifted her off the floor. With a throaty whimper, Lauren slipped frantic hands around his neck and plunged her tongue into Paul's open mouth, tasting him deeply. Her mind felt drugged, lethargic, useless. But her body was vibrant, passionate, hungry; and her heart full of ecstasy.

Paul carried her into the bedroom, meeting her tongue, thrust for thrust. She heard him sigh as he lowered her to the bed. She cried out as their lips parted. But then he was beside her, their mouths again joined.

Paul was never quite sure how they'd gotten their clothing off, for it seemed they never drew apart. But soon they were lying there, gloriously naked, and Paul ran his hands greedily over Lauren's wonderfully curving body. He could feel need emanating from her skin in waves. He loved seeing her lost in passion like this, wanted to tell her so, but was afraid even a single word would fracture the mood.

Entwining his fingers in her hair, which now tumbled loose from its chignon, he rained soft, trembling kisses on her cheeks, the curve of her jaw, her neck. Her fingers roamed his back, stopping, pressing, moving on, each touch evoking incredible sensations in Paul's body.

Lauren wanted to tell Paul how much she'd missed him, but words would intrude now, bring back common sense. Common sense was her enemy. Paul's touch, Paul's kisses, Paul's marvelous body, were her allies now. And she wanted to savor this perfect moment. For an instant, common sense told her that this was all it was—one perfect moment. But as Paul's mouth took in the sensitized nub of her nipple, she moaned with pleasure, and forgot the past, forgot the future.

They touched each other for aeons, exploring every inch of the other's body, shivering in ecstasy, shuddering with a need that they both wanted to delay satisfying for as long as possible.

For when it was over...when it was over—what then?

This question raced through Lauren's mind as Paul moved between her open thighs and entered her fully. Then the sweet, electric currents sweeping through her wiped out all reason. Only Paul mattered now; only their sweet lovemaking had importance.

She arched her back, pressing her flesh against Paul's, wanting more of him, wanting to be inside him, to love him with every fiber of her being. As delicious shudders shook her body, as she felt Paul tremble beneath her caressing hands, as their joining took them higher and higher, another thought entered Lauren's mind: nothing was more important than loving Paul.

She lay beneath him now, their heavy breathing the only sound. She felt so peaceful, and she remembered her thought at the moment of climax.

Sadness returned. If only it were true. Agony welled inside her as she stroked Paul's back, realizing she could not allow this to happen again. But it was happening now. And she vowed to take every morsel of sweetness from this moment, knowing it was the last.

Placing a kiss on Paul's ear, she slid from under him, then molded her body to his.

"I love you, Lauren." Wonder was in his voice, and he smoothed Lauren's hair as he spoke. "Marry me."

Lauren's peace of mind vanished and she jerked away, waving a nervous hand. "Marry?" she squeaked. A burst of joy exploded inside, then collided with reality.

"Yes, marry. I'm asking you to be my wife."

"I...I..." Lauren's head felt light. Her heart yelled a glad yes, while her mind told her that with marriage she'd be handing her family's company over to a pirate. Oh, he didn't brandish a sword, but he was a pirate nonetheless. She bolted upright, and with agitated little jerks, communicated her refusal. "It won't work. I can't. You're careless. Immature."

"That's what Bill says," Paul replied, sadly. "But I'll try to change. I'll really try."

Lauren gazed over at him. His eyes—blue, so blue—held guileless sincerity. He lifted a hand and placed it on her thigh. A new tremor of need almost overcame her.

She wriggled out from under him and placed her feet on the floor. Her bedroom suddenly seemed bleak.

She heard Paul sit up behind her and she responded with a little shudder when he draped his hands over her shoulders and clasped them in front of her. She wanted to pull those hands against her breasts, hold them there and let all her doubts melt.

She couldn't. Her fear was too great. Oh, she believed Paul meant everything he said. She just didn't believe he could fulfill his promise.

The lure of the game. Didn't he once call it that? It would draw him back with disastrous consequences. The game was his mistress. She had a duty to protect her family from that.

"We'll be happy. I promise." The siren song of his murmur almost pulled her in. She wanted to believe.... Oh, how she wanted to....

"No, no." With a tremendous feat of will, Lauren tore herself from Paul's embrace. She turned, refusing to allow tears to surface, and fixed Paul with a firm gaze. "I can't. Not now. Part of me wants that, Paul...but I can't forget what happened."

"I've done my best to make things right." He was concealing nothing from her now. His eyes faded in color and Lauren had never seen such hopelessness. Her heart wrenched. "It won't happen again. Please believe me."

"It's impossible." The words were a stab of pain in her tightened throat. "I can't. Too much depends on me."

She watched as he wiped emotion from his face and straightened his shoulders. He got out of the bed and began gathering his clothes. In silence, he pulled on his briefs and slacks, then put on his shirt, neglecting to button it.

Lauren remained seated, hugging herself, struggling to maintain her resolve and trying to forget she loved him. What had to be done had to be done.

Still, she drank him in where he stood, his tie loosely draped beneath his collar, his jacket in his hand. She ached from head to toe, knowing she would never see him like that again.

"I love you, Lauren. I won't give up." His voice cracked ever-so-slightly.

She turned away then, unable to look at him any longer. She didn't move, even when she heard him leave the room, even when she heard the front door open and close. A strange paralysis gripped her. She felt her body and her feelings shutting down, shutting out.

"I know," she whispered into the silence. "That's what I'm afraid of."

The silence didn't answer.

CHAPTER THIRTEEN

JESSIE LOOKED spectacular. Her hair had been cut into
a shining bob that swung becomingly around her
square jaw. Flawlessly applied cosmetics enhanced her
already striking beauty. When Lauren had commented on the change, Jessie simply waved her hand
and brushed it off by saying it was for the video, then
launched into stories of her honeymoon.

Finding it painful to look upon Jessie's incandes-
cent face, Lauren fought off remorse. Her face hurt
from the forced smile she pasted on when Jessie re-
counted the joyful experiences she'd shared with Bill.

She *was* happy for Jessie, she told herself. But it was
just the night before that Paul and she had . . .

"Anyway, we were at a blackjack table, and I—"
Jessie's smile turned to a frown as she paused. Lauren hardly noticed.

"What's wrong, Lor?"

"What?" Lauren snapped back to attention. "Oh,
nothing."

Jessie got up and stood beside Lauren, touched her
arm. The soft gauze of her sleeve brushed against the
crisp gabardine of Lauren's suit.

"You keep too much inside," Jessie said. "But I'm
here for you if you decide to talk."

Lauren looked into Jessie's eyes and the love she
saw there pierced her protective envelope. She wanted

to break down and cry, but her tears were blocked deep inside, unable to flow.

"Paul asked me to marry him last night." Lauren turned her head away from the flash of happiness she saw on her sister's face.

"You refused," Jessie said flatly.

"Yes."

"Why?" Jessie brought her hand to Lauren's cheek, turning her face forward. "I know you love him."

"It just can't be. Not after what he's done."

"Don't do this to yourself, Lor. Bill was involved, too. If I could forgive him, why can't you forgive Paul?"

"It's not the same." Lauren could almost feel something dragging down the muscles of her cheeks and mouth and making it hard to talk. "Bill became caught up in something he couldn't stop. But this was all Paul's idea. I owe it to the company to—"

"Make sure it never happens again." Irritation edged Jessie's voice. "When are you ever going to realize there's more to life than Cheri Lee Cosmetics?"

"Don't!" Lauren's hands flew in front of her face and she shrank back in her chair. "I can't.... Not right now."

"Oh, Lor. I'm sorry."

Jessie drew Lauren into her arms. Lauren sank into her sister's comforting embrace. They were silent for a long time, and Lauren felt Jessie's soothing hands stroke her hair as sorrow seemed to squeeze the life from her.

Finally Lauren lifted her head, sat back, and smoothed her hair into place. "What's done is done," she said.

"I suppose," Jessie replied, without conviction in her voice. She went back to her chair and bent over, taking a packet from her purse.

"Before I forget, here are the shares."

"Thanks." Lauren took the packet from Jessie's outstretched hand. Funny, how she'd almost forgotten about them.

"What are you going to do with them?"

"Vote Paul out. Then I'll figure a way to buy him out." It was what she had to do. Seeing Paul, lunching with him daily, was becoming more than she could bear. She had to close this chapter of her life so she could carry on. But then a thought struck her. "This won't cause trouble between you and Bill, will it?"

"No. Bill doesn't like it, but this is what we figured you would do." Jessie slipped her shoulder bag on and gazed at Lauren with undisguised pity.

"Don't feel sorry for me, Jessie!"

"I feel sorry for both of you," Jessie said sadly. "You and Paul. The two of you are so alike."

"Alike? We aren't at all alike." The idea outraged Lauren and she almost welcomed the anger.

"Yes, you are. You're both consumed by your purposes. His is power. Yours is duty."

For a moment Lauren wanted to blacken her sister's eyes, but then reason returned. Jessie was only trying to help, and the last thing Lauren wanted right now was to be estranged from any member of her family. She needed each and every one of them.

"Since when did you become a psychologist?" she asked dryly.

Jessie smiled an ethereal, sublime smile. "Guess a little of Bill is rubbing off on me."

"Guess so," Lauren replied. Then she asked Jessie how the taping had gone the day before. They discussed it for a while before Lauren finally said, "You'd better get home to your hubby. Newlyweds shouldn't be apart too long."

Jessie laughed, made a bawdy wisecrack, then scampered off.

Lauren picked up the share packet on her desk and opened it, staring for a while as if she'd never seen one before. Should she reconsider what to do with them? Had Jessie's observation been amazingly insightful or amazingly stupid?

Stupid, Lauren finally concluded. She and Paul were nothing alike. She worked for order, harmony, institutional permanence. Paul created chaos, discord, and disruption.

Having decided that, she picked up the telephone to take the first step in severing her relationship with Paul forever.

MONDAY AGAIN. PAUL HAD spent a miserable, lonely weekend in the Coronado Island condo that he'd always hated. Now, at nearly ten in the morning, he and Galahad entered his plush suite of offices and he realized he hated them, too. Nothing seemed important, nothing seemed worth doing.

"You have several messages, Paul," Carol said with a smile as he entered. Wanly, he returned her greeting, took the message slips she held in her hand and walked listlessly to his office.

His broker had called. One of his prime backers had phoned—several times. As he glanced at the last message in the pile his heart gave a glad jump. Lauren! Lauren had also called.

But the happy lurch quickly vanished. Lauren's call undoubtedly concerned business. Nonetheless, he couldn't contain the tiny spark of hope he felt. He decided to quickly dispatch his first two callers so he could concentrate fully on Lauren.

His broker predictably reminded him that he had until tomorrow to come up with the hundred thousand dollars. Paul told him he'd get back with an answer, then went on to his next message. Franklin Jessip. Paul's most important venture capitalist.

"I've heard distressing news," Frank said after their initial greetings were done.

"Oh?" Paul supposed word of his tumbling investments had already reached the grapevine. "Well, stay calm, Frank. I've got things under control."

"It's not about your stocks. And I'm hoping my information is wrong."

"What've you heard?" Why wouldn't he just get on with it? Paul wondered, tapping his desk with a pen, waiting impatiently for Frank's response.

"That you no longer own controlling interest in Cheri Lee Cosmetics. Say it isn't true, pal, and I'll take your word for it."

Pal? Only as long as Paul kept Frank's money safe. He almost laughed until the full significance of this news struck him. How had Frank known?

Realizing that the truth was his only option—glossed-over truth, anyway—Paul said, "Yes, some of the shares have been returned to the family. But I've an excellent working relationship with the Aftons and don't anticipate any problems."

"Yeah." There was a long pause, then Frank spoke again. "I'd like to believe that, but I need something more than assurances. I've got to ask for more security. You understand, don't you, pal?''

Yes, Paul understood. Oh, he understood all too well. How many similar conversations had he had with businessmen he'd backed?

"What would it take to make you comfortable?''

"Sign over the Cheri Lee Cosmetics shares to me. I might get enough for them to get us both out of this mess.''

"No!'' Paul struggled to soften his response. "No, you can't sell them. Not yet.''

"What are you waiting for, Paul? That foxy blonde who's got a ring through your nose? You, of all people, should know not to mix business and pleasure.''

Foxy blonde. Ring through your nose. Suddenly, Paul knew exactly where Frank's information had come from.

"How much does Mitch Cotton have to do with this, Frank?''

"Cotton? Nothing, nothing.''

"Don't snow me. I know Cotton's tactics better than anyone, and he's behind this. I can smell him.''

"Uh, er, well, he made an offer for the shares—double what you paid. He instructed me to keep it quiet, said you wouldn't sell if you knew.'' Frank coughed hard before he continued. "I laughed. I said, 'Paul Sherwood turn down a profit?' But I guess he was right. Regardless, I gotta have more security. Our deal gives me the right to call for repayment of my investment at any time. So it boils down to this: I get the shares or I call the loan.''

Paul's mind raced and twirled; he felt like a rat trying to find its way through a maze. How to negotiate? How to delay? What to offer?

And how had Cotton known that Bill had returned Jessie's shares? Who was passing on the information?

"Look, Frank," Paul began haltingly, then filled Frank in on Cotton's steady efforts to destroy him. What he didn't tell Frank was that he'd fallen in love with the cosmetic firm's beautiful owner and had grown increasingly fond of her family. That he couldn't sell what they valued so highly.

Still, as Frank quickly pointed out, the shares were Paul's only asset. Selling them was the fastest way to prevent an impending bankruptcy. Besides, as much as Frank sympathized, he had to protect his own investments, his own investors. This was bigger than both of them; bigger than a few lousy shares of a faltering cosmetics company.

But was it bigger than Paul's love for Lauren? The question danced unanswered though his consciousness. Finally, Paul made an offer—the only compromise his beleaguered intellect could conjure up.

"What if I sign over the shares to you with the provision that you hold them for ninety days?"

"That company could go broke in ninety days."

Patiently now—there was so much at stake Paul couldn't afford to blow it—he explained how the new product line and the value of the firm's assets would prevent any loss. "Cheri Lee Cosmetics will show a profit that will double your money within six months, Frank," Paul assured him. "I've worked with the company so I have an inside track. Surely you can trust me on this."

With that statement, Paul wagered the only asset he had left: his reputation for good business judgment.

"Okay, pal. Ninety days."

They made arrangements to sign a contract the next day and Paul hung up, feeling drained beyond repair. He picked up the pink message sheet with Lauren's name written on it. Deciding not to phone—he'd go there instead, speak to her personally—he laid it back down and stood.

Throughout the weekend, he'd attempted to borrow money to cover his margin call. He'd had no success. Maybe Mike Armstrong had been luckier. He started out of his office, then heard Galahad whimper. Turning, Paul saw the dog attempting to climb to his feet and realized arthritis was troubling him badly. He walked back, propped his hands under Galahad's hindquarters and boosted the animal up.

"You need some aspirin." He stroked the dog, then went to the bathroom off his office, rummaged through the medicine cabinet and picked up a bottle of aspirin.

It was empty. Maybe Bill had some in his bathroom. Tossing the bottle into a wastebasket, Paul headed for his partner's office. As he reached Bill's door, he heard a hushed conversation inside. The door, slightly ajar, muffled the words, but Paul knew the voice wasn't Bill's.

He grasped the doorknob and slowly pushed the door open. Carol sat at Bill's desk with the phone at her ear, looking at a notepad.

"Ninety days," Paul heard her say. "But they won't sign the contract till tomorrow."

Suddenly Paul remembered he'd heard a click on the line while he'd been talking to Frank. He'd thought it odd, but had soon forgotten about it. Meanwhile, Carol had overheard the entire discussion and was now relaying it to...whom?

Cotton! It could only be Cotton.

Crossing the room in long, angry strides, Paul was beside Carol before she had a chance to look up.

"Paul!"

He snatched the phone from her hand.

"It won't work, Cotton. I've just discovered your mole."

"Paul, what a pleasure." Cotton's slippery voice fairly oozed over the wire. "And what a surprise. Here I thought I was talking with your lovely employee."

"She's not my employee any longer." Paul glared down at Carol as he spoke, watched the tears pool in her eyes, and didn't care. This woman had ruined him. "I've caught you both now, and your game is over."

"Yes, it is over. Because, my boy, you're finished. Nothing you do will pull you out now."

"Don't underestimate me, Cotton." Anger brought Paul back to life.

"That's your failing, Paul, not mine. Tell you what, though. I'll forgive your rude refusal and extend my offer again. Come back to work for me, bring those precious shares with you. I'll bail you out, kid, give you new worlds to conquer."

"My, my, what unexpected generosity." But even as Paul delivered the dry comeback, a sinking sensation engulfed his stomach. This might be his only salvation. Cotton was right: he was all but finished. "Exactly what's prompting it?"

Cotton's sarcasm vanished. "Our war isn't doing us any good. If you can't beat 'em, join 'em, I always say."

"I'll consider it, Cotton, and let you know."

"You have until the weekend, Paul. No longer. Otherwise I'll pull out my heavy artillery."

An elephant gun to kill a mouse, thought Paul as he lowered the receiver onto the cradle. Why such an ominous threat? Paul was already on his knees—or so Cotton said.

Deciding to deal with Carol first, Paul set that thought aside. He looked at the crestfallen woman, dreading what he knew had to be done.

"Why?" he asked, the anguish on her face eating through his anger.

"It's Jim, my husband." Carol brought her hands up and buried her face. "He needs a bone-marrow transplant." Carol began sobbing softly. "He's been in the hospital so much, had chemotherapy, other treatments. The doctors say the transplant is his only hope—"

Huge, racking sobs shook Carol's body. She lowered her hands and gazed up at him. Red blotches surrounded her eyes. Paul found he wanted to comfort her, that he almost understood her actions. But he did nothing, said nothing, just waited until Carol brought her sobs under control. "The insurance has almost run out," she continued. "We couldn't afford the operation until—"

"Until Cotton offered you this way." Paul already knew the rest. Cotton had searched hard for Paul's weakest link, learned of Carol's personal tragedy and exploited it. "Why didn't you come to me—or Bill—for help?"

"You...you...you're going broke, and Bill doesn't have that kind of money. At first Mr. Cotton didn't want that much from me—just a list of your stock holdings. But he held back the payment, asking more and more. Oh, Paul, I'm sorry."

"I know," Paul said, nodding. Carol was sorry for doing what she felt she had to do. And he, too, would be sorry when he did what he'd probably have to do with his Cheri Lee Cosmetics holdings. "You understand, though, I have to let you go?"

Carol bobbed her head up and down with big gulping sobs. Paul leaned over and helped her to her feet. "Get your things from your desk. I'll write your final check."

As Carol made her way to the front office, Paul entered the bull pen. He felt like an executioner, yet he couldn't keep a traitor on his payroll. As he started to cross the room to the company wall safe, he saw Mike and remembered his original purpose.

"Any luck, Mike?"

"None. And you?"

Paul shook his head. Mike looked grim. Paul felt grim. He patted Mike on the shoulder and said, "We'll both keep trying," then he went to the safe, opened it, and pulled out a ledger. As he made out a check for Carol's severance pay, he realized he'd almost forgotten how to use a checkbook.

Damn Carol! She always did this stuff. He'd depended on her so. Remembering that, he added to the sum he'd calculated in his head, filled out the amount on the check, then carefully detached it.

When he entered the front office, Carol was placing the last of her personal belongings into a cardboard box. Paul stopped to wait as he saw her gaze at a photograph of her husband, then kiss it before putting it into the box.

A flurry of tears stung his eyes and he was glad for what he had just done. He handed Carol the check and, still sobbing quietly, she took it, started to fold it, then stopped and gaped at Paul.

"This is nine months' salary."

"Yes." He knew he sounded cold, yet he felt... unable. Unable to tell Carol how important she'd been to him, how betrayed he felt. Unable to say that even through his pain he understood hers. "I'll also pay your medical insurance until you get a new job. And this won't affect your reference. You're a damned good manager."

She didn't say anything, just tucked the check in her purse, then bent to pick up the box. Paul walked with her to the door and opened it for her, watching her bowed back as she trudged through the elaborately landscaped courtyard. When she reached the archway leading to the parking lot, she stopped.

"Thank you, Paul." The words were whispered, yet they carried to his ears and nearly broke his heart.

"You're welcome," he mouthed, the words sticking in his throat. He turned and closed the door behind him.

"ARE YOU REALLY SURE you want to do this, Lor?"

Lauren, who'd been flitting from desk to window to love seat like a restless butterfly, stopped at her sister's question.

"It's not a question of want." Moving again to the window, Lauren asked querulously, "Where is he? He's always here by ten." She spun toward her mother. "What time is it?"

"Almost noon, dear. Just like the last time you asked." Cheri allowed a frown to cross her face. "Are you *sure* you want to do this?"

"Yes. It's the waiting that's killing me."

"We know." Jessie went over to Lauren. "That's why I wondered if you're having second thoughts."

"No. None."

But she did have doubts. Was this an act of revenge? Tit for tat? She'd told herself again and again it wasn't. She was acting in the best interests of the family, the company. Yet no one was pushing her into it but herself. Not Jessie, for sure. Not Cheri Lee, who'd counseled Lauren to wait awhile. Not even E.J.

"He's here," Jessie announced, pointing to Paul's Mercedes. Lauren's misgivings vanished and she was consumed by a need to get this behind her.

She sped to her phone, dialed Paul's extension, and told his assistant she'd like to see him in her office. She then dialed E.J., saying Paul was on his way.

A few minutes later Paul walked through her door, and she waited until he was seated, then said, "This is an impromptu board meeting. E.J. will be here shortly. We'll start then."

"I don't suppose I have to ask what the subject is." He squeezed into one of her chairs, placed an ankle across his knee, and absently plucked some nonexistent lint from his cuff. There were no critters on his socks today, no youthful swagger in his movements, and Lauren wondered when the boyish Paul had vanished.

He looked up then, and stared directly into Lauren's eyes. For an eerie instant, catching the misery in his blue eyes, an odd sensation overcame her. It was similar to the way she felt when she caught an unguarded glimpse of herself in a storefront window or an unexpected mirror. Perhaps Jessie had been right. Perhaps she and Paul were very much alike. She found herself holding his gaze, unwilling, unable to release it. Her resolve wavered, and something inside her screamed a warning to stop.

Then E.J. came in, and Lauren tore her eyes away from Paul. Her brother seemed unusually subdued. He nodded a greeting to Paul and took a seat. Lauren's moment of uncertainty vanished, and she set forth to do what she'd intended.

"Since controlling interest of Cheri Lee Cosmetics has returned to our family," Lauren began, all eyes fixed upon her, "we feel that authority over its future should come back to us, too."

"I move that Paul Sherwood be removed as chief executive officer and that Lauren Afton be named in his place," E.J. said.

"Second," Jessie murmured.

"All in favor?" Lauren called for the vote.

Cheri, E.J. and Jessie all responded with ayes. Paul remained silent, then stood.

"Short, sweet, merciful." Without another word, he left the room.

"Well, that's done." Cheri stared down at a perfect fingernail.

"Done," echoed Lauren, hardly able to speak over the lump lodged between her throat and her heart. It was almost as if Paul had been expecting this. She hadn't anticipated his quiet acceptance; had expected him to try to sway them, battle until the end. She had thought she knew Paul—knew him well. Now it seemed that she'd never understood him at all.

Her family firm was safe from marauding hands. Victory was hers. Why did it feel so empty?

PAUL WANTED TO FEEL angry, he wanted to feel betrayed. None of those emotions came over him. Instead, a lethargy much like the kind he'd felt upon his mother's death, engulfed him. His brain waves appeared to have gone flat. No solution, no brilliant inspiration, snapped across his synapses. Worse yet, he didn't care.

Listlessly he removed files from the shabby wooden desk that had once been E.J.'s. Paul had never gotten around to redecorating, and the office still reflected E.J.'s personality. The furnishings had obviously been chosen with comfort and function in mind, not looks. Two easy chairs, their upholstery wearing in spots, flanked the desk. Simple plastic bookcases, where E.J. had once stored his piles of chemistry books, were stacked against one wall.

Voices filtered through his closed door, and footsteps sounded on the tiled floor beyond. A phone rang, a computer beeped. Life went on.

He placed the folders into a cardboard box, thinking of Carol and what she must have felt while doing the same. He didn't really have to clear out the office, of course. He was still a primary stockholder. But there seemed no point in staying.

His options had narrowed. True, he and Mike were continuing to look for funding sources. But Paul had already exhausted his resources, and he didn't think Mike was having better luck.

All he had left were his shares of Lauren's company, and he didn't even own them—Frank Jessip and a host of lesser investors did. Now they wanted control of their property. Hell, Paul wanted control of their property, but Lauren had just wrenched it from him in her bloodless little coup.

Finished packing, Paul got up, lifted the box, and called for Galahad to follow.

The dog rose slowly and trudged after Paul without much enthusiasm. As they entered the parking lot, it occurred to Paul that the day seem to reflect his feelings—and Galahad's. Everything around them seemed sluggish, lifeless, dreary.

When they reached the car, Paul opened the door, placed the box in the back seat, and waited for Galahad to get in. But the dog just stood there, so Paul bent over.

"You're getting heavy, Galahad." He hoisted his pet's hindquarters onto the leather seat. But as he closed the door, he frowned. Actually, Galahad was getting lighter, and Paul was glad he'd decided to head for his ranch to sort things out. His trainer would prescribe a high-nutrient diet, get Galahad out of this slump.

Pulling his car from the complex and onto Highway 8, Paul remembered the first time he and Galahad had made this drive. How different things had been, then. Today, the top was up in deference to the angry bank of clouds hanging low over the city. And Galahad, instead of lifting a proud head to be whipped by the breeze, hung his muzzle over his paws, looking dejectedly down over the edge of his seat.

His throaty whimper caused Paul to lean over and stroke his coat. Maybe Rutledge would inject some cortisone. Galahad needed attention badly.

As he took the ramp onto Highway 5, an earsplitting explosion of thunder sounded overhead, followed by furious streaks of lightning. Fat drops of rain spotted the windshield. Galahad wearily lifted his head, arched his neck, and licked Paul's hand. Paul stroked the dog's soft chin, then turned on his wipers, settling back for the long drive home.

Yes, home. San Luis Obispo—the only place he'd ever felt completely comfortable. Once they were there, Rutledge would fix Galahad up. Perhaps a day or two in front of the fire would burn out Paul's lethargy. Maybe the flames would even bring with them a burst of illumination to solve his problems.

Except his problems with Lauren. There appeared to be no solution to them. Her lovely face, with its high cheekbones and chiseled nose, haunted him. She'd looked sad, enervated, during that brief, to-the-point meeting.

He'd known why Lauren had called even before he'd entered her office. The pile of little "While You Were Out" notes stacked on his desk—all with Lauren's name and extension scratched upon them—had started his sluggish mind working. The conclusion came quickly.

As had the conclusion of their relationship. He'd made some grievous errors in judgment. He'd misjudged Lauren, misjudged Bill. Even misjudged Cotton.

But it was Lauren who had hurt him the most deeply. He'd thought she understood what he was trying to do, realized he was truly ready for a change in direction. Perhaps he should have discussed it with her before he'd marched in with Bill. *Perhaps?* Of course he should have. But surprise had always been his ally. Until now. This time it had backfired.

Why couldn't he hate her for letting him down? Hating would make what he had to do so much easier. . . .

He had two choices now. Turn the shares over to Jessip, or return to Cotton, his tail between his legs and the Cheri Lee Cosmetics in his mouth. Either way, Cotton would get the stock.

Yes, Paul was whipped. As whipped as Galahad looked. When he glanced at his dog, a frisson of alarm shot through him. Galahad lay on the seat, his tongue lolling, his breathing irregular.

Paul reached out a caressing hand. "Rutledge'll fix you right up, boy. Just hang on." He pushed his foot viciously against the accelerator. Already doing seventy, he pressed on to ninety. Everything was slipping away. His power, his wealth, and Lauren—sweet, sweet Lauren.

He'd be damned if he'd lose his dog, too.

CHAPTER FOURTEEN

THE RAINSTORM FOLLOWED them relentlessly, slowing their progress, and when Paul pulled into the shimmering driveway, he didn't stop at the house. Instead, he drove to the rambling group of buildings where his staff made their homes.

Galahad's breathing rasped now—making a terrible noise that was painful to Paul's ears. Upon reaching his destination, Paul hit his brakes so forcefully that tires squealed and rubber burned. He leaped out, rushing to the passenger door and yanking it open.

"We're here, Galahad." It was dark outside now— dark as it can only be at dusk on a rainy day, and the car's interior lights reflected the gold and white tones of Galahad's coat. But the collie barely turned his head at Paul's voice, and didn't try to stand. As cold raindrops dampened Paul's hair, he called again, "Get up, boy. We're here."

Galahad struggled to get to his feet and failed. Terrified, Paul reached down and gathered the animal into his arms. Heavy and uncooperative, the dog shifted repeatedly in Paul's arms as he awkwardly made his way to his trainer's door.

"Rutledge! Rutledge!" Paul kicked at the door, willing the man to appear instantly.

After an apparent eternity, the door opened.

"Paul, what—?" Rutledge reached forward and

pulled Paul out of the rain. Gently, Paul lowered Galahad to the floor.

Paul's breath came in gasps now—big, heaving gulps that carried the threat of tears—and he struggled to control himself. Galahad would recover. Jerry Rutledge would fix him up, as he'd fixed up any number of other dogs that Paul had owned. But those dogs hadn't been Galahad, and right now Paul cared about none of them.

"Get some medicine, Jerry. Something!"

Jerry nodded, grabbed a raincoat from his closet, and disappeared through the front door. Alone again, tremors shook Paul's body and his knees turned rubbery. He slipped to the floor to sit beside Galahad. He took the dog's head in his lap, wrapping his arms around his neck.

"Hold on. Hold on." The words began a tuneless melody as Paul repeated them again and again, trying to ignore the fact that Galahad's labored breaths were growing less frequent.

Rutledge returned, carrying a box of medicine and some syringes. Kneeling, he gave Galahad an injection and said, "This should help him breathe. Let's take him down to the kennel."

"No, no. To the house. You stay there tonight. Keep an eye on him."

"But the wife and—"

"Forget it! Galahad's sick. You can't leave him now!" Hot, angry tears bit at Paul's eyes. He blinked them back.

Jerry Rutledge had never been a man Paul could intimidate, but this uncharacteristic reaction apparently made Jerry reconsider. He nodded. "I'll tell Dora we can go tomorrow."

A few minutes later they had loaded Galahad into the back of a small pickup with a camper shell and were on their way to the big house. "Paul," Jerry said quietly from his place behind the steering wheel, "I know you've had Galahad since you were a kid, and you're attached. But he's suffering. We need to think about putting him down."

"No! He'll pull through. We'll make him pull through."

"I'll do my best," Jerry answered. "But at his age... Dogs die, Paul. That's just the way it is."

Paul's head bobbed listlessly as though he understood, agreed. But he didn't. Sure, dogs died, but Galahad had a lot of good years left. Holding on to that thought, Paul didn't respond and the conversation ended. Rain still drizzled, creating large pools on the driveway that eerily reflected the headlights of the truck. Off in the distance, a lightning bolt danced across the sky.

The night cried death, and as Paul stepped from the truck the loamy smell of wet soil assailed his nostrils; it was as if an open grave was waiting... waiting. All around, Paul saw death. The death of his financial empire. The death of his relationship with Lauren. Now Galahad.

But they'd beat it, he and Galahad. They'd beat it. And he clung to this thought as he and Jerry carried Galahad into the house.

"There," Paul directed. "In my bedroom."

Once inside the large suite, Paul headed toward the bed. "Put him here. I'll sleep with him tonight."

Jerry looked at Paul's hand-sewn down comforter with obvious misgivings. "Are you sure? He's drool-

ing now, and might soil himself. This is an expensive
spread.''

''Doesn't matter. Nothing matters. I want to be here
with him.''

''You're the boss.''

When Galahad was comfortably settled, Paul
turned to Jerry. ''Take the bedroom next to mine.
There's toothpaste and stuff in the bathroom. Paja-
mas in the bureau. Make yourself at home, fix a
drink.''

''What about you, Paul?''

''I'm staying with Galahad.''

Jerry looked sympathetic, but puzzled, too, as
though he didn't quite understand all the fuss. His lack
of comprehension stirred Paul's anger.

''He was a gift from my mother!''

''Oh, yeah.'' The man rubbed his jaw, then turned
to leave. ''I'll check with you every so often, but call
if you need me sooner.''

Paul went to the television set, turned it on and set
the volume low, then got a blanket from a brass chest.
Carrying it across the room, he lay down and wrapped
an arm around his dog, covering them both.

''You'll make it,'' he whispered into Galahad's ear.
''I know you'll make it.''

There was no other acceptable outcome, and assur-
ing himself of this, Paul fell asleep.

WATER DRAINING SLOWLY down a clogged opening.
Gurgling, sputtering. Paul attempted to figure out
where the sound was coming from even before he
opened his eyes. They popped open and he glanced at
the television, wondering if a Liquid-Plumr commer-
cial was playing.

Then the deep shudder beneath his arm shocked him awake.

Galahad! Paul shot straight up, turned on the light.

"Rutledge!" he called, but Jerry was already there, medicine box in one hand, a plastic tube in the other. Coming quickly to Paul's side, the man cut an incision in Galahad's throat, inserted the tube, then placed tape over the opening.

Galahad's breathing returned—a shallow, labored sound that tore at Paul's heart.

"Give him something, Jerry. Something to make it easier for him."

"Can't. I've given him everything possible. It's out of my hands now."

Out of my hands. Wasn't that what the doctor had said as Paul's mother rapidly wasted away in her hospital bed?

"Let me put him out of his misery, Paul." Jerry already had a syringe in his hand. "Please. He's suffering."

"No!" Paul's hand shot out, swatted Jerry's, and sent the needle flying across the room. It hit the floor, then rolled to rest at the base of the brass chest.

He'd expected Jerry to curse him, as the man had often done when they'd disagreed about dogs, but instead he walked patiently over to the chest and picked up the syringe.

The deadly tip glinted ominously before Jerry lowered it out of sight. "A person should never get this attached to a dog. Attachment clouds judgment. Look at him, man. He's dying, and it's going to be real rough on him."

Paul wanted to clamp his hands over his ears, shut out what Rutledge was saying, but instead he did look.

Saliva matted the coat around Galahad's mouth; his once-bright eyes now stared dully up at Paul. A scarlet streak of blood from the tracheotomy stained his snow-white chest. This animal had been a major part of his life for so long. The idea that he'd no longer be there tomorrow was more than Paul could bear.

In the midst of his grief, he saw Lauren's face. How long had Cheri Lee Cosmetics been in her life? Longer than Galahad had been in his. She loved that company just as he loved his dog.

He understood Jerry then, because the man was just like him. His trainer had handled so many dogs—show quality and badly flawed, young and old, healthy and sick—that he saw them only as belongings.

He went to Galahad, lifted his silky ears, stroked them. The animal tried to lift his head, but he had no strength left. His tail lifted a mere fraction of an inch, then dropped back on the bed.

Raindrops still splattered intermittently on Paul's window, and a thunderclap told him more rain was coming. The ground would be soft, easy to dig.

Paul looked at his dying dog, hot tears dampening his face.

"Do it," he said to Jerry.

"Go on out, Paul. I'll call when it's over."

Paul shook his head. "I want to stay with him."

Jerry didn't argue, just inserted the needle. Paul gathered Galahad in his arms and rested his head on top of the warm, furry body. As he felt the dog's shallow breathing diminish, sobs hammered at his chest, yet he fought them back. Finished, Jerry withdrew the needle. Paul remained where he was and Jerry silently left the room.

Only then did Paul allow his sobs to break loose, and he held the lifeless body, rocking back and forth, back and forth.

"Galahad," he whispered, with a wild hope that his pet would lift his head at this invocation. "Galahad, Galahad, Galahad . . ."

Later—he had no idea how long he'd been there— Paul released his desperate hold and sat up. A clock said it was nearly seven in the morning.

His eyes swept his surroundings. The ranch had once meant so much to him. This bedroom with its lavish furnishings, the grounds, the stables, the kennels—all were visible signs of his success. It was all slipping from his grasp, and he no longer cared. He'd gladly trade everything to bring Galahad back. And he'd chop this place into kindling, burn every last piece of furniture, to hold Lauren in his arms once more.

He remembered what he'd thought during his mother's funeral—that he'd built it all for her, and she hadn't wanted it. Sharon had only wanted his companionship and happiness. That was all Lauren had wanted, too. But he had realized this too late. Then and now.

Pushing to his feet, Paul went into the bathroom. He took off his rumpled suit and shirt, dropped them carelessly to the floor, then pulled a plush terry robe from a hook. Turning on a crystal faucet, he listened to the running water.

Yes, he'd give it all up, without thinking twice. Galahad had been more important. Lauren *was* more important. Leaning over, he splashed his face, symbolically washing cobwebs from his brain. Suddenly he knew what he had to do.

Paul turned off the water with a quick jerk of the faucet and headed for the telephone. When an efficient voice answered, he said crisply, "Tell Mitch Cotton that Paul Sherwood is on the line."

"Certainly, Mr. Sherwood. Hold, please."

As he waited, Paul silently composed what he'd say. He would be quick, succinct. Next he would write the letter. When both these tasks were complete, he'd bury his dog.

And say goodbye to his last link with the past.

"YOU WERE DYNAMITE, baby!" Bill lifted up Jessie's slight body and twirled her around. "Dyn-a-mi-i-te!"

Jessie squealed and peppered Bill's face with kisses. She'd never considered herself an unhappy person, but since marrying Bill, her happiness had swelled to such enormous proportions that her past seemed bleak in comparison.

Bill set her back on her feet, gave her one of those long, drugging kisses that she'd grown to adore, then released her with a peck on the tip of her nose.

She smiled at him lovingly and headed for the huge conversation pit that dominated Bill's living room. She'd been glad to find Bill's house so comfortable, and even lively. She'd suspected it would be so, ever since she'd seen the Bentoni paintings in his office, which had led her to believe there was much more to Bill than what one saw on the surface.

Patting the space beside her, she looked at him wickedly. "Come here, you gorgeous man."

He complied eagerly, pulling her into his arms, and for a long while they sat like that. Quiet, grateful to be together.

"It did go well, didn't it?" Jessie said, interrupting their comfortable silence. Bill kissed her forehead as a sign of agreement.

They'd just come back from the corporate viewing of her promotional video. It had been shown to the employees in shifts, then to Cheri Lee, E.J. and Lauren. The response had overwhelmed her.

"You knocked 'em dead, dear," Cheri Lee had commented afterward, giving Jessie a giant hug in full view of their staff.

"The best ever," someone called from a back table.

"If every woman in America doesn't want to look like you, I'll eat my hat." E.J. delivered a resounding swat on her back as he spoke, slamming Jessie forward and causing everyone to laugh.

"You *are* the Minx," Lauren said. "It couldn't be more perfect."

And Jessie had melted under all the adoration, the compliments. Yet, through it all, she'd been concerned.

"I just wish Lauren seemed happier," she now said to Bill.

"What do you mean? She acted as if she loved the video."

"No, not that. Personally, I mean."

The truth was, Lauren looked like hell. Oh, she put on a good show—was as beautiful as ever. But her eyes had lost their sparkle, were a deathly pale gray, and there were little lines around her mouth that had never been there before.

"Paul really hurt her, didn't he?" Bill lifted her chin and gazed into her eyes. He always loved looking into Jessie's multicolored eyes, seeing the devotion in them.

"She asked me about him at the video showing. I could see it in her eyes. But it's partly her own fault."

"How?" Jessie pulled out of Bill's arms and stared at him indignantly. "Paul just walked in and pushed her out. That's not Lauren's fault."

"Don't get mad, Jessie." Bill drew her back against him. Jessie allowed herself to be mollified by his oblique apology. "Paul is brash, headstrong and way too secretive. But afterward, he really tried. From what I've heard, he's been nothing but accommodating. Lauren didn't give him a chance."

"I didn't give you much of a chance, either. That didn't stop you."

As Bill watched his wife hotly defend her sister, it occurred to him that nothing could have kept him away from Jessie. She was perfect for him in every way, even in the ways she was different.

"No. But I'm luckier than Paul. I've got family, friends," he tried to explain. "If I take a cuff to the chin, there are people to support me. Paul has no one. He has always gone it alone. It's hard for him to show his love. Still, I know he has it. Anyone watching him with that damned old dog of his can tell that." Thinking about Paul and his affection for the dog saddened Bill, especially in light of what he'd just learned. "I got a call from Paul's dog trainer yesterday. Galahad died Monday night."

"Oh, no." Jessie gazed off. How awful for Paul to lose his beautiful animal along with everything else that had happened. Suddenly an idea formed. She turned back to Bill.

"Why don't I talk to Lauren? Tell her to cut Paul some slack. You can call Paul. Kinda bring up the subject of Lauren. You know, matchmake a little."

Jessie's voice became animated as she grew fonder of her idea. She was deliriously happy with the man she loved. She wanted the same for her sister.

"I'll try..." Bill said hesitantly, dampening Jessie's enthusiasm. "But I haven't talked to Paul in weeks. And there's something I haven't told you. Rutledge also said he was out of a job, said the ranch was being sold. When I hung up, I tried to contact Paul, without any luck."

"Keep trying, then." Jessie nibbled at Bill's lower lip, glorying in the feel of him. "He can't have disappeared from the face of the earth."

"Guess not," Bill breathed into her parted mouth. "Okay, baby, I'll try."

Then he captured her lips and Jessie slipped her arms around his chest, aching to get closer.

"I love you Bill," she murmured, deep in her throat.

"And I love you," he answered, gently pushing her body against the couch.

The joy Bill brought to her life was sometimes overwhelming. They simply had to get Paul and Lauren back together so they could experience this same joy. Somehow.

With that final thought, Jessie submitted totally to the wonderful sensations her husband's touch created in her body.

ALMOST TWO WEEKS. Lauren hadn't heard from Paul for almost two weeks. When she'd stopped at his office after the meeting, he was gone, and his few belongings had been removed. But Lauren had been sure he was sulking, would be back.

But Tuesday had passed, then Wednesday, Thursday and Friday. Now, on this following Thursday afternoon, as Lauren toured her plant—speaking to a maintenance man, the sales-office secretary, a production worker, getting a feel for the pulse of the company—she wondered if he'd ever return.

Of course he'd be back, she assured herself. He still owned a large chunk of stock. And the staff missed him. When she'd sent out the memo announcing that Paul's other interests were demanding more time and that she'd resumed her position as CEO, many employees had said they hoped he'd still be around. The Aftons had assured them he would be.

"Will Paul be in next week?" the cheerful copy-center clerk asked as Lauren passed the center's Dutch door. He spoke loudly, competing with the whir of his equipment.

"We're expecting him." Lauren hoped her answer wasn't a lie.

"Good. He made some suggestions for streamlining my work, and I wanted to let him know they worked."

Lauren forced a smile. It wasn't the first time she'd heard such a comment. "I'll tell him when he calls," she replied, continuing her tour down the bright, tiled halls.

But would he call?

Maybe it was time she reached out. For the first time since Paul had ripped her company out of her hands, Lauren openly questioned herself and her actions. Why had she thought she had no option but to remove Paul from his post, snatch back control? Had she ever really lost it? It seemed not. Everything Paul had done during these past months had enhanced the

With a decisive gesture, she picked up the phone and dialed. When an unfamiliar voice answered, she asked for Paul.

"He isn't in at the moment."

"Where's Carol?"

"She doesn't work here anymore."

"Oh." *Why?* she wondered. Then, deciding people left jobs all the time, she went on. "Well, when do you expect Paul back?"

"His, er, his return is unknown." The woman sounded evasive, making Lauren uneasy. When she asked for another number where Paul could be reached and learned there was none, her uneasiness increased.

She thanked the woman and hung up, trying Paul's condominium next. No answer. Where was Paul? He couldn't have simply vanished. Should she try him at the ranch? That number wasn't in her office files, only at home.

She got up, gathered her raincoat and marched from her office. "If I'm needed," she told her assistant, "you can reach me at home."

When she pulled into her garage a while later, planning to rush to the phone, she saw that her mailbox was open, with a large brown envelope jutting from its mouth.

The envelope resisted her first effort to remove it. She tugged, then bent to pick up a flurry of white envelopes that tumbled to the ground. Clutching them in one hand, she studied the brown package, curious.

Both the mailing and return addresses were hers. There was no clue as to where the package had come from. It was postmarked San Diego. She hurried inside, eager to open the envelope, but not so eager as to forget her original purpose.

Placing the mail on a polished wood shelf in the entryway, she went into her living room, looked up Paul's San Luis Obispo number and punched in the digits.

"Hello," answered a deep voice on the other end.

"May I speak to Paul Sherwood?" Lauren's heart pounded. She was sure he was there. Now she could tell him. Tell him she loved him, tell him how wrong she was. Love was never lost, she assured herself—not if the lovers cared enough to work things out.

"Mr. Sherwood no longer lives here." The man's well-modulated voice reminded Lauren of a picture-show butler. "The estate is on the market. Are you interested in viewing it?"

"No...no." Not live there? Paul loved that ranch. He'd never give it up. "This is a personal call. Do you know where Mr. Sherwood can be reached?"

"All calls are being directed to his San Diego office."

"I see," Lauren replied, lowering the receiver slowly to its cradle. But she didn't see at all. She'd come full circle, trying to reach him. Suddenly the tears she'd wanted to cry all day burst forth with an angry misery that fed on itself.

No one knew where he was. Not his own office. Not his real-estate broker. Not even Bill. Worse, no one seemed to care.

Still sobbing, Lauren stumbled to her bedroom, flung herself on the bed, tried to weep out her pain, but with every chest-wrenching sob it just increased.

Finally exhausted, she drifted into a fitful slumber. She dreamed she was trying to get to Paul, saw him in the distance, but he was always out of reach.

She didn't awaken until the next morning. She climbed out of bed, her eyes swollen and hard to open. Trudging to the bathroom, she grimaced at her reflection. Her hair hung in limp strands around her blotched face. Her expensive suit had wrinkled beyond repair.

It didn't matter. Nothing mattered. She considered calling in sick, then discarded the idea. She'd never, ever, missed a day of work. Besides, dwelling on her despair would only make it worse. Yet nothing made things better—not the hot shower, not the steaming cup of coffee. She only nibbled at her toast.

She dressed. Ready for work, she headed for the garage door. The knob already in her hand, she stopped, remembering the package that had arrived the day before. A minute later she held it in her hand, carefully peeling the flap away. As she pulled out the contents, she gasped.

Her shares of stock!

And a letter, a letter from Paul. Certainly it would tell her where he was. Her heart skittered gladly in her chest as she started reading.

Lauren darling,
Perhaps this can in some small way make up for all I've done. I know it can never be enough to erase the pain I've caused you.

I love you, Lauren, more than I can say. But you were right. I'm not good for you, although you were kind enough not to put it quite that way.

I'll never forget you. Never. You were the best part of my life.

                                        With love,

"Paul," it ended. Lauren ran her finger over his bold signature, imagining his face as he wrote it. A large moist drop appeared on the linen-weave stationery, spreading, absorbing. The paper wobbled, and another stain appeared.

Gently placing the packet back on the shelf, Lauren walked slowly, trancelike, into her living room where she picked up her phone and called in sick.

She wasn't sure she would ever go back.

CHAPTER FIFTEEN

POUNDING. WOULD IT ever stop? Lauren lifted a groggy head and tried to focus. Once again she had fallen asleep on top of her covers. Sitting up, she clutched her chenille robe around her. A brown stain ran down one lapel, but she barely noticed.

What *was* that pounding? Someone at the door. Reluctantly, Lauren dragged herself into the entryway and peered through the peephole. Jessie, her face distorted by the tiny lens, frowned, then looked left and right. Lauren opened the door.

"God, Lauren, you look awful!" Jessie stomped over the threshold, holding the Sunday paper, and grabbed Lauren's shoulders. "Have you been sick?"

"How nice of you to come by and pick me up with your cheery words." Lauren turned, pulling herself from Jessie's grasp, and plodded into the kitchen.

Jessie stayed right at her heels. "I called your office Friday. They said you weren't in. I've been phoning every day since then and all I got was your recorder. What's going on, Lor?"

"Want some coffee?" In the kitchen now, Lauren shoved aside an already-ajar cabinet door and plucked out the two remaining cups. The others sat unwashed, in the sink.

"Yeah," Jessie replied absently, looking around. From the corner of her eye, Lauren saw Jessie peer through the opening to her living area. Newspapers, magazines, and half-eaten bags of junk food littered the room. "This place is a mess," Jessie commented.

"Look who's talking." Lauren poured stale coffee from a cold pot into the cups, then placed them in the microwave.

"That's me. You've never lived like this. Jeez, Lor, it's almost two in the afternoon. You look like I got you out of bed."

"Matter of fact, you did." Lauren moved a few feet, plopped on a stool, and rested against the counter. The microwave's timer buzzed. "Get that, will you?"

Jessie laid the Sunday paper on the counter, got the cups, and carried them back. Perching beside Lauren, she gazed at her intently.

"I may not resemble a cover girl today, but would you stop staring at me like I have a wart on my nose?" Lauren picked up the cup Jessie had placed in front of her, took a swallow, then gulped as the hot liquid burned her tongue. The pain made her feel like crying, but she couldn't find the energy.

"Have you spent the whole weekend in bed?"

"Just about." What was the use in lying? Lauren had never been able to fool Jessie, anyway. She blew on her coffee, then took another cautious sip.

"Do you want to talk?"

"No."

That was one of the things Lauren had always liked about her sister. Jessie never pushed, didn't demand explanations. Now, she got up and began putting cups and glasses into the dishwasher. A few minutes later she went into the living area, came back with an armload of half-empty cola cans and bags of snack food, most uneaten, then began dispatching the mess with quiet efficiency.

"Marriage must agree with you." Lauren had never seen her sister so domestic. "It's turned you into a neat freak."

"Now we have another thing in common." Jessie left again, carrying a damp rag and a paper bag. Lauren heard her rummaging in the next room, then heard the noise stop.

"Oh, Lor." Her sister's words came on a hushed breath. Seconds later, Jessie appeared, holding Paul's brown envelope in one hand, the contents in the other. "I'm so sorry."

"You shouldn't read my mail." Lauren tried to sound accusing but couldn't.

"Why didn't you tell me?"

"What could you do?"

"Exactly what I'm doing now." Jessie came next to Lauren and embraced her. Lauren laid her head on her sister's shoulder, absorbing her warmth, her vitality. "Cry on my shoulder, Lor. It's okay. I've cried on yours lots of times."

"He's gone, Jess. Gone. I can't find him anywhere." Jessie's tenderness comforted Lauren, and she allowed herself to be held for a while before adding, "I'm all cried out."

"Tell you what." Jessie leaned back and looked into Lauren's face. "Let me fix you something to eat. How 'bout breakfast? Then we can drive to the zoo and feed peanuts to the elephants. That always makes me feel better."

Lauren smiled wanly, then nodded her head. Her pity party needed to end. She couldn't just crawl into a hole and die, even though she wanted to.

"Good." Jessie beamed. "Now go take a shower, fix yourself up. You look like death warmed over."

"Thanks." But Lauren's smile widened. "I'll take you up on that. It'll be fun leaving you to do the drudge work."

"My hands will probably be work-worn and red by the time you return."

"Poor baby," Lauren shot back as she left the room.

A hot shower, a shampoo, clean clothes and a little makeup did much to lighten Lauren's spirits. When she stepped back into the kitchen, she no longer wanted to die, although she wasn't yet sure she'd be able to go on.

Jessie gestured to a stool, then dished up scrambled eggs, bacon, hot buttered toast and fresh coffee. Lauren discovered she was hungry; she supposed more than two days without a decent meal could do that to a person. She opened the newspaper, took out a section and offered the rest to Jessie, then dug in to eat.

At a sudden choked sound from her sister, Lauren lifted her head from her paper. "What?"

Jessie's face was full of horror. "I don't know if I should show you this." She held the business section in her hand. "But you're bound to find out. Better if it's when I'm here."

Lauren reached over and took the section. The headline leaped out like a neon sign.

J. Mitchell Cotton Accuses Paul Sherwood Of Securities Fraud. Separate pictures of both men accompanied the article.

Lauren's scrambled eggs turned to lead in her stomach as she rapidly scanned the article.

Mitch Cotton was accusing Paul of setting up a junk bond deal while in his employ and directing their staff to assure brokers that the bonds were fully secured. Hundreds of people on fixed incomes had lost their investments. Paul had allegedly done this without Cotton's knowledge. The article finished by stating that Paul had been unavailable for comment.

As Lauren continued to read, she began to understand the extent of the pressures on Paul. But he hadn't done—*couldn't* have done—what Cotton accused him of. Of that she was certain. Paul might be mesmerized by the glamour of his game, but he would never do anything this dishonest, this illegal.

"You okay, Lor?" Jessie reached out to touch her hand.

At first, all Lauren could do was bob her head up and down. Finally her voice returned. She looked up at Jessie, her eyes shimmering.

"It's terrible. But I know this accusation isn't true. I just know it." And what Lauren also knew was that it wouldn't have mattered to her if it were. She loved Paul, with a depth of commitment she hadn't known she felt. If he were guilty, she still would gladly stand by his side. She needed to find him, tell him. "If only I knew where he was."

"Yeah," Jessie replied. "If only. He needs you now. Paul's had more than his share of bad times lately. I wasn't going to tell you, Lauren, but Galahad died."

Lauren's tears finally flooded over. Although she had none left for herself, she found there was an abundance left for Paul.

THE NEXT FEW WEEKS rushed by in a blur for Lauren. She'd continued to hunt for Paul, but to no avail. Not a soul had heard from him.

Reporters had contacted her—had contacted Cheri, E.J., Bill and Jessie—asking about Paul's whereabouts, asking for comments. The Aftons closed ranks to protect Paul. They had no comment or opinion about the investigation, nor about his association with them.

Lauren searched every newspaper she could get her hands on for news of the fraud investigation. Each article gave her more insight into Paul. Through an attorney, Paul gave a statement in his defense. Yes, he'd worked for Cotton when the bonds had been issued, but he had taken no part in the fraud. He had, in fact, filed an opinion paper with the Securities Exchange Commission stating his belief that the bonds were extremely high risk.

An SEC official, however, stated there was no record of the paper. Mitchell Cotton continued to claim that he knew nothing about the fraudulent representation of the bonds, that he had been duped by his ex-employee.

Not one paper, one article, one line had given Lauren the information she craved: Paul's whereabouts.

Amid all this, and despite her despair over Paul, Lauren handled the final details for the spring sales conference. The lavender sedans always awarded to Cheri Lee Cosmetics's top producers had been delivered. So had the mohair jackets, the pendants and rings, and all the other lesser awards. Menus, housing arrangements, meeting facilities—all were approved.

Now, two days before the convention, Lauren sat in her living room and stared at "Wheel of Fortune," not absorbing a word of it.

The doorbell rang. Her heart jumped in anticipation, as it did every time the phone rang, an unfamiliar letter arrived, or an unexpected visitor knocked. She quelled her tremor of hope and walked sedately to the door.

Peering through her peephole, she saw a swarthy man wearing a uniform. She flipped on her intercom. "Yes?"

"Are you Ms. Lauren Afton?"

Puzzled, Lauren answered that she was.

"Mr. J. Mitchell Cotton would like to speak with you." The man stated his message as though it was a command and he had no doubt Lauren would welcome it. "He's waiting in the limousine."

"What makes him think I want to talk to him?" But she did, she did. Hope rippled through her breast again. Maybe Mitchell Cotton had news of Paul. Still, this messenger, who was obviously a chauffeur, acted as if he expected Lauren to trot to the street like a commoner being summoned by royalty. He also didn't respond to Lauren's question. "Tell him to come in. I have a few minutes," Lauren finally added haughtily.

"Er, Mr. Cotton prefers not to be seen. Reporters, you know. He would prefer it if you came to the car."

Lauren chuckled darkly. Who did Mitch Cotton think he was? While she did live in a decidedly upscale neighborhood, people here drove their own cars. A chauffeured limousine wasn't an everyday sight. Undoubtedly, some of her neighbors were already spying from behind their silk drapes.

"He should have come in a BMW if he wanted to be inconspicuous."

But she opened the door anyway as the driver was replying, "Yes, ma'am, if you say so," and went outside, following the man down the curving path to the street.

The limo was more modest than Lauren had expected. The windows were dark-tinted, yet when the driver opened the door, Lauren still couldn't see inside. Thick, pungent cigar smoke filled the car. As it drifted out the door, Lauren saw a squat, round man dressed in an obviously expensive suit. The suit was a colorless gray. So was the man.

"Mr. Cotton, I presume," Lauren said.

"So kind of you to come out, Ms. Afton. Please sit inside."

Hadn't she seen this once in a movie? But she complied, despite her distaste at the cigar smoke. However, when the driver started to close the door she waved her hand in refusal, leaving one foot on the ground. She mistrusted this Mitchell Cotton person. He'd caused Paul so much grief.

The man leaned forward, opened a console on the floor, and pulled out a fluted glass. "Would you like a drink?"

"No, thank you. Would you please get to the point?" Lauren coughed as Cotton drew on his cigar and exhaled smoke.

"We have an acquaintance in common. Paul Sherwood. I believe he once owned a considerable share of your company."

So Cotton knew Paul had returned the shares. Lauren wondered how much more he knew. She would let him go on, wait for the right moment to ask if he knew where Paul was.

"I doubt you have much fondness for Sherwood. We can bring him down, Ms. Afton, ruin him totally. And I'm prepared to give you a sizable gift that would help your company out of its current problems if you help me. Are you interested?"

Lauren quickly concealed her shock. Unless she was jumping to conclusions, this man was about to do something highly illegal. Running a finger over her lower lip, she replied, "Might be. What do you have in mind?"

"It's my understanding that you and Paul were once . . . close. Perhaps he confided in you, told you how he arranged the bond deal . . . told you enough to seal his fate." Cotton lifted a pale eyebrow. "Interesting premise, eh?"

"Interesting." *String him along,* Lauren told herself. *Let him talk himself into a hole.* "Although, from what I understand, Paul has disappeared. How can we hurt him if we don't know where he is?"

"Ah, yes. He ran off to lick his wounds." Cotton sat forward, his voice coming in short, staccato bursts. "The fool's in Mexico. He's got some shoestring operation that I hear he's running himself. But we can draw him out, Ms. Afton."

"How?"

Cotton pulled a leather-bound book from his inside pocket, opened the cover, and plucked out a card. "Write him a letter, long and mushy, and ask him back. As soon as he sets foot on American soil, the feds will arrest him. Poof! No more Paul Sherwood."

Lauren wasn't sure whether her nausea came from the soupy smoke or from Cotton's words. All she knew was she wanted to spit at him. But he held the key to her happiness. She reached out casually and took the card from his hand, trying to conceal both her excitement and her disgust.

"How will I benefit if I do this? Revenge isn't enough."

"A line of credit, my dear. Big. Big enough to solve all your problems." A syrupy smile crossed his face. "The beauty is, you never have to pay it back."

"Let me get this straight. You want me to lure Paul from Mexico, then you want me to testify that Paul told me about the bond deal."

Cotton nodded, then took a puff on his cigar.

"What about the opinion paper Paul says he filed?"

"Oh, yes, the imaginary paper. Funny how easily small packages get lost."

"So the paper does exist?"

"Not to my knowledge. It would be foolish of me to say anything else, wouldn't it?"

"You realize, of course, that Paul told me no such thing. That such a testimony would be false." Lauren leaned back casually, but still kept her foot firmly on the ground outside. "If I'm going to perjure myself, I need assurances that I won't be exposed."

"I've heard you were a smart woman, Ms. Afton. It seems my information is correct. Just let me say that the matter is taken care of. The paper has vanished and it will stay that way."

Cotton had just given her the key to Paul's acquittal, and a huge smile crossed Lauren's face as she realized this. Cotton's mouth also curved into a self-satisfied grin, and he settled against his seat, appearing confident of Lauren's agreement.

"So, my dear, since all bases are covered, may I assume you're accepting my offer?"

"You mean your bribe?" Lauren's smile vanished, and was replaced by scorn, but Cotton didn't appear to notice.

"*Bribe* is such an ugly word."

"Very ugly." Lauren squared her shoulders in outrage. "Just like you. You think everyone can be bought, but my loyalty isn't for sale. And one hint: Next time you invite a lady into your car, put out your damned cigar!"

She wanted to draw back, slap this loathsome creature, knock him to Pluto. Instead, she snatched the cigar from his hand and ground it out on the plush carpet.

"What—!" Cotton uttered a shocked, sputtering sound, then a curse. Leaning forward, he tried to grab Lauren's hand, but she'd already scooted out of the vehicle.

"No deal, Cotton!"

She slammed the car door, ran into her house and quickly turned the lock. Inside, she leaned against a wall, her chest heaving, her thoughts racing. With deep, gulping breaths, she strained to calm herself. Finally her breathing leveled off, her thoughts became more orderly, and she stared down in wonder at the small card in her hand.

She clutched it to her breast like a precious jewel, giving thanks for these few handwritten words that offered everything she needed: Paul's address.

Then she walked to her telephone. It would be a long night, full of explanations, full of objections. But worth every second.

First she called the police. An officer would be sent to take her statement, she was told. Then she called her travel agent. Next she called Jessie.

Jessie responded with oh-my-Gods and I-can't-believe-its as Lauren told her about Cotton's visit. When Lauren was finished, she broached the real subject of her call.

"I want to fly down there tomorrow, Jess."

"Yes!" Jessie cried. "Go."

"I'll miss the opening day of the convention. And there's so much left to do." Lauren knew she would go anyway. The call to Paul's side was much, much stronger.

"Most of it's done already. I'll phone Mom. We'll take care of the rest."

"How do you know what's been done? You've never even known the names of our product lines, much less the details of our convention."

Jessie laughed. "Shouldn't Cheri Lee Cosmetics's new spokesperson know what's going on?"

"Oh, Jessie." A wave of relief flooded through Lauren as she realized her burden had been lifted. She'd never again have to run the company alone. "You're the greatest."

"So are you, sister dear. So are you. Now go get your man and let me worry about the convention."

Lauren thanked Jessie and hung up.

As she began packing for her trip, she wondered if Paul would be glad to see her. Cotton had implied he would be, and as much as Lauren despised Cotton, she suspected his information was accurate. She wondered how long he'd been hounding Paul, exactly how much havoc he'd caused. Enough to send Paul into seclusion, it seemed . . . although she might also have been a reason for his sudden departure.

As she took out some underwear from a lingerie drawer, she spied the black nightgown she'd found so many weeks before. Bringing the cool, smooth fabric to her cheek, she wondered if Paul would like her in it.

She could picture him now, walking along a Mexican beach, Galahad at his heels. It was then she remembered that Galahad was dead. Paul must have been devastated by his loss. The dog had been like his child.

She lowered the gown, folded it, and placed it in her suitcase. Then she went to the phone. She had one more call to make.

CHAPTER SIXTEEN

PAUL SAT ON THE DECK of the *Gypsy Rose,* bathed in temperate sunshine under a gloriously clear afternoon sky, and reading a news story that should have had him jumping with joy.

Yet it didn't. He might as well be stranded in a frigid snowstorm with no food in the larder, no hope for escape.

Cotton had been indicted for bond fraud. Paul had been cleared. He'd been expecting this story to break any day. True, the SEC had no record of his opinion paper, but Paul had—a registered-mail receipt that his attorney had delivered to the case investigators. Today's articles contained a mention that a minor clerk at the SEC had been charged with obstructing justice and taking a bribe.

As Paul perused the story for details, he thought about how this incident had revealed why Cotton had pressed so hard to get Paul back in his employ.

The truth hurt. Cotton needed a fall guy. If Paul had returned to his organization, he would have been set up, would possibly have landed in prison. This answer brought a painful realization.

Deep inside, Paul had hoped Cotton viewed him fondly, hoped his behavior stemmed from hurt feelings, and that the man had really just wanted their relationship restored. The ugly truth meant Paul could no longer kid himself that anyone cared whether he lived or died.

He smiled grimly as he read how Cotton had been arrested, fingerprinted and jailed like a common criminal. Bail was set at several million dollars and Cotton was still behind bars, rotting away. The knowledge gave Paul no joy. Nothing did.

He ached for Lauren. Her absence left a gaping hole that couldn't be filled. So immersed was he in these thoughts that when he saw Lauren's name in the article, he first thought he'd imagined it.

Cotton had approached *her!* The thought of his former boss anywhere near Lauren, sullying her with his sleazy presence, incensed him. Then he smiled, reading about how she'd led Cotton on until he'd admitted his connection to the missing opinion paper, then had openly attempted to bribe her. Did this mean Lauren still cared?

Paul put down the paper and sighed. Probably not. Lauren had so much integrity she would have done this for anyone.

He got up and went below, where his cook was frying *fajitas* for lunch.

"Buenos días," the woman said as Paul picked up a steaming strip of beef and nibbled at it.

"Good-day," Paul answered, eating the rest of the *fajita* without enthusiasm. After the first tasty bite, it had lost its appeal, just as all food did these days. He'd lost weight, and as he left the kitchen for his quarters, he pulled up the waistband of his slacks.

He supposed he should buy some pants that fit. It wasn't as though he were poverty-stricken. The sale of his San Luis Obispo estate, the Coronado Island condo and most of his securities had generated enough money to give him leverage. He certainly had enough funds for new clothes. He just had no interest in buying any.

Inside his cabin, he changed into a suit, planning to go to the factory. These days the business was the only thing that kept him going. The difference was, he no longer cared about building an empire—only about keeping his people employed and making a decent profit to pour back into the company.

Topside, he started down the ramp to the shabby dock. He paused a moment, looking around. At one time, he wouldn't even have considered docking here among the chipped pilings and the splintering planks. But all he needed was a place to moor, and this place was dirt cheap.

He lived in a paradise these days. Too bad paradise was hell when you had no one to share it with.

LAUREN SAW HIM, standing on the ramp of his polished yacht. It looked out of place among the other boats, with their leaning masts and tattered sails.

Something skipped around her chest as she watched him. Her heart, she supposed. She was taking the biggest risk of her life, taking a flying leap with no parachute to catch her. What if Paul told her to bug off? Asked where she'd been when he needed her? What if she was wrong and he didn't love her?

She'd never been so terrified in all her life.

Resolutely, she continued forward, juggling a shifting basket in her hand. She reached the bottom of the plank. Paul hadn't yet seen her, and his hand rested on a rail as he gazed out toward the sea. His blond hair, grown longish during this time, danced in the breeze. His profile was as rugged as she remembered. He seemed, to her, like a Viking.

A Viking in a business suit.

Then Lauren frowned. When had he gotten so thin? The luxurious suit hung on his frame like a potato sack. His skin appeared sallow beneath its golden tan.

"Hello," she called softly, wanting to rush to him, smooth away the lines of fatigue on his face. But fear wouldn't let her. She stood, waiting for his answer.

"Lauren." His voice was soft also, somewhat apathetic. Where was the joyous greeting Lauren had hoped for?

In truth, wonder and joy had spread through Paul upon hearing her voice. He had wanted to race down the plank, pick up Lauren's glorious body, and twirl her around insanely. But he had caught those emotions before they burst through to his face.

How had she found him? Why was she here? Maybe she had brought some documents to sever their association for eternity. He couldn't blame her if that's what she wanted.

"Aren't you going to invite me on board?" The basket tilted and she shifted it again, feeling foolish, berating herself for coming.

"Oh, yes, please." Paul came down the plank, took the basket from Lauren's hand and guided her up. "Sit there," he said, pointing to a table.

She sat obediently and Paul bent to place the basket at her feet. It tipped, nearly overturning, and he quickly grabbed it. He looked at Lauren questioningly. "What's in here?"

"Oh." Lauren had almost forgotten, so stunned was she to be in Paul's presence. She opened the basket and lifted out a wrinkled cream-colored bundle.

Paul stared. "What is that? It looks like someone's dirty laundry."

"Oh, no." Lauren lifted the puppy to her face and made little kissing sounds. "Not dirty laundry, are you, sweetpea?" Lowering the pup to her lap, she smiled up at Paul. "She's a Shar-pei. She'll grow into her skin."

"You named it Sweetpea?" Paul squatted down and scratched the dog's floppy ears as he talked. "What kind of name is that for a dog?"

"I just call her that. She doesn't have a name. I thought I'd let you pick it," Lauren answered breathily. Having Paul so close filled her up, sent her blood racing.

"Me? Why?"

"Because she's yours." Lauren was feeling more and more awkward. The puppy squirmed on her lap, then teetered off before she could catch it, landing with a little yelp. "If you want her, that is." She watched the wrinkly bundle right itself and begin sniffing around, giving her an excuse to avoid Paul's eyes. "I heard about Galahad. I'm so sorry. I know another dog can't replace him. But maybe it could be a new start."

"Is that what you're here for, Lauren? A new start? Or a final ending?" He fixed his eyes on her coldly; there was no warmth or invitation in his expression. Lauren shivered.

Her courage wanted to desert her, take tail and run, leaving her to face Paul with only her doubts and fears. But she refused to let it go.

With a big gulp of air, she began. She told Paul how she'd tried to find him even before the stocks had arrived at her home. She confessed that she'd failed him—failed to listen, failed to trust. Once, during her continuous stream of words, Paul stood, and Lauren, afraid he was going to escort her from the boat, began talking even faster.

But Paul simply went to the rail and rescued the puppy, who'd strayed quite near the edge. He brought the pup back and sat down. She curled happily on his lap and allowed herself to be scratched. Paul said, "Sorry, go on," as Lauren paused suddenly to stare at him.

"Lord, haven't I said enough? I feel like a babbling idiot." She stood and turned her back to him, angry, hurt tears stinging her eyes. "What I'm trying to say is I love you. I want you."

She whirled then, and stared at him. "Isn't that enough?" she shouted. "I love you!"

Paul lowered the puppy. He'd liked feeling the animal's warmth in his lap, but not nearly as much as he liked Lauren's angry confession. He'd heard every word Lauren had said, but had been afraid he was reading between the lines; he'd been waiting for the ominous "but" that always followed these discussions.

Now, as she shouted at him, the bubble of bliss he'd squelched since her arrival burst forth.

"Oh, dear Lord, Lauren, I love you too!" He got up and took her in his arms, drawing her close, feeling the heat of her body, smelling her delicious lilac scent. "I thought you were gone, darlin'. Gone for good."

He felt her sudden shudder, her gentle sobs against his chest, and his own tears flooded his eyes. "Does this mean you'll marry me?" He tilted her chin, kissed the tears streaming down her cheeks and watched the glowing smile spread across her face.

"Yes." Her answer was a bare whisper on an outward breath, but it said everything that was in her heart. Lowering her head, she pressed it against Paul's chest, hearing the steady beat of his heart, now realizing that beneath his boyishness Paul was steady, dependable.

"It hurts me that you've lost so much. It's all my fault."

"No. It's not your fault." Paul stroked her hair, his fingers strong and firm. "Besides, it's only money. I made it once. I can do it again."

"Is that what you want?"

There was a long pause. Paul's hands stilled as though he were deep in thought. "I don't think so. It's been gratifying running my little company here."

Lauren tilted her head and glanced at him. "Are you saying that we'll be living in Mexico?"

Paul's laugh rumbled through the air, hearty, healthy and happy—music to Lauren's ears. "No, darlin'," he said, planting a kiss on her brow. "I've got good people here. Besides, I love San Diego almost as much as I love you."

"Good. Then let's cruise back." As Lauren spoke, a tug on her foot drew her attention. She looked down to see the puppy chewing on her shoe.

"Goodness, and the shoe's still on my foot. I shudder to think of what she'll do to the ones in the closet." She picked the dog up, holding it between her and Paul. "You don't have to keep her, Paul. I know she can't replace Galahad."

Paul rested his chin on Lauren's head, staring at the living mass of wrinkles. The puppy tilted her head, her flopping ears lifting, her bright eyes curious. "No, she can't replace him. But she does have her own charm. Besides, Galahad was a gift from a woman I loved. And so is Sweetpea."

Lauren's face lit up. Sweetpea was only the first of many things she'd planned to help Paul recover from his losses. She tipped back her head and, parting her lips, she captured Paul's mouth. A sharp spurt of desire reminded her how long it had been since she had tasted him.

Slowly lowering Sweetpea to the ground, she leaned into his hard frame as he deepened the kiss with a hunger that matched hers. His tongue darted dizzyingly over the edges of her lips and deep inside her mouth, creating that wonderful, exquisite longing she had not forgotten. Time and space *were* forgotten now: it was just her and Paul. Together again.

"*Sí, Señor! Sí, Señorita! El amor.*" The voices brought Lauren back to reality. She turned, as did Paul, toward their source. A group of Mexican fishermen stood on the dock, their fists raised in encouragement.

"*El amor!*" Paul shouted back.

The fishermen cheered.

"*El amor,*" Lauren whispered to Paul. "And privacy. We need privacy!"

Paul laughed, swept up the puppy, and grabbed Lauren's hand. Pulling her along, he ran pell-mell for the stairs. She giggled with delight, knowing exactly what marvelous wonders were in store for her.

As their heads disappeared below the upper deck, the fishermen cheered again.